KILLERS
OF THE TRUE
HOLY WAR

KILLERS
OF THE TRUE
HOLY WAR

PETER ABRAHAMS

The Book Guild Ltd

First published in Great Britain in 2017 by
The Book Guild Ltd
9 Priory Business Park
Wistow Road, Kibworth
Leicestershire, LE8 0RX
Freephone: 0800 999 2982
www.bookguild.co.uk
Email: info@bookguild.co.uk
Twitter: @bookguild

Typeset in Minion Pro

Printed and bound in Great Britain by CPI Group (UK) Ltd, Croydon, CR0 4YY

ISBN 978 1911320 845

British Library Cataloguing in Publication Data.
A catalogue record for this book is available from the British Library.

To God, Countries and Continents

To Julie
With all the Love in my
heart.

[signature]

1

THE BOY'S NAME was Deji-Vita. He was surrounded by killers in the name of religion. Around the killers in the name of religion were preachers who preached peace. The preachers preached peace in the name of God weekly. The killers killed people in the name of God daily.

The preachers said they believed in Judgment Day. The killers, too, said they believed in Judgment Day. Yet the killers killed people as they pleased without waiting for Judgment Day. And the preachers did nothing about it.

So the boy said to himself, "Let's go and check the Scriptures for answers, for this is a big, big madness that medicine cannot cure."

Upon checking the Scriptures, the boy found God began a relationship with man through breath. And God exercises power through that breath.

Breath is spirit, so God's breath is Holy Spirit.

Holy Spirit speaks through prophets and sages. Prophets and sages take God's messages to men on Earth. Then it is up to each man to believe or not believe the message, until Judgment Day.

According to the law that governs Judgment Day, no one is

allowed to judge, except God. Yet God does not pass judgment until Judgment Day. And Judgment Day only takes place after death.

"Why then are the killers killing people in God's name without waiting for Judgment Day," the boy asked himself. "And why are the preachers doing nothing about it?"

The boy checked the Scriptures again.

Then he discovered a sideshow – a big fight – that had been going on since man and the devil first met: the devil will trick man into doing what God had asked man not to do. Then God will get angry with man and punish him.

The devil first tried the trick in the Garden of Eden and it worked wonders for him. He got Adam and Eve to do what God had asked them not to do, and God punished them severely.

The devil has been using the same tricks ever since: he tried it on King Saul and it worked. He tried it on Samson and it worked. He tried it on the Israelites in the wilderness and it worked.

So the boy said to himself, "The law that governs Judgment Day says no one is allowed to judge, except God. Those who kill people in God's name are therefore playing with fire. They are destined for nowhere but hell. I'm sure they were taught through the prophets. Then the devil stepped in fast, like he did to Adam and Eve in Eden, and tricked them into disobeying the law that governs Judgment Day.

"But how on Earth did the devil manage to achieve such a staggering feat? How did the devil manage to get man, God's greatest creation on Earth, to start killing his fellow man in God's name without a care?

"I will search into how the devil achieved this astonishing feat. Then I will tell the blinded to the law that governs Judgment Day by the devil's trick to stop the killings in God's name at once. Else they will face the severest of consequences in the fire of hell. And they will have no one to blame but themselves."

The boy's maker had a different idea.

He gave the boy life to tackle the problem of poverty, and he wanted the boy to focus fully on that task.

Besides, someone was already on his way to do what the boy was thinking about doing for those who kill people in God's name.

So the maker of the boy decided to use spiritual powers to change the boy's focus.

One day, while fast asleep in the middle of the night, the boy dreamt of a mysterious spray that could kill poverty outright. Unaware that his maker had used the dream to focus his mind on what he was given life for, the boy became so obsessed with finding the spray that can kill poverty outright he started fasting monthly because of it.

While fasting monthly and praying to God to show him how he could bring the spray that can kill poverty outright into existence, the boy had another dream.

This time, he dreamt of a crying child, who had just learnt how to walk. Three times the crying child tried to run. Three times the crying child fell flat on his face. After the third fall, the crying child became extremely angry and started beating the ground with his fist.

Thousands of pigs were busy feeding on a hill close to a lake nearby, but the crying child showed no interest in them at all. All he did was beat the ground. And the more he beat the ground, the more he cried.

Owners of the feeding pigs caught sight of the crying child and started talking about going to his aid. Then a wise-looking man appeared from nowhere and stood before the crying child.

"Why are you crying?" the wise-looking man said.

The crying child ignored the question and kept doing what he was doing.

Not too far away, was a bleeding man, who was busy cutting his own skin with stones in a tomb.

To the astonishment of the crying child, the bleeding man came and fell before the feet of the wise-looking man.

Then, with both bleeding arms raised in the air, he yelled, "Please don't torment us. Send *us* to the pigs instead, *we* beg you."

"Why is he saying 'us' when he's only one?" the crying child wondered.

All the thousands of pigs that were once busy feeding rushed down a steep bank into the lake nearby and drowned one after the other, which visibly shocked the crying child to no end.

Owners of the pigs took to their heels and fled.

Then the wise-looking man turned to the bleeding man and said, "You are now cured of your illness. Go home and sin no more."

"Who is this man?" the crying child wondered.

Then, while the bleeding man was on his way home, the wise-looking man turned to the crying child and said, "That man was made ill with madness by demons. Demons made him live in a tomb. Demons, which are also known as Legion, made him cut his own skin with stones. Demons spoke through his tongue and begged me not to destroy them.

"Demons know I have power to destroy them, so his demons begged me to send them into the thousands of pigs instead, and I did. That's why all the pigs rushed into the lake and drowned, one after the other. They couldn't cope with the powers of demons that flew into their flesh."

The crying child became more attentive at this juncture.

Then the wise-looking man said, "I did as the demons asked because of you… I wanted you to see for yourself how wasteful demons are. When they lived in a man, they wasted all his talents. When they flew into thousands of pigs, they wasted all their lives. The same demons, which wasted a man's life and talents for years, wasted meats of thousands of pigs in less than one minute. I made you witness that because of what God has decided to do with your life, which will become clear in good time."

The crying child frowned deeply now and hardened the look on his face.

Then the wise-looking man added, "I know who you are and where you are from. You come from a world in which poverty and illness does not exist. God put you to sleep in that world and woke you up in this one, which you hated so much because of its poverty. You wanted this world to disappear from your gaze at once but it did not.

"In your previous life, you could fly like a bird and you could command things to do whatever you wanted. So when the shocking poverty of this world met with your eyes, you tried to propel your wings and fly away at once but found you can no longer fly. You commanded the ground to open and swallow you up but the ground did not yield to your commands. Both experiences shocked you greatly and made you very angry.

"Not knowing what else to do after those two shocks, you threw yourself on the ground in anger and started crying; not able to make sense of what had happened to you and your previous powers.

"Take heart. God clipped your wings and curtailed most of your powers before sending you down on Earth through birth, knowing otherwise you will fly out of this world at once and leave humans to their many problems."

The crying child wiped tears off his face now.

Then the wise-looking man said, "Humans are born with a minimum of five talents…"

"Only five talents?" the crying child almost blurted, looking visibly stunned by what he'd just heard.

"I know, I know…" the wise-looking man said. "For what God made this world for, and for what God created humans for, five talents minimum is sufficient for every human. But any human can have up to twenty talents while forming in the womb, if his or her parents obey certain rules set by God."

The wise-looking man continued, "Demons destroy talent. Demons can waste any human's talents. Yet humans have no idea how dangerous demons are to their lives and wellbeing. They don't realise that demons are behind the reasons why so many of them are wallowing in abject poverty.

"So God wants you to go amongst demons in disguise and learn things to help humans. With the help of angels, you will learn how demons enter humans; how they destroy talents; how they grow in humans; what they eat; why they eat them; and how they cause poverty to abound on Earth.

"Your gatherings shall make you *Gift Bearer of Great Significance to All of Mankind*. Gifts you bear shall serve as the final warning to mankind in this generation and many to come.

"Your suffering shall be long and hard. Your pain will be excruciating and often unbearable. Once your work is done, however, you will awake from another deep sleep to find yourself back from whence you came. Then you will be glad that you did something to help God's creation that is mankind."

With that, the wise-looking man bowed solemnly and vanished. Then the crying child bowed solemnly before the sacred ground and left.

Minutes after the boy Deji-Vita awoke from the dream, he thought to himself, "This dream is very important. It has opened my mind to why poverty abounds in this world. But who was the crying child in the dream? And where can I find him to learn things from him?"

Years later, while busy philosophising at an isolated place by a riverside, an old man appeared before Deji-Vita from nowhere.

"Be warned, child…" the old man said in a husky voice. "The

devil is after the treasure to have it destroyed. He has enough powers to turn himself into whatever he wants, the devil. He will turn himself into anything that can help him get the treasure and destroy it."

With that, the old man vanished.

Then Deji-Vita thought to himself, "The spray that can kill poverty outright must be the treasure that the devil is after. But why did the old man not tell me where I can find it before the devil gets his evil hands on it?"

Days came to pass.

Then a courier appeared out of the blue and handed Deji-Vita a letter from America, which turned out to contain a flight ticket to Frankfurt and one thousand American dollars.

The letter was from his only brother, whom he had not heard from since days before his fifth birthday. The brother wanted to meet him at an address in Frankfurt as a matter of urgency, which he found curious.

"My brother never wrote to me since he left home over ten years ago," he thought to himself. "Now he wants to meet with me as a matter of urgency? This meeting must have something to do with the treasure."

Deji-Vita became so excited he took to going for long walks twice or thrice in a day.

Three days before he was due to travel, he returned home from a walk to find the flight ticket and his one thousand American dollars had disappeared.

"The devil must be behind this," he thought to himself.

He was a boy who lived with his grandfather. And his grandfather was the only person on Earth who knew where he had hidden the flight ticket and the one thousand American dollars. So he went and told his grandfather what had happened.

Then, looking at his grandfather, he said, "My brother must

have found the treasure that the old man said the devil wants to steal."

"Who knows?" his grandfather replied.

"The devil knows something and wants to keep us apart," he insisted.

Then, desperate to see his only brother again, he broke down and wept bitter tears until his grandfather promised to borrow money and send him on the trip.

The grandfather honoured his promise. But the amount of money he was able to borrow could only buy the cheapest of flight tickets from a poor former French colony, which was hours drive away from where they lived, so it was that he travelled hours by road in a van to the former French colony and slept on a bench at the airport.

The next day, he flew to Frankfurt and rode in a taxi to the given address; only to find the place was the huge vicarage of a German priest of the Lutheran church. His only brother was nowhere to be found. And the German priest said he spoke very little English.

First thing the next morning, the German priest put him on a train and sent him to an English priest in Cologne. The very next day, the English priest put him on another train and sent him to an American priest in Wiesbaden. After one night in Wiesbaden, the American priest took him back to Frankfurt International Airport in a car and put him on a flight to Heathrow.

"A priest will be at the airport in London waiting for you," the American priest had told him.

"How would I recognise him?" he asked the American priest.

"You'll see him holding a white card aloft with your name boldly written on it," the American priest said.

"What on Earth is going on?" he almost blurted on the plane

that was about to take him to London. "Why am I being sent from one priest to another like this?"

Moments later, the plane took off.

Then his mind turned to a dream.

He dreamt the same dream in each of the three priests' house in Germany. And, on all three occasions, he awoke at the same point in the dream to find himself sweating like water had been poured on me.

"Why was that?" he wondered.

He arrived at Heathrow Airport to find the priest who came to meet him at the airport had a terrible stammer. This astonished him greatly because he had never come across a stammering priest in his life, until then. The priest's stammer was so bad it took him almost a minute just to say hello.

2

THE STAMMERING PRIEST took Deji-Vita to his house in Central London and made him a cup of tea. Deji-Vita had many questions on his mind, but he could not bring himself to ask any of them because of the priest's terrible stammer.

Thankfully, there was a dog in the house called Smokey, which became very fond of Deji-Vita at first sight.

Moments after finishing his tea, the stammering priest jumped to his feet and took ages to say he had a meeting to attend with the Bishop of London. Then he left Deji-Vita with the dog.

"How can a bishop drag a man with such a terrible stammer into any meeting?" Deji-Vita wondered.

Hours later, the stammering priest returned.

He gave the dog a pat on the back for being a good host to the boy. Then he put Deji-Vita in the car while Smokey was barking and drove him to a white mansion in Primrose Hill in North London, where a very beautiful lady called Habiba and her husband, John, lived.

Living in the house with John and Habiba, were Fiffy, Holly and Anoushka.

John was away on a business trip. Holly and Anoushka were at a friend's house. Fiffy was watching Deji-Vita's every move from a hiding place in the mansion.

It was about twenty minutes before midnight. And Habiba knew in advance that the boy was coming to stay with them for a day or more. So she showed the boy to his room on the first floor of the mansion, and then left him to make himself at home.

The next day, Deji-Vita awoke from a deep sleep to find he did not dream on his first night in London.

"Why did I dream the same dream in every city I visited in Germany but not in London?" he wondered.

A few hours later, he was drinking tea in his self-contained room on the first floor when a blonde girl with striking blue eyes knocked at his door.

She introduced herself as Fiffy, and she looked fourteen in his eyes. But she was nineteen and three years older than him.

While they were talking, a brunette joined them and introduced herself as Holly. Moments later, a black girl joined them and introduced herself as Anoushka.

During the course of conversation, the girls asked him to do them a favour. They wanted to buy presents for a young Arab prince in Dubai, they said. And they wanted him to try clothes on for size before they bought them.

He agreed to help, so the girls called a cab, after breakfast, and took him to Bond Street in Central London.

To his astonishment, he tried on four terribly expensive suits and the girls bought them all. He tried on different shirts, shoes and ties and the girls bought them all. They asked him to wear a gold watch for them to see and they bought that, too.

Moments after the returned home to Primrose Hill, he was on his way back to his room on the first floor when he heard a highly disturbing scream. The girls called for his help yet again and he ran fast to help.

This time, they said a huge spider had just crawled under the bed in Fiffy's room, and they were all very scared of it.

"Please help me get it out," Fiffy said.

He crawled under the bed and searched every nook and cranny of the room but found no spider.

He later returned to his room to find he had been deceived. Fiffy used the spider story to keep him out of his room. Holly and Anoushka went and dumped all the shopping from Bond Street on his bed while he was busy looking for a spider that did not exist.

There was no Arab prince, he soon discovered from a note that Holly and Anoushka left behind. All the terribly expensive shopping from Bond Street was for him. And he was not allowed to say a word about it when they next meet.

Shocked, Deji-Vita cast a gaze towards the ceiling.

"What's going on, Lord?" he wanted to say. "All I'm looking for is my only brother. Yet this journey is getting stranger and stranger at every turn. Cost of the gold watch alone could send thirty boys to secondary school for a year in some parts of my country. The four terribly expensive suits could sponsor fifty children to primary school for three years in any village in the region where I was born. Why would they waste such vast sums of money on me when they don't even know me? Is this one of the devil's tricks? Is the devil trying to lure me where I can become like fish out of water and finish me off because of the treasure?"

As soon as Fiffy set foot in his room to see him for a chat, he looked at her in the eye and said, "Let's take them all back."

"No," she snarled, and started brimming with anger.

"If I take any of these things to where I come from, I will be lucky to be alive the following day. Thieves will try to kill me and take them."

"Tell Habiba that when you see her," she replied.

"Habiba asked you to do this?"

"Yes. And, if you don't mind me asking, can you afford to move into a hotel tonight?"

"No."

"Then I'll strongly advice against questioning Habiba about this."

"Why?"

"She kicks people out of her house, if she buys them presents and they don't take them."

"What? Why?"

"Has it occurred to you that, if the rich of this world don't buy things from expensive shops, those who work in them will end up poor, too?"

"No. I never thought of expensive things in that way."

"Then don't question the wisdom of Habiba…"

"But…"

"Please, Deji-Vita. I came to see you about a very, very, very important dream. And I have very little time. Can you interpret dreams?"

"No."

"Have you ever had a dream that baffles you no end?"

"Yes."

"What was it about?"

He didn't want to say.

So they argued back and forth until he gave up and decided to tell her about the dream that he had years ago about the crying child.

Moments after he finished telling her about the crying child, she looked at him and said, "You are the crying child."

"No, I'm not the crying child," he replied.

"You are trying to hide who you are but it's not working," she retorted.

"Why would I want to hide from anything or anybody?"

They argued back and forth yet again.

Then she said, "Okay, listen to this: a skinny boy wearing

a golden robe was walking along a narrow path flanked by dangerous thorns. To his left and to his right was nothing but danger to his flesh. A host of angry beasts with big horns came and stood in his way and started staring hard at him. The angry beasts would not budge. The skinny boy would not beat a retreat.

"They eyeballed one another, until a whirling wind came and swept the skinny boy off his feet and lifted him high up in the air, where the angry beasts could block his progress no longer. The angry beasts jumped and jumped but could not get anywhere near where the skinny boy was now in the air.

"The wind suspended the skinny boy in the air for a while, which enabled him to look at the jumping, angry beasts for a while. Then the wind started moving him towards his destination and the angry beasts started making a turn to give chase.

"A glowing force soon appeared before the eyes of the beasts like a smaller version of the sun. Then a stampede of the beasts ensued and blood started flowing like a river. Harrowing noise of anguish soon filled the air and many beasts were left dead on the floor. Many more got badly injured and they all gave up the chase.

"The wind took the skinny boy to the beginning of an endless stretch of beautiful lawns and placed him there. Then men, women and children started emerging from north, east, south and west and started following him, all of them singing songs of joy while waving hands.

"Three days after I had this amazing dream, you walked into this house in the company of a priest and my heart almost stopped beating."

"Why?"

"You are the skinny boy that I saw in the dream."

"What?"

"Your God put you in my dream without asking for my permission. He invaded my space. He invaded my privacy with your face, your hair, your height and everything about you when all I wanted was to sleep. Why did he do that, for goodness sake?"

Staggered by what he'd just heard, Deji-Vita stepped back and looked askance in silence for a moment.

Then he looked at her and said, "First of all, apologies from God through my tongue for putting me in your dream without asking for your permission. But I can assure you that God asks for no one's permission before putting whatever he likes in their dream…"

"Why does he do that? That's taking us for granted."

"Please, let's leave that sort of talk to one side for now…"

"Why?"

"Arguing with God is a triple top super power affair. And I'm not in the mood for that right now. A dream, at times, shows the true status of a person in the grand scheme of things. God wants me to know how big you are in spirit…"

"Don't treat me like a child."

"I don't treat anyone like a child."

"I've not slept a wink since I had that dream and you walked into this house."

"That's because you don't know what the dream means yet. I have an only brother that I'm looking for. Our grandfather says he's very good at interpreting dreams…"

She interrupted him by leaning forward to kiss him at this juncture. He yelled and runaway from her like he'd just seen a ghost.

"You see…?" she said, while staring at him.

"I see what?" he replied, while trying to keep his distance.

"That's what the skinny boy did in the dream. He did not allow anyone to kiss him. He asked all who wanted to kiss him to praise God instead."

"I didn't want you to kiss me because of what I read in a book," he sighed.

"What kind of stupid book is that?" she retorted.

15

"It's called *The Determined Man*."

"Which teaches what, stupid things?"

"It teaches why we must not joke with the power of kiss."

"Why must we not joke with the power of kiss?"

"According to the book, there lived a determined man, who wanted to save hundreds of millions of people under a spiritual siege that made them terribly poor. What he did not know was that the devil lured fathers of the suffering people into a trap some six thousands of years ago, and left them under lock and key where he could keep a close eye on them. Any soul that made the slightest attempt to help them escape was either killed or punished severely and watched round the clock by the devil and his cohorts.

"The determined man had read in a book that thinkers of centuries past freed people in Western Europe from a similar siege, and all they needed to do it was the power of philosophy from various angles, so he wanted to do the same for the suffering people before him.

"The devil came to know about what he was trying to do, and the devil decided to do something about it before he did considerable damage.

"The devil tried luring him into a trap but failed. The devil offered him bribes through his cohorts but he did not take them. The devil tried sending him abroad but he didn't go. Nothing the devil tried worked.

"Eventually, the devil despatched powerful demons into the girl with the softest lips on Earth, and she started having strong feelings for the determined man.

"The determined man was the most disciplined man that the girl with the Softest Lips on Earth had ever met, so she pretended she had no interest in him at all but kept watching him covertly from a distance.

"One day, she caught the Determined Man taking a deep nap under a tree, after exhausting himself through philosophising, so she skulked and skulked with her breasts fully exposed until she was very close. Then she planted a kiss on the Determined Man's lips and everything changed.

"The determined man enjoyed the kiss so much he did not want to let go. The more he was kissed, the more he wanted of it. He came to believe the kiss was very helpful to his mission. And the devil rubbed his hands with glee and bided his time.

"Weeks into a passionate relationship, the devil withdrew the girl from sight and sent her thousands of miles abroad, where the weather was so cold the determined man did not want to go, so the determined man felt a need for a replacement.

"In the bid to find the perfect replacement for the softest lips on Earth, which he missed terribly, the determined man kissed girls after girls until he broke more than a thousand hearts. Spurned and embittered women cursed him every single day and night for breaking their hearts, whilst the devil was piling all sorts of pressure on him from all sorts of angles. His willpower waned, his concentration suffered badly, and he started working less and less.

"To hasten him to his grave, the devil teased him daily and called him a loser, who could have become rich beyond his wildest dreams.

"As if that was not punishing enough, the devil composed teasing songs about how he defeated the determined man with a kiss. And the devil got his cohorts to sing them to the hearing of the determined man come every day and night.

"The songs were so hurtful they drove the determined man to the brink and he turned to drink until hard liquor killed him. Instead of freeing hundreds of millions of people in captivity at the devil's hands, he died a lonely man in a place of squalor.

"Now…think about it. You are a very rich and an amazingly beautiful European girl. I am a very poor and wretched African boy, who cannot wait to return to his suffering people, after finding his only brother. Can you imagine what will happen to me, if I long for your kiss day and night whilst we're thousands of miles apart on different continents?"

"No."

"I could end up like the determine man."

"How do you know it can end up like that?"

"How would I know it couldn't end up like that?"

They argued back and forth yet again. Then a knock came at the door and they stopped talking.

The man behind the door, it turned out, was an Egyptian doctor, who was the last person on Earth that Fiffy wanted to see.

She hated the sight of the man so much she became disorientated in his presence and fled the room without saying goodbye.

3

THE EGYPTIAN'S NAME was Dr Farouk Al El Majid. He was a man in a hurry and he said so from the very onset. He sat on a chair behind a desk to face Deji-Vita and waved Deji-Vita to a chair.

Then he hardened the look on his face and said, "I'm the bearer of a very bad news, I'm afraid, and my mission is about a protection of a treasure that the devil wants to steal. The treasure has rare powers for solving extremely complicated problems, and it was meant to be inherited by the only child that God himself said must be named Deji-Vita; he was given a second life that made him the only person that can use the treasure to maximum benefit.

"The devil came to know about the treasure and what its successful deployment could do to his empire and he went mad with rage, feeling attacked by God. To hurt God back before doing anything else, the devil despatched countless demons into the House of Abraham to bring down as many Jewish, Christian and Islamic clerics as they could conquer.

"Synagogues, churches and mosques came under unprecedented spiritual attacks and relatively few Jewish,

Christian and Islamic clerics fell. The few that fell attacked other clerics in spirit constantly, and they used every opportunity to confuse matters at meetings to spread their wings. This enabled them to bring more and more bad people into the priesthood. Consequently, paedophile priests came to abound in the Christian Church. Phony mullahs, terrorists and breeders of suicide bombers became ten a penny in hijacked mosques of Islam around the world. Knife twisters in the backs of the downtrodden sprang from the Wing of Judah like mad.

"To cut a long story short, God kept His cool and moved the treasure to safety. The devil searched everywhere in fury and came to know the treasure is somewhere here, in London.

"Last week, a boy came here, to London, claiming to be Deji-Vita: the only boy born to inherit the treasure. Days later, you came to London claiming your name is Deji-Vita. Yet God asked for only one child to be named Deji-Vita. In other words, one of you two boys, who look like identical twins, is an imposter sent to London by the devil to steal a precious treasure."

Deji-Vita brimmed with anger, as the old man's warnings by the riverside flashed through his mind at this juncture.

"Be warned, child..." the old man said in a husky voice. "The devil is after the treasure to have it destroyed. He has enough powers to turn himself into whatever he wants, the devil. He will turn himself into anything that can help him get the treasure and destroy it."

"Where's the imposter?" Deji-Vita snarled.

"It is not for you to decide who came to London as an imposter," the Egyptian snarled back.

"Who is to decide?" said Deji-Vita.

The Egyptian retrieved a book from a briefcase and placed it on a table before them. Then, pointing at the book, he said, "The Mejai, the man you will read about in this book is to decide. You will see why in the book."

"Is he here just to deliver the treasure to its rightful inheritor?"

"The Mejai is in London to deliver a message to the world and to killers of the True Holy War. No more questions."

With that, the Egyptian rose to his feet and left.

Then Deji-Vita took the book and read the blurb on the back cover.

4

THE BOOK, WHICH was entitled *The Mejai,* was about how a holy man became useful to a militant atheist and professor of medicine.

According to the first chapter of the book, the professor travelled from London to attend a summer school in Birmingham, where the history of the world's major religions was being taught. While standing in the college garden during the first lunch break to get some fresh air, a fourteen-year-old skinny boy appeared from nowhere and stood before the professor.

Then, with arms outstretched, he said, "Philosophers can change the world without leaving a room. Seers receive life-changing messages in their sleep. Why then should heaven let a friend travel around the world in vain, when all he needs to be fruitful and righteous is right here in our palm?"

The professor did not understand.

So the skinny boy continued, "Your name is Trevor Thomas Huddleston. You are a professor of medicine and a good teacher. You lost two of your three sons in quick succession to the menace of crime: one was killed by recreational drugs and the other was killed by robbers. You lost your children's mother, the love of your life, to cancer not long after you buried your eldest son.

"You contemplated suicide but could not go ahead with it. Your love for your only remaining son, your only daughter and your grandchildren made you change your mind. You decided to help make this world a better place for all children instead by becoming a writer. You wanted to write books about how we came to be where we are now with insurmountable problems. You felt you had no choice but to start by learning about the history of humans and religion. This is why you came here. I'm here to tell you that the devil is trying to send you on a wasted journey to waste great talents at your disposal."

Silence fell between them at this juncture.

Then the professor said, "How did you know everything that you said about me?"

"Angels revealed them to me," the skinny boy replied.

"Why?"

"All nations have small people, normal people and big people. Normal people enable things to be normal when they are allowed to do their normal jobs. Small People are those who lust after power and big titles but get lost when they come across the slightest test in office because they have small hearts. Such people strive to get others to join them in being small, make living together difficult, retard progress, and wastes so much to come up with very little. In short, they cause human suffering to accelerate and multiply.

"Big people, however, fight for all of mankind. They come up with big ideas that enhance progress, save lives and enable talents to flourish. They make living together sweeter because they are shepherds with big hearts.

"Sadly, they are the fewest in number, so the devil is able to target them and go after them from infancy. Where the devil cannot stop them from playing their shepherd's role, he will go after their loved ones to drive them to distraction. I'm here because you were born with more valuable talents than most

23

people living in this age. For this reason, the devil went after two of your children to distract your attention. Open your heart to me now and I will make you one of the greatest fishers of men."

"Why now? Why after I've lost so much that mattered dearly to me?"

"Nothing goes into humans' heads when the going is good, especially when they have no faith. That's why the right time to come to you is now."

"Nothing you do now can bring my wife and kids back."

"What about your two remaining children and grandchildren? What sort of world do you want to leave them in? What right have you to leave your own children, and their children's children, in a mightier mess than the one that you inherited? Who do you expect to make this world a better place for them, if you are prepared to let the devil waste your great talents?"

"What great talents? I've already decided to do something to help."

"When artists and scientists think themselves philosophers, they come up with foolish conclusions that bring waste and misfortunes to all mankind. When philosophers become too preoccupied with art and science, they waste so much to come up with very little. The journey you have in mind will make matters worse for you, your children and their children's children."

"Why?"

"It is written in the Scriptures: 'Unless *the Lord builds the house, the builders labour in vain*'. Scientists do not have what it takes to make this world a better place for children and their children's children. If they do, there will be no crime, no addictions, and no humans who get high on drugs in this world. I have what it takes to spot great talents in you that need the right soil to flourish. In only seven days, I can arm you with what will help you make this world a better place for all children."

"Start right now," the professor said, after a long silence.

"First lesson: before this world, there was another world. In that world lived a creature that we refer to as That Someone. Second lesson: the key to all materials in any world is known as ability-to-understand. Ability-to-understand enables the chosen key holders in any world to become co-creators with God in their world. It gives them wisdom to bring all material things and all creatures in their world under their care and control..."

"Where is that key?" the professor interrupted, looking curious.

"God plants the key known as ability-to-understand in the brain of his chosen key holder at the point of creation, so that it can be handed down from one generation to another through births."

"Carry on."

"Third lesson: when God finished creating this world, That Someone went to God and said he would like to be given the key to it. God declined the request because God had already decided to give the key to Adam. God gave the key to Adam at the point of creation and humans inherited the potential to know the values of gold, diamonds, emeralds, oil and all the other great resources on Earth. If not for that key, humans will be trampling on the great resources of this world without knowing what to do with them, like animals do.

"Beasts, like whales, elephants, lions and horses are all bigger and by far stronger than humans. Yet, thanks to the key known as ability-to-understand, man inherited the potential to use things on Earth to create and control things that are far bigger and far stronger than them.

"Mankind has neither wings nor feathers. Yet, thanks to the key known as ability-to-understand, humans inherited the potential to create and control things that can enable them to fly higher and faster in the air than birds, and do things in the air that birds can never dream of, such as eat, drink and sleep in aircrafts while travelling thousands of miles in the air.

"Man has neither fins nor no tail, like sea creatures do. Yet, thanks to ability-to-understand, man inherited the potential to use things on Earth to create and control things that can enable him to travel in waters and do things in waters that sea creatures can never dream of.

"Man has no powers for controlling day and night. Yet, thanks to ability-to-understand, man inherited the potential to use things on Earth to make extra lights by day and extra lights by night to do his work or entertain.

"Ability-to-understand gave mankind so much it drove That Someone mad with jealousy. Adam's beauty alone drove him insane, so he refused to bow before Adam when God asked him and all angels to bow before Adam."

"Why did God want angels to bow before Adam?" the professor asked.

"To bow before a creature in Heaven means you accept to serve that creature for life. Hence angels serve mankind to this day by bringing messages from Heaven down to men on Earth. He, That Someone, refused to serve Adam and vowed to fight God and Adam and his offspring to the bitter end..."

"Why did God not kill him there and then?" the professor interrupted

"Typical human in the tiny world of science," the skinny boy sighed, shaking his head in disgust. "Truly powerful and fair-minded fathers do not kill their offspring or creation because of a dispute. They let them go and learn. God is the creator and father of all living things in existence, the devil known as Satan included.

"So God said to That Someone, '*I will not kill you for taking a stand. I will give you until the end of time to show me how you came to be right and I came to be wrong. Then I will decide what to do with you.*'"

"I see," the professor sighed. "So it was God who gave the devil licence to kill."

"What do you mean by that?" the skinny boy frowned.

"God gave the devil licence to do whatever he wants, until the end of time, so it was God who allowed the devil to harass us, torture us, maim us and kill us at will. God left us to pay for His fight with the devil, right?"

"No. God gave you, humans, everything you will need to protect yourselves from the devil. It was you, humans, who failed to heed God's advice and the devil started beating you for fun."

"What did God give us to protect ourselves from the devil?"

The skinny boy retrieved a pen and drew the shape of the heart in his left palm.

Then, showing his left palm to the professor, he said, "The heart of man contains everything that God gave man to protect himself from the devil."

"How is that the case?" the professor said.

"Nothing can subdue man, until it succeeds in subduing him at heart," the skinny boy replied.

"Why?"

"Because God made the heart of man the seat of power that will control all things on Earth. Whatever takes control of the heart of man shall take control of the whole Earth. Hence the heart of man became the battleground on which the three breakers and the Three Energisers fight relentlessly. The three breakers are ugliness, defeat and injustice. The Three Energisers are beauty, justice and victory."

"Why?"

"Ugliness, defeat and injustice are known as the three breakers because they break the human heart like nothing else is able to do. Beauty, justice and victory are known as the Three Energisers because they energise the human heart like nothing else can."

"Who's in charge of the three breakers?" the professor asked.

"The devil, of course," the skinny boy replied. "The devil vowed to spread the three breakers wherever he could find man to destroy. In reply to the devil's threat, God gave men Commandments to help them."

"The Ten Commandments are for those who believe in God."

"There were Commandments before the Ten Commandments. But look again and you'll find none of the Ten Commandments does anything for God. The Ten Commandments were meant to help mankind through believers. Its goal was to help man stop the devil from spreading ugliness, defeat and injustices everywhere, as the devil threatened to do."

"Why did Ten Commandments not achieve their goal?"

"Free will is the answer to that question. Individuals use their free will to ignore the Ten Commandments. Consequently, the devil succeeded in spreading ugliness, defeat and injustices through human hands, which waste talents to make people suffer and doubt the existence of God."

"In that case, religion failed," the professor said.

"The Ten Commandments are not about religion," the skinny boy replied. "They're about spiritual duties owed to ourselves and to others. Fulfilled spiritual duties make us stronger than evil spirits."

"What's the difference between religion and spiritual duties?"

"Singing and dancing are not the same things and do not always need each other. You can sing without dancing. And you can dance without singing. Same applies to religion and spiritual duty; they do not always need each other. You can fulfil spiritual duties you owe to yourself and to others without being religious. And you can be rich in religion but very poor in spiritual duty. The church deals in pluralities. Spirituality deals in singularities.

"The Church needs worshipers; individuals need spiritual strength in depth. Spiritual strength in depth is what makes a man difficult to corrupt. He who is religious but deals in drugs and substances that destroy talents of others is a pauper in spirit; he's nothing but an empty barrel that makes the most noise. Religion is supposed to encourage man to strengthen himself in spirit, not to replace spiritual duties that man owes to himself and to others."

"So you are saying religion is not what we need to fight with the devil."

"I told you the devil is trying to send you on a wasted journey."

"Yes, you did."

"Evil spirits can only be fought with spiritual strength in depth. Spiritual strength in depth depends not on church, mosque or synagogue. Religion can help, but it has no power to take over what is required to fight the devil."

"What exactly is *spiritual strength in depth?*"

"Spiritual strength in depth can be found on production lines, as well as in the personal lives of individuals."

"Can you give me an example? Just one will do."

"That comes in the fourth lesson. Men produce less when they fight more amongst themselves, and produce more when they fight less amongst themselves. Where people fight amongst themselves more than the amount they produce with their talents is where the *weakest* people in spirit are on this earth. No matter how religious they are, such weak people in spirit help the devil more and do not worship God, as they may think."

"Carry on."

"The three breakers – ugliness, defeat and injustice – cause men to adopt beastly conducts to become less and less users of their God-given talents. The biggest question for the societal man therefore is 'peace or beasts?' The society which prefers peace to beasts will do everything to organise themselves in a manner that refuses to allow one man's exercise of his free will to impinge on the God-given rights of others. The majority therefore carries the vote in peace or beasts."

29

"In what sense?" the professor interrupted, looking curious.

"The *heaviest* around cannot be pushed around by the *lightest* around."

"Meaning what exactly?"

"Meaning the more there are of those who want peace, the more they cannot be pushed around by those who want to embrace beastly conducts for ugliness, defeats and injustices to spread everywhere. In others words, you need the numbers to spread peace and prosperity."

"Can we force the numbers to swell?"

"No. Swelling of the numbers requires wisdom, which you'll find by studying human behaviour: humans regress in both mind and spirit to embrace conducts and behaviours that are preserves of beasts of the wild the longer they are denied peace. The more those who embrace beastly conducts swell in number, the more peace will elude those who need peace to prosper.

"Peace lovers will then dwindle to become *the* insignificant minority that can be pushed around and ignored. Then more and more people will migrate to join masters of beastly conducts than peace lovers. The question, peace or beasts, must therefore be answered first and foremost by all of the people in every nation on Earth; else they will face constant chaos and vast waste of their talents."

"Carry on."

"Lesson number five: man is made of spirit and matter. The spirit gives life. Matter that is the flesh manifests what's going on in spirit. Spirit cannot be seen, but can be engaged. Spirit cannot be touched, but can be felt. Spirit cannot be held, but can be used and wanted. The spiritual life of man is thus not just when he's at prayer. The spiritual life of man includes his yearnings, desires and aspirations and dreams. Until dreams are aired and aspirations are made manifest, man is at home in spiritual realms, where battles are fought before they are manifested in the flesh in the following guises:

"Beauty will tell the heart one thing.
Then ugliness will turn up and tell it another.
Victory will fill the heart with joy.
Then defeat will come and drench it in gloom.

Justice will strengthen the heart.
Then injustice will come and weaken it badly.
Opportunities will open doors to hope.
Then threats will come and slam them shut.

Charity will cheer the heart.
Then crime will come and turn it cold.
Kindness will bring joy.
Then cruelty will come and choke it to death..."

"Okay," the professor interrupted. "I can now see why you deem the human heart a battleground. But, if God exists, why can't He interfere to give the heart a break?"

"God is everywhere so God cannot be in a rush to go anywhere."

"Meaning exactly what?"

"If you already know where everything will end up, you have to allow those who don't believe you to see it through experience. All God needed to do, after granting free will to man, is to advise and warn, and he did. Interference is a rush on the part of the divine. Man lives under the breath of God known as air, so God is already everywhere and cannot be in a rush to go anywhere. Should God rush to interfere in the life of man, it will mean God cannot wake man from the dead and punish or reward him on Judgment Day. Free will requires rules. God set the rules. And God does not break rule."

The professor gave the boy a look, as if to say, '*What a child?*' Then he said, "What does Judgment Day mean?"

"Judgment Day means the day you will be woken from

the dead to be confronted with the amount of talents that you collected from the womb and the amount of talent that you could have collected before birth, the generations of humans that your talents served and should have served, and all the generations of humans that your talents and actions and inactions should have helped but hindered."

"What will happen after I'm judged?"

"If you are judged to have done well with your talents during your days on Earth, your soul will be rewarded with eternal life in Paradise, where you will live forever. Bad use of talent and waste of talent causes people to suffer in this world. So, if you wasted your talents or used them badly during your days on Earth, you will be sent to the fire of hell."

"Carry on."

"There are three beauties, three victories and three justices; each of which contains a division of labour. The three beauties are a division of labour between the heart, the skin and the ground.

"The first beauty was meant to make mankind sweet, so God placed it in the heart. The second beauty was meant to lift mankind in spirit, so God placed it in the skin made of clay. The third beauty need to be firmly in place before man is born, if children are to retrieve talents from their mind, body and spirit to thrive, so God placed mankind in the beautiful Garden of Eden to set an example for every people to follow, if they are to prosper.

"The three victories arise from a division of labour between God, state and individuals. A society attains the first victory when it creates environments in which humans can retrieve talents from their minds, bodies and spirit with relative ease. Individuals attain the second victory when they realise their potentials. The third victory is attained through the Eternal Life, which God and God alone can bestow."

"Are the three justices part of the division of labour between God, man and states, too?"

"The three justices are a division of labour between states and man alone. God does not need to play a part in that. The first justice demands provision of equality in opportunities for all to prevent waste of talents. The second justice demands fair pay for hard work to avoid low morale, as well as provide means of gauging lacks in efforts. The third justice demands helping hands to those left behind, the biggest test of all in spirit."

"Why?"

"The devil, metaphorically speaking, drives around in his truck looking for those left behind, so that he can pick them up, give them his food and drink, and use them against the rest of mankind. Every crime and illness can be traced back to those who were left behind and the devil went and picked them up and used them against the rest. Friends of mankind come to this world from time to time to help people like you, so that they can go and help others."

"Who are the friends of mankind?"

"Friends of mankind are partly human and partly something else. They come into this world like humans but they are not pure humans."

"Why?"

"If they come into this world as pure humans, they will not have the minimum spiritual strength required for fighting the devil on certain fronts. If, on the other hand, they come into this world with too much spiritual strength than required, they will be far too superior to humans and fail to understand humans. That which cannot understand man cannot help man at all. The human side of their nature enables them to understand human weakness better and how best to help man in his fight with the devil."

"And how do friends of mankind fight the devil?"

"Friends of mankind are first and foremost spiritual detectives. They take peeks at what the devil is doing in the dark to harm man. Then they tell man what is happening and what he can do about it. The devil and his cohorts battle hard to stop them, and so they endure levels of pain and suffering pure humans cannot endure."

Intrigued, the professor asked question after question about the friends of mankind and the skinny boy answered them all.

On their sixth day together, the professor looked at the skinny boy and said, "Last night, a spirit revealed unto me that you are the Mejai, meaning *Gift Bearer of the Greatest Significance for the people of this age and beyond*."

On their seventh and last day together, the professor unfolded an emblem and placed it on a table before them.

Then he said, "This is it, Mejai… *the blue bird emerging from the skies with its gaze fixed at the red rose that shields the human heart*; emblem of the BEJAVE Movement; the organisation that I'm going to form as soon as I'm back in London. BEJAVE is the acronym for Beauty, Justice, and Victory Eventually. The blue bird emerging from the sky is to remind us constantly that we bring our talents to the face of the Earth from the heavens, and we have no right to waste them."

"Why is the bird in the emblem blue with its gaze fixed at a red rose?"

"You said talent is a command of God through which men live or die. Commands of God don't come in humans' skin colour and they take precedence over everything, you said. I therefore want talent, the command of God, to dominate and drive thoughts and acts of the movement, like the blue sky overwhelms and dominates all things on Earth; hence the bird in the emblem is blue. *Talent Above All Else* shall be our motto. The red rose symbolises essence of the third of the Three Beauties."

"Superb," the Mejai said.

The professor continued, "Talent, you warned, is easily diluted and destroyed in cruel and inhumane environments, like crammed conditions, overcrowded homes, filthy and ugly towns and cities filled with stench, and places with little or no beauty in them. Man has an obligation to avoid all such diluters and killers of talent, you said, because talent is a command of God.

"The red rose is to remind us constantly of the need to create and live in beautiful environments for children's talents to flourish. The red rose is also shielding the heart in the emblem to remind us of the need to protect the Three Energisers – beauty, justice, and victory – from the harmful three breakers – ugliness, defeat and injustice – which cause poverty, hunger, disease and conflict to spread and accelerate throughout the world."

"Now you will be first amongst fishers of men in this age," the Mejai said, looking greatly delighted. "I am full of joy in the nature of man, who can rise and fall and rise again."

With that, the two embraced warmly.

Then the Mejai stepped back and said, "Today we are brimming with joy. Tomorrow we'll become fire fighters."

"What fire, Mejai?" the professor said, looking a little perturbed.

"Satan wants to burn down the House of Abraham, and he wants to use hands of children raised in the House of Abraham to do it, knowing it will increase doubts in the existence of God. Every Jew, Christian or Muslim is at risk of being conquered by the devil's demons, unless he does not fail in spiritual duties that he owes to himself and to his fellow humans.

"Whether he has faith or no faith, every man, woman or child with a Jewish, Christian or Islamic background is at risk of being conquered, if he fails in spiritual duties that he owes to himself and to his fellow humans. That's how he likes it, Satan. He likes destroying things that were built with God's blessing, knowing the alternative will always prove a nightmare for mankind. He's already despatched powerful demons to do the groundwork.

"So, from tomorrow, we start fighting Beelzebub Fire. Woe betide the Beelzebub warriors that Satan uses to set the fire; woe betide those who give them succour. Woe betide the homes from which Beelzebub warriors spring; woe betide the tongues that praise them. Woe betide the pockets that fund them.

"We build ceaselessly. Demons destroy relentlessly. We must therefore make haste to deliver laws that are fit for purpose urgently, else fire for fire will burn the whole House of Abraham down before men know where they are. Then they will find the alternative a horrible nightmare."

With that, the two embraced warmly for the second time.

Then soon the Mejai was gone.

Deji-Vita put the book down after reading the first three chapters.

He frowned and thought deeply about what he had just read.

Then he said, "The Mejai is qualified to resolve the matter. He has enough spiritual powers to overcome the devil's tricks and expose the other boy as an imposter. He can determine who the real Deji-Vita is."

"I hear the devil hides in things," he later thought to himself. "And all my life I've begged God in secret to let me meet the devil face to face, no matter what would be the outcome. Is this is it? Is this God's answer to my prayers? Will the Mejai question me and the other boy together so that I can meet the devil face to face? It will be very interesting to see how the devil will behave in my presence, while hiding in a boy that he made to look like me."

The phone in the room rang moments later.

Then, after a slight hesitation, he answered the phone to discover it was Fiffy. She was preparing desserts for them to enjoy together in his room and she wanted him to know that in advance.

5

FIFFY'S DESSERTS, HE later discovered, were very delicious. He enjoyed them so much he licked the plate with his tongue, which made her laughed, until tears welled in her eyes.

Minutes later, while she was making tea, he looked at her flat stomach and laughed.

"What's going on in that head of yours?" she said.

"You won't believe this, but God put a miraculous pyramid in your stomach," he replied.

"What?"

"There's a miraculous pyramid in the stomach of every woman, which copies itself to perfection each time a girl is born."

"Did God tell you that?"

"No. I read it in *The Mejai*, which the Egyptian left for me to read."

"You're kidding, right?"

"No. Listen to this. According to the Mejai, God created four different means of acquiring human gifts at the point of creation and named them Rarest Gifts, Rare Gifts, Great Gifts, and Good Gifts. Then He put Eve, the first woman that ever lived, to sleep and lined her stomach with the four means of acquiring human gifts in a pyramidal format.

"Rarest Gifts are the greatest in value but the least required in number, so God placed them at the tip of the pyramid. Rare Gifts are required in a larger number than Rarest Gifts, so God placed them below Rarest Gifts in the pyramid. Great Gifts are required in greater numbers than Rarest Gifts and Rare Gifts combined, so God placed them third down in the pyramid. Good Gifts need to overwhelm the other three gifts put together in number, so God placed them from bottom up to more than the middle of the pyramid."

"Why no lower than Good Gifts in the Pyramid of Human Gifts?"

"The Mejai said there is nothing lesser than Good Gifts in the Pyramid of Human Gifts because every gift in a human has the potential to aid Great, Rare or Rarest Gifts in others to bear fruit or larger fruit. Every human gift is thus a Good Gift, unless it is placed higher in the Pyramid of Human Gifts."

"Why did God do that in the first place?

"God did it to be fair to all children. Children forming in the womb therefore get their talents without any interference on the part of God."

"What determines the kind of gifts that a child would acquire?"

"Strength in spirit determines everything when children are forming in the womb. The stronger you are in spirit, the higher you will climb the Pyramid of Human Gifts while forming in the womb. The further you go, the higher the levels of talent you will accumulate. The higher you climb, the more the spiritual strength you will require to keep going. Most children cannot climb high enough in spirit to reach Rare Gifts, let alone Rarest Gifts. Hence the world of humans is teeming with Great and Good Gifts, but has less in Rare and Rarest. But that's okay because Good Gifts, are required in vast numbers because of a major role that they play."

"You will say God is fair and impartial, right?"

"Yes."

"So what determines the level of strength in spirit that each child would acquire?"

"According to the Mejai, parents' blood and other factors surrounding a pregnancy will influence the level of strength in spirit that the child forming in the womb will end up with. God does not interfere in that process for two reasons: fairness to all children and the free will of would-be parents."

"So luck played a part in the different talents, as well as the different levels of talents, that you and I ended up with?"

"Luck plays a tiny part. Spiritual strengths of parents, good hearts of parents and spiritual state of the mother during pregnancy, spiritual awareness, diligence and hard work on the part of would be parents; all play important roles in the kind of talents and levels of talents that we get."

"Does religion plays a part in it?"

"No."

Silence fell between them at this juncture.

Then he said, "The most astonishing part of it all is that God, designed the Pyramid of Human Gifts to move people from humble beginnings to the ideal society or the best human community imaginable, so the way we live now is wrong. All nations are lagging behind God's plan."

"And why did God need that plan?"

"God wanted every human, without exception, to play a part in the movement toward the ideal society or the best human community imaginable so that all men can be equal; none can get there without the other."

Fiffy frowned deeply for a moment.

Then she said, "How did God intend to attain such a feat, after giving us free will?"

"Good question. God designed the Pyramid of Human Gifts to work in practice like the lives of molluscs. Let's take three molluscs – snails, mussels and clams – as an example. Like all molluscs, snails, mussels and clams have *shells* and *muscles*: the shells give warmth and protection to the muscles, so the shell has to be made bigger than the muscles. Muscles give life and prevention of corrosion and waste to shells, so the muscles have to be made smaller to fit into the shell. By fitting into shells, muscles are able to take shells around for both of them to thrive. Else both will die.

"God designed the Pyramid of Human Gifts in the same format. Good Gifts are the shells of any human community, so God made Good Gifts easily acquirable and vast in number. Rare and Great Gifts are the muscles of a people, so God made them more difficult to acquire and smaller in number. Rarest Gifts are the oxygen that all molluscs needs, so God placed them at the very tip of the pyramid."

"Wow," she sighed. "How does it work in practice?"

"Rarest Gifts provides the *oxygen* through extremely rare creativity. The *muscles* that use the oxygen are professionals in the fields of arts and science and in all trades and their professionalisms. The *shells* that were designed to protect the muscles are the overwhelming majority of people who use their Good Gifts to work in offices, factories, workshops and shops."

"How are the shells supposed to protect the muscles?"

"The ballot box is where they are supposed to offer protection. The shells are the greatest in number, so they can change governments or systems of government through the ballot box. Their role is most crucial in the movement toward the ideal society or best community imaginable."

"Okay, what is the ideal society or the best community imaginable?"

"The ideal society or best human community imaginable is where no human has any reason to feel bad about his life, let alone starve or be homeless. Everybody has something to contribute.

Each wakes up to enjoy what he does for the objective. No one is left behind to feel useless or stupid."

"What happens after you get to the ideal society?"

"Those who get to the ideal society are to be left with one task: to maintain the ideal society for others to inherit. Those who are yet to reach the ideal society are to have two tasks: to maintain progress made to date and keep moving toward the ideal society through trades and professionalism. That's what God wanted to see when He divided the Pyramid of Human Gifts into three: oxygen, muscles and a shell."

"Is there one ideal society or best human community imaginable in this world?"

"No. It all went wrong when broken shell countries started emerging."

"How do you get broken shell countries?"

"If I give you an egg and you choose to break it underfoot on sandy grounds, what will be the outcome?"

"The shell will shatter to pieces and its yolk will waste in the sand."

"That's how you get broken shell countries – the biggest problem of this world. Break the shell of a nation, the overwhelming majority of the people, and you'll get a broken shell country. Get a broken shell country and brutal dictators and evil lawmakers will rise from it like maggots rise from dead meat. This is why no one ideal society or the best human community imaginable exist in this world. People break shells that God designed to protect their professions and professionalism. Then problems come to abound."

"Where's the breaking point in practice? I can't see it?"

"The Mejai said that the breaking point of shells of a nation is poor education delivered to the overwhelming majority of the people, some countries don't provide state education at all to get a broken shell country. Poor education lowers voices of the people in the ballot box. Lowered voices in the ballot box keep

41

standards of living of the majority down. The lower you can keep the standard of living of the overwhelming majority down, the easier it becomes break shells of a nation underfoot.

"Nations, the Mejai observed, have different methods of breaking their shells underfoot. The poorer the nation, the worst the tactics required. The worst the tactics required, the more brutal the dictatorship. In rich countries, the tactics are subtle. In rich countries, the tactic used is to frustrate and keep frustrating the overwhelming majority to prevent them from participating in the voting process."

"Now I see why many people don't vote in Britain," Fiffy said.

"Knowingly or unknowingly, the more you frustrate the shells from voting, the more a handful of people will emerge as bad lawmakers or dictators, who will, consciously or subconsciously, strangle professionalism through coercion and corruption and bad laws. Where you get in broken shell countries depends not on what you have in talent and hard work but who you know."

"I guess it would be worse in developing countries?"

"Yes. Africa, Asia, Latin America, the Middle East and large swaths of Eastern Europe are teeming with the worst of broken shell countries. Brutal dictators rise from them like mad. Some people think religion is responsible for broken shell countries in such places. They are wrong. Ignorance and demons are the problem."

"What?"

"God did not put a soul on this earth to starve or beg in the street. Ignorance and demons will cause people to break shells of their nations for problems to abound. Then they will start using plights of their broken shells to question the existence of God."

Fiffy laughed.

Then he added, "According to the Mejai, owing to ignorance and demons, the poorer a people or a nation, the more those who acquire professional qualifications in the country or community tend to regard themselves as superior to the vast majority. Yet the vast majority of the people are the shells that should protect their professions and professionalism through the ballot box for all to thrive."

"It happens here," she said. "I've come across people in the legal profession in this country who think they are superior to the rest of us."

"Can the muscles of a mollusc be superior to its shell?"

"No."

"The muscles need the shell and vice versa, so they are *equal*, right?"

"Yes."

"Professionals who regard themselves as superior to the vast majority of the people are therefore the most stupid of a nation, said the Mejai. Through their stupidity, they break shells that should protect their professions and professionalism through the ballot box. Then corrupt politicians, cruel lawmakers and brutal dictators will rise and make them part with ethics of their professions through coercion and bad laws."

"I'm glad we had this discussion," Fiffy said.

"Why?" he asked.

"I used to think culture is the reason why people are so unprofessional in poor and developing countries."

"I'm glad you said that. Because, according to the Mejai, culture has nothing to do with it. Yet rulers of broken shell countries in Africa, Asia, Latin America and the Middle East want people to think that a lack of professionalism is part of their culture. It is not. Ignorance and demons are their problem."

"Why are ignorance and demons their problem?"

"They are totally ignorant of the reason why God made people with Good Gifts to be in the overwhelming majority. And their demons don't allow them to treat people well, so they look down on people and treat them with appalling disrespect, until they break them in spirit to stop voting."

"Now I understand," she sighed. "I didn't know the many were meant to be the shells of our professions. The whole world is ignorant of why the overwhelming majority of humans are born with no more than Good Gifts."

"Sadly for all of us, bad scientists exacerbated the problem of broken shell countries and poverty multiplied and got worse."

"Why?"

"Bad Scientists, said the Mejai, looked at the ways animals get their food and protection and imposed them on humans in the guise of survival of the fittest. Men who had no talent for running a Sunday school, let a country, were emboldened by the concept of survival of the fittest to take power by corrupt means and the problem of broken shell countries multiplied. The whole world started going backwards instead of marching towards the ideal society. Once made aware of the problem, Professor Huddleston girded himself with the Mejai's teachings and travelled around the world to change minds."

"What did he do, Professor Huddleston?"

"He travelled all over the world and opened minds to the Pyramid of Human Gifts. He laboured to show how broken shell countries make people poorer and poorer for cruel dictators to multiply, and make this world a horrible place to live for the overwhelming majority of billions of people.

"He took snails and mussels, as well as chicken and eggs to every country he visited. He showed students and professionals why it was in their best interests to help raise standards of living of the overwhelming majority of people in their countries. He made people see why professions and professionalism cannot be protected without high standards of living of the majority, whom God made the shells of countries and communities.

"In country after country, he told students that *'the destitute are nations' invertebrates with no backbones. Monstrous rulers and brutal dictators need little pressure to crush them.'*

"Wherever he went, he showed how molluscs, like snails and

mussels, die the moment their *shells* are crushed. Eventually, people started calling him the Chicken and Eggs Prophet."

"Why?"

"At every gathering, he will hold a hen in one hand and crush eggs under his foot. Then he will say, 'Out of one crushed egg countless chickens die. Through every nation's crushed poor, professionalism dies like chickens die when eggs are crushed.' Thanks to his hard work, the BEJAVE Movement that he formed in London gained hundreds of millions of members within five years…"

"No wonder," Fiffy interrupted.

"No wonder what?" he replied.

"Thousands of members of the BEJAVE Movement are in London from all over the world. It was on the news yesterday. The Mejai will deliver a message to the world and to killers of the True Holy War tonight…"

The phone in the room rang at this juncture and she answered the call.

Then she turned to him and said, "I must go at once."

"Why?" he asked.

"I'll tell you later," she replied and hurried away.

"Why did her mood change so suddenly?" he wondered.

6

WHAT HE DID not realise was that, London was bombed at two ends while he and Fiffy were discussing teachings of the Mejai. Habiba was at work in Paddington when the news first broke. And she called home at once and told Anoushka about it. Then she asked Anoushka to tell the others to keep the news from Deji-Vita for as long as possible.

"Why?" Anoushka asked, looking surprised.

"Dr Majid left him a book to read. I want him to learn as much as possible about the Mejai before he meets him."

So it was that Deji-Vita was in London reading about the Mejai, while the world was watching shocking scenes of terror in London on TV.

The girls could not believe what they were watching on the television set in the living room. The East End and the Heathrow area were bombed at the same time. Terrified men, women and children ran in all directions, most of them in tears. Tearful eyewitnesses gave account of roads covered in scores of dead bodies and badly injured people. Body parts were said to be everywhere. The public transport system was shut down. Roads leading to and from the Heathrow area were closed. Helicopters were in the air. Armed police officers could be seen looking for terrorists and their cohorts.

There was a television set and a radio in Deji-Vita's room but he never went anywhere near them. He was extremely busy learning more about teachings of the Mejai when Fiffy burst into the room and asked him to hurry.

"Why?" he asked.

"We've been bombed; London has been bombed," she replied.

"What?"

"Religious lunatics did it. They were caught on CCTV bragging and promising us mayhem in the name of Allah."

"What?"

"Habiba is on her way home from Paddington to get you. She wants you to dress smartly in one of the new suits from Bond Street at once and wait for her downstairs…"

"Why?"

"She's taking you in a limousine to the Royal Albert Hall, no matter what, to hear the Mejai speak. The dress code for the event is suit and tie…"

"Oh."

"She's coming to get you early because so many roads have been closed. And the public transport system is completely shutdown, so it could take a long time to get where you're going."

Visibly shocked, he said, "Did the terrorists call God's name in Arabic?"

"Yes."

"Did you see terrorists staining God's name on TV yourself?"

"Yes."

"This is what the Mejai said the devil wants to use some people who were raised in the House of Abraham to do," he said.

Then he dressed up in one of the brand new suits from Bond

Street, as the dress code demanded. And Fiffy helped him fix the tie. He was so strong in spirit he did not allow her to turn on the television in his room. They went downstairs and watched on the television in the living room with the other girls, while he waited for Habiba to come and get him.

7

ACCORDING TO A prophecy, after he had finished all but one of his works on the face of the earth, the Mejai will deliver a message to the world from the city of London. He will address questions that had not been answered since the Tower of Babel. He will reveal something that God has never revealed to people of any religion before. He will take questions from believers and non-believers. And he will spend two nights in a famous hall to deliver his message to the world.

On the third day, he will perform his very last duty to God's creations on Earth. Then he will depart to a place in the Americas, where he will honour Christ before his soul departs the earth to return from whence he came.

The Mejai was in a hotel room near Heathrow when the area was bombed and the police had to seal all roads leading to and from the place.

So the Mejai was stranded, unable to travel to Central London to deliver his very important message to the world.

Professor Huddleston and others were thus hard at work, trying to get the Mejai special permission to travel to the Royal

Albert Hall and deliver an important message to the world.

The professor went all the way to the top in government because he wanted to see the message delivered in London, as it would put his home city and his country on the map, when it comes to holy matters.

For decades, the Mejai did all his work in private. He taught a chosen few in private. And the chosen few went around the world and taught people, like Professor Huddleston did.

His pupils were not allowed to take pictures of him. He never spoke on tape. He did all his field research in disguise. And he never made a public broadcast. His work on Earth required great discipline and he never faulted.

Consequently, the overwhelming majority of members of the movement did not know what he looked like, and they had no idea what his voice sounded like, some say he cannot be a real person, because everything they knew about him was either from books written by him or from books written about him. And his teachings were all about heaven, life after death and how to make this world a better place, especially for little children.

This was the only chance people would get to see what he looks like and what his voice sounds like, and they were all eager.

Members of the movement came to believe the devil was behind the bombing of London. The devil, they believed, was scared of the message that the Mejai was about to deliver and wanted to stop it from happening, hence the devil used his hexed captives to bomb the city.

They wanted to show the devil and his cohorts how strong they were in their beliefs, and how efficient they were as organisers, so, despite the bombing, they organised themselves fast, after coordinating with the authorities, and flocked to the Royal Albert Hall way ahead of schedule.

Deji-Vita and Habiba later entered the Royal Albert Hall to find people praying hard, asking God to thwart the devil and let them see the Mejai with their eyes and hear him deliver his message with their ears.

At around nine at night, Professor Huddleston mounted the rostrum with a huge smile on his face and the whole place erupted with joy.

"The Mejai has arrived," he announced, after a deafening ovation.

8

DRESSED IN A simple blue robe with gold trimmings, the Mejai waited until the hall had become dead silent. Then he bowed his head and mouthed a little prayer and went straight to work due to lack of time. Delivering the message of his Lord and maker, he said:

"I begot the fed to feed as well as the feeder.
And I made objective the ruler king.
Objective gives me reason to create.
And objective begets what my creation is to feed upon.

Objective dictates what my creation is to avoid.
Objective resolves how my creations are to be armed.
Objective decides how long my creation can live and die.
Objective determines the fate of everything that came out of me.

I begot the objective behind the creation of man.
And I created man in my own image because of the objective.

Nothing I placed on Earth needs man to be.
Nothing I placed on Earth gets anything back from man.
Water needs not man to be. Rain needs not man to fall.
Water gets nothing back from man. Rain gets nothing back from man.

The sea, sun, stars and the moon get nothing back from man.
Plants, trees, fruits and flowers need not man to rise.
The air that I placed on Earth gets nothing back from man.
The sun, sky, moon and the stars need not man to glow.
Man is thus born indebted to things that I placed on Earth to serve him.
Yet man now growls a lot. And man now boasts a lot.

The only thing I owed man as his creator is objective.
And I gave man objective.
The objective that I gave man begot man's rights and talents.
Rights and talents determine whether interference is necessary.
I gave man rights and talents that require no interference on my part."

The Mejai paused and continued, "In the beginning, humans had only one language. They all spoke in one tongue and understood each other to perfection. Then they threatened the objective behind the creation of man by building the Tower of Babel and they made God angry.

"God got so angry with humans for building the Tower of Babel He confused them and dispersed them throughout the face of the Earth. Humans lost their original language as a result and had to learn different languages in different places. Different groups came up with different languages. Different languages brought misunderstandings, different groups and new problems.

"After God took their original language from them in anger at Babel, humans started saying to themselves in their confusion, *'Who are we? And why are we here?'*

"Then, in their confusion, they started ascribing supernatural powers to things around them, which caused them to become idol worshipers who worshipped strange things in their panic throughout the face of the earth. Study Jews, Christians and Muslim and you will find many of them still worship idols – things created from their hands – through Judaism, Christianity and Islam than they obey God.

"To this day, humans have failed to answer the questions *Who are we?* and *Why are we here?* The confusion that God imposed on humans at Babel still rules human minds.

"So, today, we are going to begin a journey. For the first time since God confused humans and dispersed them throughout the world for building the Tower of Babel, the correct materials for answering the questions, 'Who are we?' and 'Why are we here?' will be laid before you.

"We will begin with objective, then vacuums and lendables, and then, finally, the mother of all reasons.

"What a creator owes its creation is objective. Objective begets talent. Talent begets rights. Rights and talents are therefore fused in nature.

"Our first task, therefore, is to look at the objective behind living things surrounding mankind, starting with the fact that nothing is in this world for nothing. Everything is here to serve a purpose. And food is always the starting point. Why is food always the starting point?

"No living thing can live without living food. Every living thing needs to feed on living foods right from the womb or it will die. The foods of every living thing therefore have to be in existence before it is created or it will not survive.

"So God would create all the foods that a living thing will need to eat right from infancy. Then He would create what would eat that living thing itself.

"God created foods for one living thing after another, until He ended up with countless plants and animals. The objective behind every plant and animal can therefore be found in what it provides as food for other living things.

"God created man last, because man was not meant to be food for anything. Nothing was meant to depend on man for food to survive.

"Since man was not made to be eaten by anything, the objective behind the creation of man – in other words, 'Who are we?' and 'Why are we here?' – is first and foremost tested through comparison with creature endowed with higher talents than humans, namely, angels:

"Men age, angels do not.
Ageing gives men pressing needs, angels have none
The inferior thing about men is ageing and pressing needs.
The superior thing about angels is lack of ageing and pressing needs.
That which has pressing needs cannot worship God to perfection.
Man has not what it takes to take the place of angels.
God had no need to replace man with what only angels can do best."

The Mejai continued, "There are those who think God created humans because of religion. Religion is not a living food. In other words, religion is not even a creation of God. Religion is a creation of man, which embodies what humans feel or think about God.

"Like all human creations, religion has Dangerous Limitations. And religion has three Dangerous Limitations, which are as follows.

"The first dangerous limitation of religion can be found in the lives of Cain and Abel. Cain and Abel made different offerings to God. Each made his offering according to what he thought of God. Cain was a farmer. Abel was a shepherd. Cain thought God will not eat farm produce, so he took less than the best of his farm produce and burnt them as offerings to God. Abel, on the other hand, felt God deserved to be offered the best food, whether God would eat them or not, so Abel slaughtered the first lamb of one of his sheep and offered the *best* part of it to God.

"God did not impose thoughts on Cain and Abel. God let them think for themselves. But, upon looking at their different offerings, God praised Abel for making the most respectful offering. Cain became jealous and bitter as a result, and he went and killed his brother Abel. God did not kill Cain even after Cain killed Abel, because God waits for Judgment Day to reward or punish.

"From the jealous and murderous act of Cain, we get the first dangerous limitation of religion. The first dangerous limitation of religion is that it is shaped, moulded and impinged on by differing points of view: Cain and Abel saw things from different points of view.

'The second dangerous limitation of religion is that it begets superiority complex; mainly because religious points of view are shaped by different levels of visions, different levels of talents, different tastes and professions, as well as different circumstances and environments.

"Different points of view in religion lead to different understanding of exegesis. Different understanding of exegesis leads to different sects in the same religion. Consequently, humans have never practiced any religion in exactly the same way.

"No religion can be practiced in precisely the same way by all its followers. Each sees their way of worship as the best way. Then superiority complex, the second dangerous limitation of religion, will creep in and cause humans to start killing each other for nothing.

"Every religion excludes some people in one way or another due to human nature.

Cain's view of God differed from that of Abel.
Pharisees' view of worship differs from that of others in Judaism.
Protestants' view of worship differs from that of Catholics in Christianity.
Sunnis' view of worship differs from that of Shiites' in Islam.

"God had absolutely nothing to do with the differences that have emerged in Judaism, Christianity, Islam, or any religion. Every division in every religion was created by humans, shaped by humans, and impinged on by superiority complex, the second dangerous limitation of religion.

"The third dangerous limitation of religion is that it can be highly wasteful of human talents.

"Superiority complex has caused generations of humans to try and impose their view of God and way of worship on others and failed. They all failed. They all wasted human talents vastly. They all killed husbands and created widows. They all murdered parents and created orphans. They all created the problem of poverty for human suffering to accelerate and multiply.

"God has never imposed one form of worship on humans. God has never asked any prophet to impose one form of worship on humans. Any attempt to impose one form of worship on all humans will therefore fail and waste human talents vastly. Those responsible for the waste will then pay dearly for it, come Judgment Day.

"The purpose of this journey is to answer the questions, 'Who are we?' and 'Why are we here?'

"I can now tell you that, whatever excludes one human, let alone millions of humans, in any respect from anything cannot help answer those two questions. Judaism, Christianity, Islam and every religion excludes some humans in some respects, so religion cannot tell us who we are and why we are here on Earth.

"In a world full billions of humans, only what excludes not a single person in any respect whatsoever can tell us who we are and why we are here on Earth. Religion is therefore the first subject to be eliminated, if we want to answer the questions, 'Who are we and why are we here?'"

With that, the Mejai ended the first part of his message.

The whole hall responded with a thunderous applause on their feet, until the Mejai left the stage.

Minutes later, a fifteen-minute break was announced.

Then people throughout the hall started talking about the Mejai and what they had just learnt.

9

HABIBA HAD BEEN stealing looks at Deji-Vita throughout the speech. She caught him taking notes in shorthand, like a journalist; it surprised her no end and distracted her attention.

"Where did he learn to take notes so fast in shorthand at such a young age?" she had wondered. "What made him feel a need for such skills? And why did he carry a notepad with him like a journalist?"

"How did the note-taking go?" she asked him, after the Mejai left the stage.

"Fine," he replied, and changed the subject.

He was born short-sighted but he was shy to tell her. He lost his glasses on his travels and had been struggling to see things from a distance ever since. Sadly for him, they were sitting on the third tier of the Royal Albert Hall, the farthest from where the Mejai was delivering his message to the world. He squinted long and hard but could not see what the Mejai looked like, so he concentrated on taking notes.

"The Egyptian will take me to him later anyway," he had thought to himself. "I'll see what he looks like then."

Habiba engaged him in a conversation throughout the break.

Then fifteen minutes came to pass and the Mejai returned.

A thunderous, welcoming applause subsided and the Mejai bowed his head and mouthed another little prayer.

Then, turning to the crowd, he said, "We've eliminated religion from what can help us answer the questions, 'Who are we?' and 'Why are we here?' Let's now see whether religion's good friend, atheism in its militant form, can help us answer the question."

The hall burst into laughter and became dead silent again.

Then the Mejai continued, "There once lived a man, who fell from a mountain. His injuries were so bad he wanted death to take him from his pain and suffering but did not get his wish.

"While writhing in pain, a herd of elephants came and looked at him and went their own way. Then monkeys, moose and deer came and went their own way. Wildebeest, zebras and all sorts of animals came and looked at him and did exactly the same.

"His eyes soon fell on three huge approaching lions and panic gripped him to no end. Fearing the three lions would make him suffer more by eating him alive, he tried dragging himself into a hole nearby to hide but he could not move. To his great, great astonishment, the three lions did not even bother to give him a look. They just walked pass him and went their own way. He considered the occurrence a miracle and started wondering why.

"Then he caught sight of his fellow man and his hopes soared to the zenith. He was so lifted in spirit he yelled and flailed his hurting hands repeatedly to attract his fellow man's attention to where he was lying injured.

"To his bewilderment, his fellow man walked passed him and went his own way, like the animals did. But then, on this occasion, he lost his temper immediately and started yelling curse and abuse after his fellow man for failing to help him. He was so busy yelling abuse in fury when he felt a sharp pain in the chest and died of heart failure.

"Death came to him but not in the manner that he had wanted. He did not know the man that failed to help him. Yet his heart made demands of the man. And when the demands of his heart were not met, his blood boiled naturally and caused him to yell, curse and abuse, until he succumbed to heart failure

"Note that his blood did not boil when so many animals did nothing to help him. Note that he could not even feign hope when he caught sight of the animals. Yet everything in his blood changed when his eyes fell on his fellow human. The sheer presence of his fellow human raised his hopes so high it resulted in heart failure and death when those hopes were dashed.

"But then his blood boiled naturally, and it boiled badly enough to be able to kill him. He did not feign hope.

"More importantly, he did not die in vain. The manner of his death revealed truths about blood-boiling points.

"Blood-boiling points reveal deep-seated bonds. Blood-boiling points tell us how closely one is related. The closer the bond the higher it can raise hopes. The higher it can raise hopes, the deeper the wounds that can it inflict when the hopes are dashed. Hopes raised high by a deep-seated bond can kill.

"Deep-seated bonds come from shared breath or shared blood. Shared breath and shared blood give hope and stir passion.

"What lacks a deep-seated bond through shared blood or shared breath cannot give hope, cannot get blood to boil and cannot kill through disappointment. In other words, the unconnected cannot stir passion, cannot give confidence and cannot bring about disappointment. Disappointment cannot occur without a link to something.

"The manner of the death of the man who fell from the mountain, therefore, gives us a glimpse of militant atheists' link to God. Subconscious injuries arise from subconscious disappointments. Subconscious disappointments lead to lurking anger.

"Militant atheism is a sign of subconscious injuries inflicted by subconscious hopes raised too high dashed by the world of experience. But where is the bond between God and man? Where is the unbreakable link that stirs passion?

"The unbreakable link between God and man that stirs passion is borrowed breath. As is written in the Scriptures, God lent His breath to Adam. God breathed into Adam's lungs and gave Adam life. Shared breath is the link between God and man.

"High expectations of God, through shared breath, led to militant atheism. But then militant atheism is stirred by blurred vision, a deep disappointment that this world is not as good as it should be, which betrays link to a higher moral force. Hence you get passion and lack of passion in militant atheists when it comes to God and apes.

"Militant atheists can see apes but cannot see God. Yet tell a militant atheist that he owes his existence to God and his blood will boil and cause him to speak in anger. Tell the same militant atheist that he owes his existence to ape and he will feel nothing to speak in anger.

"A human cannot have higher expectations of God, if there is no deep-seated connection between God and man that came through shared breath.

"The man who fell from the mountain had low expectations of animals due to lack of direct link. Low expectations are not potent so low expectation cannot kill. High expectations are potent so high expectations can kill. Both low and high expectations, however, comes from nature. One is connected. The other is unconnected. Connection is the key to behaviour.

"Religion and militant atheism are thus two sides of the same coin; both speak of God but via different routes: Militant Atheism speaks of God *via negativa*. Religion speaks of God *via positive accoutrements*. To the militant atheist, life on Earth should be better than what it is. To the religious, life on Earth could not have been better structured.

"What religion and atheism have in common above all else, however, is the fact that they both exclude some people in thoughts and deeds. Like religion, atheism and militant atheists exclude some humans in their point of view. Consequently, since only what cannot excludes a single human on Earth can tell us *who we are and why we are here on Earth*, we have to eliminate atheism, too, from what can help us answer the question. Atheism, like religion, cannot answer the questions, 'Who are we?' and 'Why are we here?'"

The audience leapt to their feet and started applauding long and hard.

Not long after the crowd became silent again, he looked at them and said, "Let's now look at the mind of man."

Deji-Vita looked at Habiba and Habiba looked at him.

Then the Mejai went on, "What is universally true about the mind of man that applies to every soul, without exception?

"The mind of man is a container first and foremost, which transports *thoughts* and *values* from classes to classes and from one age to another; starting with messages, creations and ideas imparted by one or a few.

"One human will have an idea. Then other humans will *contain* the idea in their minds and start transporting it from classes to classes and from one age to another.

"Another human will deliver a message as a seer or storyteller. Then the mind of man will *contain* the message and start transporting it from classes to classes, and from ages to ages, using utterances, writings, teachings and acts after acts. What keeps making sense in this transportation of ideas exclusive to humans will be retained and transported by the mind of man. What stops making sense at any stage will be dropped by the mind of man and consigned to history.

"See the mind of man as the container and transporter of ideas that it truly is and the inevitable question that will arise is, 'Who is the third agent?'

"The inevitable question, 'Who is the third agent?' will arise for the following reasons. A container and its contents cannot bring themselves together without acts of a third agent. This fact of life applies to wines in wine bottles, as well as the logic of Newtonian physics in the minds of teachers of physics.

"Wine cannot enter bottles without acts of 'the third agent' that is man. And man will not take the trouble to make bottles and put wine in them, if not for the need to consume them on demand. Similarly, Newtonian physics and teachers of physics cannot bring themselves together without acts of a third agent that is totally independent of them and their nature. And the third agent here will not bother to bring the creator of Newtonian physics and teachers of physics together, if physics cannot fit perfectly into other science subjects and combine perfectly with art subjects to give Man a meaningful life on Earth on demand, namely, where man obey rules that make talents retrievable from his head. Here philosophers speak of God:

"God, the supreme third agent that makes all things fit perfectly, apportioned talents in a manner that makes all the Arts and Sciences fit perfectly together to give mankind a meaningful life, except where men fail to obey rules that make talent retrieving possible. Look carefully, if you know what to look for, and you'll find Man only fails to make progress where rules helpful to talent retrieving are either not in place or are not followed.

"What you've just heard today is the ternary intelligible order, which God, the Supreme third agent, imposed on the mind of man.

"God imposed the ternary intelligible order on the mind of man for self-governance to take place among humans on Earth without interference on His part. The ternary intelligible order forms part of what is known in the Bible as 'the Earth is fixed.' The Earth is fixed means immovable rules put in place to govern things and all of God's creations on Earth, so as to avoid constant interference on the part of God.

"Your fathers failed to understand what The Bible meant by 'the Earth is fixed' and they started talking nonsense after nonsense, until it led them into self-misdirection and costly mistakes, which generations of humans are now paying for.

"Angels laugh whenever they are reminded of your fathers' interpretation of 'the Earth is fixed.'

"I therefore feel obliged to give you some examples of what The Bible means by 'The Earth is fixed.' How animals are to get their food is fixed. How humans are to make progress is fixed. Where every journey will end is fixed. It is fixed that humans and animals can only start life through birth. It is fixed for death to follow life. Every aspect of life on Earth was fixed to avoid constant interference on the part of God.

"When it comes to humans and humans alone, it was fixed through the ternary intelligible order that the mind of man must work as follows: only a handful must be creative in a subject; a few more must be capable of teaching the subject; and, finally, the overwhelming majority must be able to benefit from the subject, unless it did not come from the ternary intelligible order imposed by God.

"Look at any subject or field of trade or profession and you'll find the ternary intelligible order rules. God imposed the ternary intelligible order on the mind of man but not on the minds of animals. Hence a handful of animals cannot play music for many animals to dance; one animal cannot compose music for a handful to play or teach; one animal cannot write books for many animals to read and learn from it.

"Until you get a good understanding of the fact that, unlike animals, the ternary intelligible order was imposed to rule the mind of man for a good reason, you cannot answer the questions, 'Who are we?' and 'Why are we here?'"

With that, the Mejai ended the second part of his message for another fifteen-minute break.

Then the whole hall rose and started cheering to the rafters.

10

HABIBA STOLE ANOTHER look at Deji-Vita during the break and smiled to herself. Then it occurred to her to test him.

So she turned to him and said, "I'm starving. Let's go outside and find something to eat."

"No, please endure," he replied, looking shocked.

"Why?" she asked.

He checked his notes.

Then he said, "The Mejai said we need objectives, vacuums and lendables, and the mother of all reasons to answer the questions, 'Who are we and why are we here?' He's still on objectives. And I want to be here when he talks about vacuums and lendables and the mother of all reasons. I want to hear them from the horse's mouth."

"Why?"

"London was badly bombed today by religious terrorists…"

"Yes?"

"If we can answer the questions, 'Who are we?' and 'Why are we here?', it will expose the foolishness of those who kill people in the name of religion. Support for terrorism in the name religion will dwindle, like it did in Europe centuries ago. Then money spent on fighting terrorism can be diverted to education and children's recreation."

"I couldn't agree more. But the Mejai has already proved that religion is *not* the reason why we are here on Earth. He said religion is not even a creation of God."

"That's not enough. We need to answer the questions, 'Who are we?' and 'Why are we here?'. That's the only way ignorant brutes can be put in their place."

"Okay, I'll do my best to endure," Habiba said, feigning disappointment.

"Thank you so much for that," Deji-Vita replied, unaware that he was being tested.

Moments later, the Mejai returned.

Again, he waited, until a welcoming applause had subsided. Then he bowed his head and mouthed yet another little prayer.

Looking at the crowd now, he said, "The next step is vacuums and lendables. And the last step is the mother of all reasons.

"So where did vacuums and lendables come from? They came from a visiting angel that dwelt briefly on Earth. Upon returning to the angels' realm, he said this about humans to his fellow angels:

"Vacuums and lendables:
Every one of them is nescient. None of them has it all.
Each one of them has vacuums that need to be filled by another.
So they go round and round filling vacuums."

The Mejai continued, "There are three vacuums in the lives of humans, namely, obvious vacuums, semi-visible vacuums and concealed vacuums.

"Obvious Vacuums can be found in the differences between male and female bodies. What male bodies lack but can be found in female bodies and vice versa are obvious vacuums. They are known as obvious vacuums because they are before our naked eyes from infancy, and little or no effort are required to detect them.

"Semi-visible vacuums are different. Effort is required to detect them. Effort is required to remove impediments in their way. And effort is required to make them more useful.

"Semi-visible vacuums can be found in every trade and profession. For instance, we cannot tell who is a doctor in our midst, until we are told or seen him or her practice medicine. We cannot tell who is the more gifted or hardest working amongst a group of doctors until we've been presented with results of their work. We can also not tell which individuals are more gifted in different branches of medicine, until we are presented with results of their efforts. Finally, we cannot tell which areas of medicine require more funding, until we are presented with facts and figures.

"Same applies in the field of education. We need comparative studies and data to determine which schools and educational approach are failing pupils. We need to scrutinise resources and environments in which pupils and teachers work to improve standards in education. Efforts are required on our part to know why some countries and communities are more productive than others. That's the nature of semi-visible vacuums: they don't lend themselves to detection. We have to detect them. But there are good reasons for it.

"Visible vacuums and semi-visible vacuums highlight the fact that every human is essentially a Container-that-is-half-empty. And the great difficulty of containers is that *a* container cannot detect its own vacuums.

"The great difficulty of containers applies to barrels containing oil, as well as human minds containing Newtonian physics or Mosaic Law.

"In the world of humans, the great difficulty of containers – the fact that a container cannot detect its own vacuum – has many meanings and manifests itself in different guises.

"The fact that we cannot tell what male bodies lack without female bodies and vice versa gives us one meaning of a container cannot detect its own vacuum.

"The eyes of a man cannot tell him what his own face looks. We need the aid of a mirror to see what our own faces look like. That's another meaning of *'a container cannot detect its own vacuum'*, which leads us to the nature of human talents.

"Human talent has a mirror-effect. Your gifts as an individual act as a mirror to what others have or lack in talent and vice versa. No human can detect his or her vacuums or limitations in talent without talents at the disposal of other humans. This fact is known as the Divine Divide.

"We call it the Divine Divide because God imposed it to separate humans from animals. Humans' gifts have a mirror-effect. Animals' gifts have no mirror-effect. All claims that humans are animals are thus born out of ignorance.

"Owing to the lack of mirror-effect in gifts at the disposal of animals, all animals have the following in common:

"*What one lion cannot teach, every lion cannot teach.*
What one elephant cannot know, all elephants cannot know.
What one cow cannot understand, every cow cannot understand.
What one horse cannot explain, every horse cannot explain.
What one moose cannot make exist, every moose cannot make exist. One lion cannot teach medicine for other lions to become doctors.
One donkey cannot open shops for other donkeys to shop.
One animal cannot play music for many animals to dance."

The Mejai continued, "God denied animals gifts the mirror-effect because the objective behind the creation of man is hugely different from the objective behind the creation of animals. You cannot answer the questions, 'Who are we?' and 'Why are we here?' without understanding the mirror-effect nature of human talents.

"Humans can behave like animals at times. Animals have to behave like animals at all times.

"For humans to behave like animals at times, cruel and unfortunate events and circumstances have to conspire against them (in their past or present) consistently and for a considerable length of time. Cruel and or unfortunate events and circumstances that cause humans to embrace animal-behaviour for long or short periods of times are known as *Clippers*.

"The full name is Clippers of the Human Wings. Because God gave humans two wings to fly that are completely different from the wings that God gave birds to fly:

> "*God gave unto birds wings to fly by way of feathers.*
> *And God gave unto man wings to fly by way of minds.*
> *One of the two wings of the mind is known to man as humanities.*
> *The other wing of the mind is known to man as science.*
> *The scientific wing was meant to prevent the Humanity wing from knowing corruption. And the humanities wing was meant to prevent the scientific wing from knowing corruption. Through both wings, man was expected to rise from humble beginnings and soar in achievements.*"

The Mejai continued, "Clip one of the two wings in the mind that God gave unto man to fly in any community, and humans in that community will degenerate to adopt and embrace conducts and behaviours that are preserves of beasts of the wild.

"Clip the scientific wing of any human community and humans in that clipped-community will degenerate to dwell excessively on religion and fail to soar in the achievements God intended for man. Such a clipped community of humans will harm more, kill senselessly, and tell mindless and harmful lies to their offspring to the detriment of all mankind.

"Conversely, clip the humanities wing and humans in that clipped-community will get blurred visions through warped scientific lenses. They will engage in self-misdirection and selfishness beyond reason for corruption and insanity to abound in their midst. Such clipped-community of humans will sooner or later face a total collapse in humanity. Then they will waste more in talent, harm more in spirit, kill senselessly without a care, and tell mindless and harmful lies to their offspring to the detriment of all mankind.

"Man must learn to fly with both wings of the mind to soar in achievement or face ruin through the total waste talents that will follow. Hence God gave unto each of the two wings means of preventing the other from knowing corruption. Yet, as usual, man has managed to corrupt them both..."

The crowd leapt to their feet and interrupted the Mejai with a very long applause.

Then, after the crowd quietened down again, he looked at them and said:

"Secondary education was meant to follow primary education;
Use of talent was meant to follow training;
Earthly life was meant to be nurture;
Eternal was meant to be the ultimate reward.
Neither nurture nor the life eternal is attainable through coercion.
Heaven is thus filled with the willing, not the compelled.
Hence God imposed concealed vacuums on man.

71

Concealed vacuums test different generations of humans differently.

"Concealed vacuums are the last of the three vacuums that rule the lives of humans. Concealed vacuums are what human minds and eyes cannot detect – no matter how hard they work, no matter how hard they look – until the appointed time of God.

"Concealed vacuums are about how to test different generations differently. Concealed vacuums are therefore known as the secret weapons of God.

"On the scientific wing, a typical concealed vacuums can be found in the gap between the works of Isaac Newton and Albert Einstein. Scientists were unable to detect vacuums in Newtonian physics for over a century, until Albert Einstein came into prominence. By then, generations of humans had gone to their graves in their millions thinking Newtonian physics had no vacuums.

"On the humanities wing, concealed Vacuums can be found in the gap between Mosaic Law and the birth of Christ. For centuries, readers of the Bible could not detect vacuums in The Ten Commandments. Then Jesus came and showed how the Ten Commandments given unto Moses were not given in their fullest form. By the time Jesus came to reveal concealed vacuums in the Ten Commandments, generations of humans have died thinking the Ten Commandments had no vacuums in them at all.

"Concealed vacuums require divine intervention. Divine intervention depends on appointed time of God. However, divine intervention does not always require religious acts or religious individuals. For concealed vacuums deal with *time* and time alone, meaning people of a generation or generations, not religion. And concealed vacuums deal with time in centuries and millenniums.

"Hence, on the humanities wing, there was a huge gap

between when the Ten Commandments were given unto Moses and when Jesus was born. On the scientific wing, a century passed before the works of Albert Einstein revealed vacuums in the works of Isaac Newton.

"Centuries or millenniums are allowed to elapse before concealed vacuums are revealed in order to *test* different generations differently. Testing of different generations differently is the reason why revealing concealed vacuums is not always dependent on religion or religious individuals.

"Concealed vacuums demonstrate to humans that they cannot know God through their own volition. The mind of man cannot know anything about God through hard work. Therefore no human is allowed to impose his view of God on other humans in any shape or form.

"Minds that *failed* to detect vacuums in The Ten Commandments for centuries, until Jesus came to expose them, cannot begin to imagine what God looks like, let alone tell what God can do or cannot do. Minds that *failed* to detect vacuums in Newtonian physics for over a century, until Albert Einstein was born, cannot even begin to imagine the vastness God and what God looks like, let alone tell God why it's in God's best interest to intervene in what goes on in this world..."

The crowd interrupted the Mejai with another long applause.

Then, looking at them, he said, "Revelations are the only means by which humans can know anything about God.

"Ye are gods. And ye are also men.
There are times to speak to you as gods.
And there are times to speak to you as men.
When we speak to you as men, we speak to creations of God.
When we speak to you as gods, we speak to creators in their own right.

73

Ye men, as creators, command and make demands of your creations.

Ye men predetermine things for your creations and give reasons why.

Ye impose capabilities and limitations on your creations.

Ye predetermine needs of your creations.

Ye decide whether your creation is to be powered by fuel or by battery.

Ye decide whether your creations are to be serviced monthly or yearly.

Ye predetermined and preordained what became of every machine.

What ye men do to machines God did first to you.

God predetermined and preordained what will become of man.

God predetermined that ye men should have vacuums.

God preordained that ye men should be lendable.

God imposed concealed vacuums on your minds.

God programmed you to be dependent on the Mother of All Reasons."

The Mejai continued, "Faith rules the earth and all human journeys. Nothing begins without faith. All human achievements depend on faith. And faith comes in the guise of belief as well as confidence.

"A man of science is a man from faith heading towards reason. A man of faith is a man from reason ruled by confidence. Confidence is the first-born of faith; all talents know ruin without it. Every successful artist or scientist gives belief to others to embark on scientific or artistic journeys of their own. Faith devoid of worship is thus the mother of all reasons.

"Without faith, the mother of all reasons, men start nothing to end up with nothing. Nothing can be built or endured without faith. Hence religion gave birth to science and not the other way round.

"The mother and child relationship between faith and science thus require special attention. Progress retards to the point of madness when religion is misused or abused to stifle science. Life becomes insane and tasteless when science is misused and abused to stifle faith.

"A man of faith who wants to kill science is a deranged parent courting ruin. A man of science who wants to destroy faith is a jealous child that will self-destruct. There is no science where a claim is not governed by tangible facts.

Fact dictates that faith rules more than facts.
Fact dictates that faith conquers more than facts.
Fact dictates that faith will always conquer more than fact.
Fact dictates that faith has more followers than science.
It's thus incurable insanity to want to make science as popular as faith."

With that, the Mejai retrieved a large brown envelope.

Then, having waved the large brown envelope for all to see, he said, "I leave these shores a day after tomorrow. Before my departure, I will seal and entrust this brown envelope to the founder and leader of this movement, Professor Trevor Huddleston. I showed you my brown envelope because you'll all need one of your own and I'll tell you why.

"In my brown envelope will be how to use everything you've heard today – from objective, vacuums and lendables and the mother of all reason – to work out who we are and why we are here on Earth.

"Try and answer the questions by yourselves, using objective, vacuums and lendables and, finally, the mother of all reasons. Seal your conclusions in your brown envelope and sign where it was sealed. Then send your sealed and signed brown envelope to a friend or colleague by a date to be provided by Professor Huddleston.

"Because there are millions of you in this great movement around the world, please meet in a group of a hundred at different venues near you. Then, to the hearing of ninety-nine people, let each read his or her friend's conclusions on 'Who are we?' and 'Why are we here?' on Earth.

"Try and be systematic in how you arrive at your conclusions. And write no more than five pages. The replies of each and every one of you will be turned into a book of volumes, so that generations of humans can read what the first humans to be provided with the correct materials for working out 'Who are we?' and 'Why are we here?' did with the revelation.

"Conclusions that are similar will be placed in the same volumes to make counting of similar minds easier. Each volume will be a thousand pages long and will be called *Similar Minds*. Conclusions that are the same as mine or close to mine shall be judged as the winning volume or volumes.

"Why must we all engage in this exercise and take it seriously? And why has it now become necessary to give humans the correct materials for working out who we are and why we are here?

"The bombing of London today by terrorists is a prime reason. They cited religion, not demons, as the reason why they are bombing towns and cities across the world. That's why we must do this and do it together with those who differ in faith but have faith, as well as with those who have no faith at all. Thank you for coming and goodnight."

The whole hall went wild and cheered. Then soon he was gone.

11

DEJI-VITA THOUGHT he would be taken to meet the Mejai straight after the event, so he started praying silently in his heart, asking God not to let the devil pull any tricks and delay matters.

"Where's the other boy anyway?" he wondered. "Is he here with us in this hall? If he's here, then the devil, who was the mastermind behind the bombing of London with spiritual powers, sat in this nice hall among peaceful people and listened to the Mejai, which will not be fair."

A man came and whispered in Habiba's ear.

Then Habiba turned to Deji-Vita and said, "Let' go home."

Shocked, he replied, "I thought I was going to be taken to see the Mejai after..."

"We're coming back tomorrow," Habiba interrupted.

"We are coming back tomorrow?"

"Today was about what he must do for those who want peace. Tomorrow is the people's question and answer session with the Mejai. Tomorrow he will deliver a message to killers of the True Holy War."

Deji-Vita rubbed his hands with glee.

But he was a little disappointed. He wanted to meet the Mejai straight after the speech because of the treasure. He was, also, itching to meet the other boy and see for himself why the Egyptian said the boy looks like his identical twin. Besides, there were questions that he would like to ask the other boy right in front of the Mejai.

Fiffy, meanwhile, could not sleep. She had not been sleeping well at all since Deji-Vita set foot in the house.

The other girls said she was in love. She said, "No, no, no, no."

They insisted she was in love. She insisted she was not.

At one o'clock in the morning, Habiba and Deji-Vita returned home to the mansion to find her watching television in the living room all alone.

Holly and Anoushka had since told Habiba that they believed Fiffy was madly in love with the boy. And they strongly recommended a large dose of 'leave them alone' for Habiba.

So Habiba took one look at her and the boy and said goodnight.

They talked, they pried, they joked, and they laughed. He read some of his notes from the Royal Albert Hall to her and told her how magnificent the Mejai was as a teacher.

Then she looked at him and said, "We are coming with you tomorrow."

"You are coming with us tomorrow?"

"We are all coming with you and Habiba tomorrow. We were sent tickets for the Mejai's last public performance moments after you and Habiba left the house."

"Who sent them to you?"

"A courier brought them on a motorbike. You and Habiba are among the lucky few to be given tickets for both the first and last public performance of the Mejai. I'm content with that. I want to ask him about God and suicide bombers."

"I bet someone will ask that question before you do," he said.

Moments later, they went their separate ways to get some sleep.

12

DEJI-VITA NEEDED no more than four hours sleep from an early age, so, after a deep four hours sleep, he made himself a strong cup of tea, after brushing his teeth. Then he started reading *The Mejai* yet again.

According to the fourth chapter of the book, there once lived a man who became unable to stop himself from committing crime. He first went into juvenile detention centre when he was twelve. And he never again spent more than three months outside a prison yard. He never got a job. He never spent a birthday outside a prison yard. And he always managed to commit crimes that left judges with no choice but to send him back to prison.

One day, only two days after he was released from prison, he decided to sample prison life abroad at the instigation of a friend. He was forty-four years old but had never travelled outside his country in his life.

During the course of his journey, he ended up in a country called Where No Human Can Be Defiled at night. He became desperate for a drink but did not have a penny. He walked into a tavern and ordered a drink. Then he tried to rob a man of his wallet and the man resisted. He broke the man's jaw badly in the tavern and waited for the police to be called.

The matter ended up in court. And he asked the judge not to waste his time and send him to prison. The judge was shocked because the prison system was abolished in the country a long time ago. And dwellers of the land – citizens and guests alike – were supposed to know that under the law.

So the judge looked at him and said, "When you crossed the border into this country, you were given a small pamphlet. Did you not read it?"

"No," he said

The trial was conducted and he was found guilty.

Then the judge looked at him and said, "What do you know about jail house tenants?"

"Nothing," he said.

"Have you heard about jail house rent?"

"No," he said,

"What about the three for one rule, do you know about it?"

"No," he said,

"Are you conversant with Victims Law?"

"No," he said,

The judge looked at the clock, calmly, and started timing what he was about to say, because it would cost the jawbreaker quite a lot.

Then the judge began, "Had you read the pamphlet that was given to you at the border, you would have known about God-given human rights. Through that, you would have realised why we abolished prisons for good in this country. What we have here are jail houses and jail house tenants.

"As a tenant in one of our jail houses, you will never be allowed to lose an iota of your God-given human rights. That means you will not be allowed to stare at toilets in your room. You will never slop out. You will not be put in positions where you could be raped or witness rape or fear being raped. You will not be put in situations where you could be bullied by anyone. You will not be allowed to be abused by other jail house tenants. You will not be allowed to be insulted or abused by any staff of the jail house."

The judge continued, "You cannot be forced to share anything that you don't want to share. You can order food of any quality that you want. You can order African food, Asian food, European food, American food, Chinese food, Australian food or Indian food. But you will have to pay for every food that you order whether you eat it or not. You will pay rent as a jail house tenant. You will pay water and electricity bills. You will pay for your transportation costs whenever you have to be transported anywhere. You will pay for everything that those who have not committed crime pay for every day and every night. Your room will be very nice…"

"I did not ask to be put in a nice place, so why make me to pay for it?" he asked the judge.

"Demons find it easier to harbour people in harsh and inhumane conditions, like prison yards," the judge replied. "If we put you in harsh and inhumane conditions, demons will find it easy to harbour you and weaken you in mind, body and spirit. Then you will find it hard to stop committing crime. You will commit crime time and time again to be housed and fed by the taxpayer. That, we say, is not fair on victims of crime and the taxpayer."

"I don't have money to pay for my food and my rent in a jail house," he said.

"We'll come to all that," the judge replied. "First of all, under the three for one rule, you owe the victim of your crime three times the amount of what you stole or tried to steal from him…"

"What?" he yelled.

"You also owe him three times the amount of what your crime has caused him…"

"What?" he interrupted.

"The victim of your crime," the judge continued, "is a senior doctor. He became unfit for work for three months due to the crime that you chose to commit. You therefore owe him *three times* his monthly salary as a senior doctor, as well as *three times* the amount of the money that you tried to steal from him."

"This is robbery," he yelled in anger. "This is so wrong."

The judge continued, "Now, I'll to tell you how you're going to get a job in a minute. Before I do that, this is what is going to happen when you start working as a jail house tenant. The Victim of your crime works for a hospital, which has to pay his salary while he's unfit for work because of your crime. Come the end of each month, your monthly salary will be paid into your jail house account, which will be affixed to your jail house tenancy number.

"Seventy-five per cent of what you earn every month will be paid from your jail house account to the hospital, because the hospital is paying the salary of the Victim of your crime while he's off sick because of your crime.

"The remaining twenty-five per cent in your jail house account will cater for your expenses but not your rent. Once the employer, the hospital in this case, has been paid in full, the seventy-five per cent payments from your jail house account will be paid directly into the senior doctor's bank account.

"This senior doctor's salary is £3,000 a month, so, under the Three Times Rule, you've come to owe him £9,000.

"£9,000 a month for three months comes to £27,000. The hospital gets back the £9,000 three months' salary that it paid the doctor while he was off sick for three months due to your crime. The doctor gets £18,000 in addition to his monthly salary due to crime that you chose to commit."

"This is a joke," he yelled, "a big, big joke."

The judge ignored him and continued, "Once the victim of your crime is paid in full, the state will start deducting jail house rent from your jail house account. Seventy-five per cent of your monthly salary will be deducted as jail house rent.

"Once jail house rent owed had been recovered in full, seventy-five per cent of your monthly salary will go directly into paying for food that you ordered, soap that you ordered, electricity bills and so and so forth, until the day the jail house landlord can say to you: '*You have now paid all rent arrears and all jail house debts owed in full, so leave now.*'"

"Whose idea was this?" he yelled.

"Our philosophers worked it all out," said the judge. "They worked out the Three Times Rule from nature…"

"What, human nature?" he sneered.

"Well, according to our philosophers, victims of crime suffer unwanted thoughts as a result of human nature. Unwanted thoughts rob people of enjoyment of life, which, in turn, adversely affects individuals' productivity. Furthermore, crime interferes in people's lives through fear of crime.

"Above all, fear of crime causes harm to health more than crime itself; this because humans are born without knowledge of crime. Crime drags minds of victims of crime into a hitherto unknown murky world of fear, which brings about numerous stress-related illnesses.

"Stress-related illnesses in turn rob governments and taxpayers of cash through rising health bills in clinics and hospitals and medications that have to be provided through the National Health Service.

"In addition to all that, humans differ when it comes to recovery from stress-related illnesses; this is because humans are born divided into different personality groups and different sub-personality groups. Consequently, doctors can seldom predict accurately who will recover fully from stress-related illnesses caused by crime and fear of crime and who will not.

"So sometimes the state pays highly for one *small crime* due to the personality and sub-personality group that a victim of crime belongs to, sometimes the state pays less in health bills for *big crimes* due to the robust nature of the victim of crime. But the state and taxpayers get hit in the pocket in health bills and lower productivity rates of victims of crime each time a crime is committed.

"A state cannot tell who will be made poorer in health and in wealth creation because of crime and fear of crime, so our philosophers decided the fairest administration of justice is to impose Standard Help for all victims of crime. Hence the Three Times Rule.

"The Three Times Rule compensates for lost peace; then what was stolen or what the crime perpetrator tried to steal; and then, finally, the dangerous consequences of detrimental distraction syndromes.

"Crime and fear of crime causes distraction syndromes – unwanted thoughts that affects people's ability to generate wealth for themselves and for their loved ones, some humans become more prone to distractions than others after becoming victims of crime. The less wealth such people generate in a lifetime due to crime, the higher the burden that their offspring and the state will have to shoulder in the future.

"Crime and fear of crime therefore causes lower collection in taxes while increasing the state's bills in education, healthcare and state benefits that has to be paid to unfortunate offspring of past and present victims of crime at the same time, so, as you can see, crime costs nations a lot, sometimes even more than war..."

"This is daylight robbery," the jawbreaker yelled.

"No," said the judge. "Taxes are payments made under communal contract. A communal contract is a pure business arrangement between the state and the taxpayer, who expects to be protected from crime and the fear of crime. Taxes to be paid upon gaining employment are a part of that communal contract.

"Consequently, whenever a person becomes a victim of

crime, the government has failed to deliver a service that the person or his guardians or relatives or loved ones had already paid for in taxes. He who paid for what was *not delivered* has right to reimbursement.

"A state cannot have its eyes and ears everywhere to deliver a crime-free society. Most crimes cost more than three times the monetary value of what was stolen or destroyed or harmed. Costs of security measures in banks and shops because of crime and fear of crime, in most cases, costs three times more than what a thief managed to steal, so our philosophers opted for standard help for all victims of crime.

"Standardised help for all victims of crime ensures swift administration of justice for three main reasons.

"Firstly, judges are humans, too; judges can suffer from human failings, just like everyone else. A judge suffering from hatred for a person or a people on racial or religious grounds could allow his hatred to influence his or her decision. Such twisted judges could lower payments due to a victim of crime or, conversely, inflate the appropriate amount that should be paid by a crime perpetrator. No society, which needs its entire people to remain strong and integrated, can let that happen.

"Secondly, it is not justice to ask victims of crime to sue perpetrators of crime before they can recover losses they incurred because of crime. It is also brutal to ask the poor to sue before getting justice, after paying taxes or expected to pay taxes to be protected from crime and fear of crime. Suing crime perpetrators causes victims of crime to suffer twice through added stress, which is no justice at all.

"Thirdly, and above all, no human can measure punishment accurately by the number of days or years spent behind bars. Hence those who are sent to jail houses in this country are told before leaving court, *'You are to stay in a jail house, until you've paid in full what you've come to owe victims of your crime, as well as your rent and bills'*. What a person has to pay the victim or victims of his crime determines the length of his stay in a jail house."

"How am I to get a job?" he asked the judge.

"Jail house tenants must be considered fairly under law for employment by all on government contracts. Any private firm, small or large, can hire your services. You are to be treated like any employee and are entitled to full pay. No one will dare abuse your God-given human rights, knowing what it will cost them under the Three Times Rule. Farmers, butchers, hotels, cleaning companies, laundries and laundrettes can all employ you to work from a jail house. We have everything in there. You just wouldn't have right to continuous employment, after leaving the jail house."

"Where am I to work?" he asked the judge.

"There are jobs that can be taken to a jail house for you to do," said the judge. "And there are jobs that you could be transported to a workplace to do, if you are assessed not to be a flight risk. I guarantee you will start work before one week is over. You will see that I'm telling the truth."

"What if I abscond?"

"If you abscond, the victim of your crime will have to be paid in full at once by the government. Then officers found responsible for your absconding will pay the government three times what the government had to pay the victim of your crime from a jail house. I will, however, advice against absconding."

"Why?"

"If you are caught after absconding, you will have to pay the officers responsible three times what they had to pay the government, in addition to three times what it cost the state to recapture you. Anymore questions?"

"No," he said.

"Good," said the judge. "Now, when you entered this country, you were given a sky blue pamphlet at the border and you were advised to read it to protect your God-given human rights and that of others. You refused to read it and became a danger to others in our streets. I therefore had to spend the time of this court telling you things that all dwellers of this land, citizens and guests alike, are required to know under law. There's a price to pay for breaking this law. The price will be spelt out at another hearing in this court. A hearing date will be sent to your new address in the jail house, and you will be brought before me for that hearing."

With that, the judge hardened the look on his face and asked for the thief and jawbreaker to be taken away.

The jawbreaker arrived at his new home to find a jail house built for five hundred tenants had less than fifty tenants in it.

"Where are all my fellow thieves?" he asked a new neighbour.

"Thieving no longer pays here, my friend, so they've all migrated," the new neighbour replied.

"I came to the wrong country for my trade as a professional thief."

"Yes. It takes about five to ten years to pay for theft here."

"Why are they so cruel to our noble profession in this country?"

"Well, according to their philosophers, if you want to stop petty thieves from graduating into big time crooks, you have to make small crime extremely expensive. That's why the jail house is so empty. No more crook graduates."

"Have you lived in a better place than this in your life?"

"No. It's the best and cleanest place I've ever lived in. From what I've seen on TV while here, it's better than some five-star hotels in this country."

"That's the thing. You choose your hotel but you can't choose this one."

"Well, you're not put here for yourself. You're put here to be in good health to work and pay what you owe victims of your crime. According to their philosophers, demons find it easier to enter humans in harsh and inhumane conditions. Demons, they say, make us see thieving as a noble profession.

"Demons, they say, make us commit crime time and time again for others to suffer and live in fear for their lives, so they abolished prisons. They protect your God-given human rights like you're a king to stop demons from entering you. I used to reoffend like a demon, until prison was abolished here."

"Are you saying you are now clean of demons?"

"I don't know whether I'm free of demons or not. But I no longer get a strong urge to steal something or harm somebody. I don't feel like a zombie anymore. I don't blame anybody for my problems anymore."

"How long have you been here now?"

"I've been here for seven years now, working to pay a nurse £21,000 for a robbery that cost her £7,000. But I live in a nice, clean place. I can order any good food I want. I just cannot be out there thieving and harming people. By the time I finish paying my owed rent and bills I would have done about ten years."

"Would you like to come back here?"

"No. I rather work and use the money to enjoy life than work to pay someone to enjoy life for me."

"We used to do that to them, didn't we? We thieves used to enjoy life at their expense."

"Now they are wise, can you believe it? Now they leave their doors open. Ten thieves walked into open doors and end up here to work for the house owners. Now you can leave the door to your house open for a year in this country and no one will go in."

"They set a trap for us?"

"There are four always busy cooks in this jail house that were stupid enough to walk into the trap. They are here now working eight to twelve hours a day to pay others to enjoy life for them. How stupid is that?"

"Maybe their demons were still in them at the time?"

"Well, no thief has come here for that sort of crime in three years now."

"Who was the last thief to come into this jail house before me?"

"A terrorist…"

"I said the last thief to come here before me…"

"I heard you the first time. In this country, terrorism is a theft war, whether it was done in the name of religion or not…"

"Theft of what…?"

"Terrorism is a theft of other people's liberty and sanity, their philosophers say…"

"So the last thief to come here before me stole liberty and sanity."

"Yes."

"What did it cost him?"

The thief neighbour fell down laughing.

"Why are you laughing?"

"Cost of all the dead was calculated. Cost of all the maimed was calculated. Cost of all the injured was calculated. Costs to the police, hospitals, ambulances and paramedics were calculated. Cost of all damages done by the bomb was calculated…"

"What did he bomb?"

"They bombed an airport and came to owe over three billion pounds…"

"What? He should have killed himself."

"If he kills himself how can he go on terrorising people? His demons kept him alive… so that they can use him to kill people and make others live in fear, said the judge who sentenced him to what he has to pay."

"How was he caught?"

"The Seventy-five Per cent Rule. Under the Seventy-five Per cent Rule, if you provide information that leads to anyone that was part of a crime, seventy-five per cent of what you'll have to pay from a jail house will move on to that person if convicted.

If he, in turn, supplies information that leads to the capture of another member of the group, he will have what he owes reduced by seventy-five per cent. Nobody declares allegiance to a terrorist group in this country because of the Seventy-five Per cent Rule."

"What will happen, if you declare allegiance?"

"You will share in the total cost of any damage that they did, and you'll end up in a jail house to start paying what will be calculated as your share."

"Who gets paid first?"

"Families of the dead get paid first; then the maimed and injured before damaged properties. But the idea behind it is not money, said the judge. The idea behind it is to stop support for terrorist groups that want to impose their way of life on the country. If you are caught with any material or thing that supports or give succour to any terrorist group anywhere on Earth, you are liable to share in the total costs of any crime that they commit. They wont allow criminals to be fed and housed for free by the very people that they want to live in fear. What skills have you got, by the way?"

"I've got no skills."

"That's the thing. Like you, I was too busy thieving things to have time for skills. I nearly beat a nurse to death in her own home, while robbing her of what she's been working hard for since her college days. Now, due to lack of skills, I'm here working in a jail house laundrette for hotels to pay her £21,000.

"The lower your earnings as a person without skills, the longer the time you'll spend in a jail house working to pay victim or victims of your crime. You have no skills and you beat up a senior doctor, after trying to rob him of his wallet? Senior doctors' salaries are huge."

"I didn't know he was a senior doctor, did I?"

"You may have to do three jobs a day, if you want to get out of here in ten years."

The two thieves chatted, until they had to go to bed early, because they both had jobs to go to first thing in the morning to pay back victims of their crimes.

Deji-Vita put the book down and became pensive.

Then he thought to himself, "I like this way of tackling crime. Everybody's God-given human rights are well protected by it."

Moments later, he went back and read the last thing that the Mejai said to Professor Huddleston in Birmingham: *"We build ceaselessly. Demons destroy relentlessly. We must therefore make haste to deliver laws that are fit for purpose urgently. Else fire for fire will burn the whole house of Abraham down before men know where they are. Then they will find the alternative a horrible nightmare."*

Then he said to himself, "The Mejai did this for Abraham, for everything he did for Jews, Christians and Muslims and the civilised world."

13

HE READ TWO more chapters. Then Fiffy called him on the phone and he went downstairs at her invitation to join the girls for breakfast. Not long after they finished eating, Fiffy rose to her feet and started pouring tea for everybody.

Then Holly turned to Deji-Vita and said, "Why did God not make us naked?"

"I beg your pardon?" he replied, looking stunned by the question.

Fiffy chuckled and sat back down. Then Holly repeated the question.

"God made us naked," he replied at the second time of asking.

"No," Holly retorted, "horses do not wear clothes yet their private parts do not become visible, until they get an erection. If God is against choice, why did He not make us like horses?"

"May I ask what prompted the question?" he asked.

"The bombing of London did," Holly replied.

"Would you be kind to tell me why it did?"

"Yes. The terrorists that bombed our country left a video message. They said they hate our way of life, especially the way

93

we dress. So, if God did not want us to have choice in how we dress, why did He not make us like horses?"

"God gave you choice," he said. "God gave every human choice."

"Then why is He allowing His people to bomb us for wearing skirts? Why give us choice and let us be bombed for choosing what we want to wear?"

"They are not God's people."

"They are. They call God's name before and after every bombing."

"It doesn't make them God's people. Anyone can call God's name anytime he wants. The time to deal with the calling of God's name in vain is Judgment Day. Not now."

"You don't know that they are not God's people."

"I do."

"How did you know that they are not God's people?"

"If they are God's people, they will know that choice starts with the eye, not with dress. Choice begins with what you choose to view with your eyes because God put every human in full and total control of his eyes. The strong in spirit exercises choice by taking their eyes away from what they consider temptation. The weak in spirit keep their eyes on what they consider temptation and keep moaning. But then empty barrels make the most noise."

Fiffy smiled and looked delighted with his reply.

Then he added, "Exercising the choice of taking your eyes away from what you consider temptation is the easiest of all to make, unless you are an empty barrel that makes the most noise. Your tormentors are the weakest men in spirit to ever walk the face of the earth, bar none."

Fiffy giggled this time. Anoushka chuckled.

Then Holly said, "Why does one God need many prophets? And why does one God need different religions that cannot agree on a lot of things?"

"God has no religion," he replied. "In fact, the Mejai proved last night that religion is not even a creation of God. Prophets are messengers sent to different people for different reasons. Prophets are not sent to all humans for every wrong that exist in this world. God does not behave like that…"

"How does God behave?" Holly interrupted.

"If God has never sent a prophet to a people before, but sees reason to do so, the first message that He will send to them through a prophet will be detailed. And the only reason for it is to give them a window into of His character and why He so behaves. If God has sent prophets to a people before, the new prophet will only deal with specific issues that came to dog the people on their travels. That's how we came to have many prophets."

"And why do they not all agree?" Anoushka asked.

"The prophets have no disagreement with each other. They were messengers who delivered what they were asked to deliver. People, who want others to think they are bigger than what they are are the ones who end up crazy to start shouting and shooting at people.

"Anyone who tries to make his religion bigger than what it was meant to be will go mad; he will become so crazy, like a man who needs to be in a mental asylum, and he will start doing crazy things all over the world.

"Why does God not kill them, full stop?" Holly said.

"God did not kill Cain when Cain went crazy and killed Abel because of an offering. God has no need to rush and punish people made crazy by religion because He can raise anyone that they kill from the dead and compensate him with eternal life, the Mejai said. God has endless time. He will wait patiently for the crazy fools to die, then He will raise them from the dead, punish them for all to see and then extinguish them from existence all together to be totally and completely no more."

"I told you," Fiffy said to Holly and Anoushka.

Before inviting Deji-Vita to join them for breakfast, Fiffy told Holly and Anoushka that there was no question about God that he could not answer with confidence to perfection. They did not believe her. They teased her and said she was only saying that because she was blinded by love.

Now she felt totally vindicated.

So she made a loud, happy noise like an opera singer, which amused everybody in the dinning room and they all fell apart laughing.

14

HOLLY AND ANOUSHKA were not finished with the boy just yet. Anoushka had a tale to tell, which she felt would test his knowledge to the limit.

Three months' rain fell in two days on a city in Africa. Every home in the city was buried under water. Homes of the good, the bad, the rich and the poor alike were taken over by a terrifying flood.

The rich took flight abroad and stayed in hotels and in their holiday homes.

The poor had nowhere to go.

The poor wallowed in mud and wailed. The poor starved and begged for food in tears because the flood took every food and property they had away.

The rich replaced everything they lost when the flooding finally ended, except what money could not buy.

The poor were left with no money, no mat, no bed, no chairs, no table, no food, no cooking facilities, and no clothes, apart from what they were wearing before the flood came and chased them out of town.

Children of the poor died of hunger and disease in their

thousands. Those who survived became so badly malnourished Anoushka found it excruciating just to look at them on TV.

Anoushka told their story with great passion, and depicted their plights like she was representing them in a court of law.

Then she said to Deji-Vita, "Why did God not send prophets to them? Why did God not stop the rain that took their things?"

"Strange you put this question to me now," he replied.

"Why?" Holy and Anoushka asked in unison.

"I read the fifth chapter, the chapter on consequences in *The Mejai*, in this very house. And it opened my eyes to things that I did not know before."

"I don't understand," Anoushka said.

"Okay," he sighed. "According to the Mejai in the chapter on consequences, we humans have birthright accounts in spirit that rules our scales of good and bad fortune, because God pays us in advance with talents prior to birth and talents paid to us in advance are for good deeds only.

"So, if you engage in good deeds, as you must with your talents, debts in your birthright account will go down. If you fail to engage in good deeds with your talents, as you mustn't, debts in your birthright account will go up. The scale of fortune thus changes with levels of debts in individual's birthright accounts.

"If your bad fortune outweighs your good fortunes on the scale, misfortunes will rise in your life and you'll know hard luck more than good luck. If the reverse is true, you'll know good fortune more than hard luck.

"The big problem here is this. We take our scales of good and bad fortune on our travels and into all relationships, ventures, communities and countries. If the combined bad fortunes of a couple or people or community or country outweighs their good fortunes on the scale, they will know bad fortune than good fortune and vice versa.

"Now... do you know where it all becomes extremely

dangerous for the poor and the innocent, especially children, like it happened in the flood?"

"No," the girls replied in unison.

"We humans are made of spirit and matter. The spirit aspect of our nature makes a part of the air that we live in. The spirit aspect of our nature forms hidden walls when we come together as a group, community or country. Hidden walls, said the Mejai, are living structures invisible to the naked human eye. They form through spirits of individuals. And they protect humans in spirit from what can come and destroy them in spirit.

"Hidden Walls form quickly. And they are strengthened or weakened by deeds of individuals within the group, community or country.

"If the combined bad deeds of a group, community or country outweigh their good deeds, it will start damaging their hidden walls. Then all sorts of bad luck will start bedevilling them. If the reverse is the case, they will know good fortune more often than not.

"Dreams and aspirations of individuals affect their hidden walls one way or another. Customs, culture and traditions affect hidden walls even more. Why? People do good and evil through customs, culture and tradition daily. If a people's custom, culture or tradition is unfair or abuses God-given human rights of others, it will weaken their hidden wall each time it is practiced. Consequently, the people will become bedevilled by hard luck and they will be unable to smell danger until danger is at their doorstep.

"Laws and decisions of rulers and lawmakers carry more weight on the scale of fortune than any other. Bad rules weaken hidden walls faster. Good rules strengthen hidden walls faster. And this is where the biggest problems of the poor and powerless of this world stem from.

"The more cruel leaders or powerful people enact laws that violate God-given human rights of others, the more they will do damage to hidden walls of the people as a whole for everybody to suffer the consequences like floods comes to town. When flood comes to town, it affects homes and properties of the good, the bad, the rich and the poor alike. But the poor always pays the highest price by far. Same applies when bad luck afflicts a people or a community or country, like a flood, due to evil laws, bad customs and traditions or cruel deeds of their rulers and lawmakers."

"Why did God structure things this way?" Anoushka asked.

"God structured things this way to make us *responsible* for our actions and inactions. God structured things this way to avoid constant interference in our lives on His part. *What you sow is what you reap.* If you allow a few cruel people to make bad laws in your name, you will pay for it through damages to your hidden walls that will ensue. If you allow cruel custom, culture and traditions to deny others of their God-given human rights, you will pay for it through your damaged hidden walls for hard luck to dog your lives, community or country, until you take responsibility to change all bad practices.

"It's unfair to interfere in the lives of humans, if you've already decided to reward or punish them after death on Judgment Day, so God did right."

"So you are saying customs, culture and traditions that violate God-given human rights of others brought bad luck to all the people in that African country, and the poor paid the highest price, as they always do," Fiffy said.

"Yes. Africa has her fair share of very nice people. God put me where I can see that for myself. But great, great evil in so-called customs, culture and traditions and evil deeds of cruel rulers breached people's God-given human rights and damaged hidden walls of countries throughout the continent."

"What great, great evil are you referring to?" Anoushka asked.

"Humans sacrificed to idols; slavery; trafficking of humans

into slavery across lands and seas; satanic female genital mutilation; customs and traditions that give brutal, unfair advantages to men. All served to damage hidden walls of Africa and brought chilling bad luck to the people."

"How did female genital mutilation form part of what destroyed Africa's hidden walls and brought bad luck to the people?" Anoushka asked.

"Please call it satanic female genital mutilation."

"Why?"

"It dilutes and destroys women's spiritual ability to protect their offspring. Whatever dilutes and destroys human's spiritual ability to protect their selves and their offspring, as God intended, is satanic, the Mejai said."

"Okay, answer the question now," said Anoushka

"Satanic female genital mutilation is a gross abuse of a person's God-given human rights. Again, it dilutes and destroys women's spiritual ability to protect their offspring. It puts children's future at risk through destroyed and diluted strengths of their mothers, and breaches children's God-given human rights in the process; all damage the hidden walls for bad luck to ensue."

"Why did they start satanic female genital mutilation?" Holly asked.

"The devil tricked them into it, knowing it will bring them bad luck in abundance. It started as a controlling device for serving interests of ignorant men. Then it was cooked up as a tradition that brings people together. Then it was wrapped in a total nonsense that it makes children belong to a community. A community that shares not income equally among children but forces them to share pain equally is a tool of the devil."

The girls chuckled.

Then he said, "The devil tricked them into so many evil customs, culture and traditions that bring bad luck to make them suffer. To this day, there are many women who suffered

Satanic Female Genital Mutilation in childhood, who want to see their kids and all kids suffer the same fate."

"That's evil," Anoushka snarled, looking disgusted.

"Such women are satanic soldiers," he said.

"Can damaged hidden walls be repaired?" Anoushka asked.

"Yes. Damaged hidden walls are repairable through laws that restore people's God-given human rights. The further you distance yourselves from what damaged your hidden walls in the first place, said the Mejai, the more you will find your fortunes changing for the better."

"Can the poor play a role in this?" Anoushka asked, looking sad.

"Yes. The poor's role in it is the most vital, the Mejai said. The poor are in the overwhelming majority, which gives them voting power. They suffer the most from bad luck flood and always will, so their most important role is to fight to earn the right to elect their leaders, monitor the behaviour of their leaders religiously, and scrutinise laws passed in their name like their lives depend on it."

"What if their rulers refuse to yield and try to bully them, like religious terrorists are trying to bully us now?" Anoushka said. "Will God help them?"

"Dealing with bullies is the responsibility of man, not God's. God helps those who help themselves. God's responsibility is Judgment Day. "

"This is hard on the poor," Anoushka said.

"It's not hard on the poor. You cannot institute Judgement Day and engage in interference at every turn at the same time. Such senseless teachings belong to teachers of terrorism in lunatic schools. God instituted what gives souls good and bad fortunes in this life. God did this to be fair to all and to avoid constant interference on His part in the lives of human beings. If you work hard and practice fairness at all times, good fortune will head your way more often than not. Then you will overcome all sorts of bullies and obstacles that make life hard in this world. That's the true meaning of '*God helps those who help themselves.*' Religious terrorists are damaging and weakening hidden walls of their communities and countries for their poor to pay the highest price in the future but people don't know it yet…"

"I was going to ask you about that," Holly said. "When will their communities and countries start getting bad luck?"

"We cannot look forward to that Holly…" he replied.

"Why?" Holly interrupted, looking serious.

"As we gathered from Anoushka's tale, when bad luck hits like a flood, it affects homes and belongings of the good, the bad, the rich and the poor alike. But the poor pays the highest price by far…"

"So?" Holly interrupted.

"So we cannot look forward to that. Their poor will suffer the most, like the poor paid the highest price in Anoushka's tale…"

"What about the price that our poor are paying now?" Holly snarled. "What about the terrible price that our poor are paying right now in higher travel costs at airports, in libraries, in cuts after cuts in public services to divert funds to fight terrorism because of their constant bullying and harassments?"

"Still, we cannot wish their poor ill and bring bad luck on ourselves. God has done his work. Nature will take its course. Then people will learn to take responsibility and change their fortunes for the better."

"Can we tell when their bad luck will start?" Holly asked.

"According to the chapter on consequences, only those whom God gave eyes for seeing hidden walls can tell when damaged hidden walls will give way for bad luck to start raining down on a people. Hence prophets are sent to guide. But then demons in people within communities and countries fight prophets hard."

"I used to think either God does not exist or He sits there

doing nothing," Anoushka said. "Now I can see that God has put everything in place for us to govern ourselves and take responsibility for our actions…"

"The process God put in place is too slow; far too slow," Holly interrupted.

"The purpose of the process is not speed but deeds," Deji-Vita replied.

"What does that mean?" Holly said.

"The process is governed by *deeds* of people within communities and countries, so… you've got millions of people within a community or country, some are engaging in good deeds more often than not; others are carrying out terrorist acts, bullying, harassments, and cruelty against innocent people at every opportunity they get. Deeds of the good and the bad alike will go into the same community account or country account. As soon as evil deeds heavily outweigh good deeds in the account, hard luck will hit the whole community or country like a flood. Then they will start questioning the existence of God."

"Let's celebrate what we've learnt with some chocolates now," Fiffy said.

15

THE MOOD LIGHTENED up in the dining room and the girls introduced Deji-Vita to a variety of delicious chocolates. He loved them so much he started cracking jokes.

Then, suddenly, Anoushka looked at him and said, "Did God tell you all the things that you taught us, apart from what you read in *The Mejai*?"

"God does not have to tell us everything," he replied. He answered the question that way because there were aspects of his life that he seldom shared, until he'd deemed it necessary.

"Why?" Anoushka asked.

"There are things that God expects us to know through search, and there are things that God has to help us know through revelation," he replied.

"How did you know that?" Anoushka said.

He hesitated for a moment.

Then he told them a story.

"One day," he began, "I was on my way back from preparatory school when I saw two younger children trying to get to rotten food on a stinking rubbish dump before a fat pig. One child tried to scare the fat pig away; the other child to grab the rotten food. The fat pig showed its nasty side and the two hungry kids lost the battle on the rubbish dump. They were both visibly malnourished. They were both clearly starving. They both burst into tears at the same time due to hunger.

"Sight of suffering little children had always crushed me. I was so crushed by what I saw I marched straight to a mango tree in a forest nearby in anger…"

"What?" Holly and Anoushka exclaimed.

"'You and I,' I said to the mango tree, 'did God make us for His personal needs or for reasons that are the highest in morals?' The mango tree said nothing back. I asked the question again and again and again but the mango said not a word.

"I hurried to a pawpaw tree, then a banana tree, then an orange tree, and, finally, a sunflower plant. I asked all of them the same questions but none of them said a word back.

"Feeling disrespected, I threatened to hit them with a curse and make them barren and fruitless but they didn't care…"

The girls interrupted him with laughter.

Then Anoushka said, "Why did you not go home and ask people the same question?"

"I never spoke to humans about God in my childhood."

"Why?" the girls asked in unison.

"They were so dead in the head they actually believed God punishes people for not worshipping Him. They claim it is God's will/Allah's will that they should be poor and wallow in abject poverty, which convinced me that they were all mad and not worth talking to…"

"That's why you chose to talk to trees," Anoushka interrupted, while laughing.

"Yes. That's why I wanted the trees to tell me whether God made us for His personal needs or for reasons that are the highest in morals."

"And how did it end with the trees?" Holly said.

"I became so exhausted and hungry after yelling at the trees without getting any reply, so I slumped to the floor and leaned my back against the mango tree to rest. Then, to my astonishment, a big ripe mango dropped right between my opened legs.

"Why I did what I did next I do not know. But I instinctively took the dropped mango, held it aloft and fixed my gaze towards the sky. Then I said, 'Teach me how to pray.'

"Within seconds, I heard, *'Father, bless this food and dine with me, Amen.'*"

"You actually heard words from a voice without a body speaking to you?" Holly asked.

"Yes. I heard the words so clearly they stuck in my head forever."

"Then what happened?" Holly asked.

"Then I discovered what plants and trees have in common with God: they do not answer questions that humans are supposed to discover through search. Their properties speak for them. If you want to know what they think, search their properties.

"If you want to know what a tree thinks, you should eat its fruits, taste its juice. If you want to know what a plant thinks, smell its flowers, sample its oil, taste its meat. Through their healing properties or the energy or refreshments or nourishments that they provide, you will know all that they have to say.

"So I looked around me long and hard and ran back home, convinced God does not answer foolish questions and questions that humans are supposed to answer for themselves through search..."

"What did you do with the mango?" Fiffy interrupted.

"I ate it," he said.

"Good," Fiffy said.

"Why did you not worship the mango for leading you to a big discovery, like some people do?" Anoushka asked.

"Worship it? I can't worship anything apart from God."

The girls found how he made his face while saying it funny.

Then he said, "I started looking at things around me long and hard. The more I looked, the more I found answers. The more I found answers, the more foolish claims of the people around me drove me crazy.

"One day, to test my ideas, I hid a whip under a table. Then I took a pair of shoes and a vest that fitted my grandfather no longer and placed them on the table. I waited and waited, until my grandfather was sitting where he could see me clearly. Then I retrieved the whip and started beating the vest and the shoes like mad.

"'You have sinned, you have sinned,' I said with every crack of the whip so that my grandfather could hear me.

"'Have you lost your mind?' my grandfather yelled.

"I pretended to have heard nothing and kept doing what I was doing. My grandfather jumped to his feet to come and deal with me and I stopped at once.

"Then, turning to him in anger, I said, 'How many of the lunatics here punish human creations that they cannot use? How many of them beat shoes that they cannot wear?'

"I was such a good boy my grandfather could not believe what he was seeing.

"The shock on his face emboldened me to continue, 'The lunatics here don't harm chairs that they cannot sit on; they don't beat shoes that they cannot use; they don't punish clothes that they cannot wear. Yet they stain the image of *my* God every day, by lying – *lying* – that He punishes people who do not worship Him. Not one of them will set foot in Paradise if I have anything to do with it.'

"My grandfather was so shocked he did not know what to say. He pretended he was going for a walk and ran to a seer. Weeks later, he evicted a tenant and gave me my own room..."

"Why?" Holly interrupted.

"Seers told him I need peace and quiet in abundance to do a very important job. Sadly, a room in Africa is not enough."

"Why?" the girls asked in unison.

"Noise makers in Africa can disturb the Pope in his bedroom in Rome, when they're in form."

The girls laughed.

Then he said, "Poor housing and bad environmental design is children's biggest nightmare in Africa. It gives children addiction to noise from infancy. It disturbs brains. It harms ability to think clearly. It harms human capacity to invent, so I kept going to the forest to do my thinking.

"One day, my grandfather sneaked into my room while I was resting. He thought I was asleep but I was not. He went through what I was working on and fell in love with one of them."

"What were you working on?" Anoushka asked.

"I was working on the differences between utilities and works of art. One is loved; the other is used, so I wrote...

"*We are not utilities. We are God's work of art.*
Utilities are created out of need.
Works of art are born out of love.

Utilities are used. Works of art are loved.
We are born to be loved.
Utilities are created to be used.
We are not utilities. We are God's work of art."

16

THE GIRLS CAME to like his teachings so much they delayed him with questions after questions, until he begged them to let him go. He was itching to go and finish the book that the Egyptian left him.

But within minutes of returning to his room, he realised he needed Fiffy urgently and gave her a call.

Fiffy was so excited she dropped everything and ran to him like mad.

To her astonishment, he led her to an open window and pointed at something blue.

Then he said, "What's that?"

"What's what?" she replied, looking puzzled.

"That blue thing there. What is it?"

"You don't know what that is?"

"No. I just opened this window for the first time and saw it there."

"You don't know what a swimming pool is?"

"Oh. Is this is what swimming pools look like?"

"Don't you watch movies?"

"No."

"But you've got TV at home, right?"

"No. We have no money for things like that. And I don't want them."

"Promise me you won't tell anyone about this."

"Why?"

"They will laugh at you."

"Are we supposed to be born with swimming pools?"

Dear, dear, oh, dear," she said

Then she turned to hurry away.

"Where are you going?" he asked.

"I'll be back in a minute," she replied.

Minutes later, she returned dressed in swimwear. And she had a pair of swimming trunks for him to wear.

The trunks were so huge on his skinny body they both fell apart with laughter, until tears started running down their cheeks.

"Let's go," she said, after she had managed to compose herself.

Then, while chatting, she took him to the steam room, then the sauna, and then the Jacuzzi. There, in the Jacuzzi, she started telling him about the health benefits of all the things around them.

"My people are ruled by counterfeit leaders," he said, after she told him that every London borough has many public swimming pools, saunas and steam rooms.

"Why did you say that?"

"You saw it yourself today. I'm sixteen years old, yet I did not know what a swimming pool was, until today. They don't build these things for us. They don't care about health. They don't give a damn whether we can compete or not. Go to Africa and count the number of countries that build public swimming pools for their people. Your jaw will drop and never close again. We are a humongous market in an enforced coma induced by zombie leadership. It is a huge loss to the world, all because of monstrous, counterfeit leaders that take God's works of art for granted to pay later in hell."

"Maybe your rulers don't know what these things do themselves!"

"Trust me, they do. I hear they drink something called champagne."

She laughed.

Then she said, "Would you like to taste some?"

"No," he replied.

Then he added, "They take our money to buy nice things for themselves and for their loved ones, but hate to see us prosper. They don't want us to have what only they can boast of."

"That's mad."

"Why else do you think we are suffering? They're all mad, our counterfeit leaders."

"How would you get a thriving economy, if your own leaders don't want to see you prosper? They're in urgent need of psychiatric help, your rulers."

"That reminds me. Talking of doctors, why is Dr Majid never here?"

"Why should he be here?" Fiffy retorted, hardening the look on her face.

"I thought he's Habiba's husband."

"What?" Fiffy gasped.

Then she laughed, until tears started rolling down her cheeks.

"Why are you laughing?" he asked.

"You called a rookie doctor and a jerk Habiba's husband," she replied, while still laughing.

"What?"

"The jerk came here and insulted us…"

"I beg your pardon?"

"He first set foot in this house five days ago. He averted his eyes as soon as he saw the three us. Holly went close to say hello. He blurted something in Arabic and walked away from us in visible anger…"

"I can't believe what I'm hearing."

"He's a jerk and a typical self-righteous religious lunatic, who think he's better than those who don't dress the way that fits dress codes in his head. Please don't mention his name in my presence ever again."

"I won't."

"The great Habiba is Anoushka's stepmother…"

"What?"

"I know. Habiba is far too beautiful for her age. Anoushka's dad is the grandson of an African-American hero and a magnate."

"Anoushka is half American?"

"Her would-be father was sent from New York to do a masters degree in law at Oxford. His eyes fell on a woman in Selfridges in London and that was it. He fell so madly in love he never went back to America to stay.

"Anoushka's mum, my mum and Holly's mum were colleagues at Selfridges; two of them worked in the accounts department. Anoushka was born first. Two years later, my mum and Holly's mum fell pregnant in the same year. I was due to be born first but Holly came ten days ahead of me. The three women spoilt Anoushka rotten before Holly and I were born. When Anoushka was five and Holly and I were three, Anoushka's mother died in her sleep…"

"No," he exclaimed.

"We found her sudden departure from life so tough that Anoushka's dad had to put all sorts of medical practitioners on standby. We were asking questions that made us sound crazy. But grief united us and made us inseparable. Holly and I could not leave Anoushka for a second. The three of us slept in the same bed every night. Anoushka's dad, who is extremely rich, was so impressed he gave us scholarships to a theatre school in Marylebone to keep us together."

"You are all actresses?"

"We are all actors. Thanks to Anoushka's dad's many companies around the world, we've been acting in films and TV adverts since we were in nappies."

"What about Habiba?"

"She's got brains like ten computers, Habiba. She's a part-time director of three huge organisations; the smallest is St Mary's Hospital in Paddington. She, also, teaches corporate strategy at the London Business School in Marylebone. Anoushka's dad is a very wonderful man with a rich history behind him. What about you? Are both of your parents still alive?"

"I was orphaned on the day of my birth."

"I beg your pardon?"

"To cut a long story short, the only two people I had left in my family on the day I was born were my grandfather, who is old, and my only brother, who disappeared from my life before my fifth birthday."

"Why?"

"I don't know."

"Did he say anything before he left you?"

"Well, he said he was heartbroken blah, blah, blah, and wiped tears from his eyes several times. Then he gave me a piece of paper and disappeared in floods of tears."

"What was in the paper?"

"Something he had written."

"What did he write?"

"It goes as follows…

"No journeys back, no great leaps forward.
Everything depends on journeys back: team building,
nation building, security and financial progress included.
Progress and lives of humans depend on journeys back.
God is the author of journeys back. And by His command
I go now."

Silence fell between them at this juncture.

Then, suddenly, she said, "Was that it?"

"That was it," he replied.

"Your one and only brother gave you just that and left you as an orphan at the age of four?"

"Yes."

"You have had a very difficult and highly stressful life, Mr."

"Please don't say such things to me."

"Why?"

"I'm here to help, not to enjoy this life."

"I see," she sighed, and changed the subject.

Minutes later, they left the swimming pool area.

"I'll choose your suit tonight," she told him before they would part.

"Okay," he said, and smiled.

17

THE EGYPTIAN CAME again. He returned to the mansion when least expected. Dressed like an Arab prince on this occasion, he made the conference room his destination and called Deji-Vita to an urgent meeting.

Thinking he was about to be taken to see the Mejai, Deji-Vita discussed the matter briefly with Fiffy on the phone. Then he hurried to the conference room.

Fiffy came to fear the Egyptian could take Deji-Vita away without him to say goodbye, so she waited, until Deji-Vita had closed the conference room door behind him. Then she went and positioned herself where she could eavesdrop.

Deji-Vita's said hello but did not get a reply from the Egyptian.

The Egyptian was sat behind a huge conference table. He waved Deji-Vita to a chair while glaring at him.

Then, suddenly, he said, "I'm afraid, I have very bad news. I want you to go and pack your things and leave this house with me now."

"Why?" Deji-Vita asked, looking shocked.

"There's no longer merit in taking you to see the Mejai..."

"What? Why?"

"I had a dream last night that proved you are the impostor."

"I beg your pardon? How can your dream determine such a very important matter?"

The Egyptian ignored the question completely and said, "I've booked you into a hotel. And I've booked you on a flight back to your country tomorrow, unless you insist on letting the Mejai decide..."

"The devil tricked you into this," Deji-Vita interrupted.

"Don't be absurd," the Egyptian snarled, brimming with anger now.

Fiffy became so angry where she was eavesdropping, she was tempted to go into the conference room and punch the Egyptian.

Deji-Vita, meanwhile, was unflustered. "The treasure is mine to inherit and I want the Mejai to decide," he told the Egyptian.

"If the Mejai confirms what I saw in my dream, the police will be called, you will be arrested, you'll put behind bars and you'll be charged with identity theft and attempt to steal a treasure. Yes, you have enough spiritual powers to turn yourself into whatever you want and escape, but I'll still do it."

"In other words, you think I'm the devil!"

"Yes."

"Okay," Deji-Vita snarled, looking increasingly angry. "If the Mejai proves you right, I will gladly submit myself to any punishment under law. And I will dance daily for Christ and *all* the prophets in the Bible and the Koran for ten years. In those ten years, I will dance in any city of your choice. And I will perform any dance that you request. But if the Mejai proves you wrong, you will do all those things. And the choice of venues shall be mine."

"And if I refuse to dance for ten years because I'm a doctor?"

"A nasty curse will fall on you for the rest of your life for calling me the devil. Then you will know the true powers of God. Do you know how much I hate the devil for causing God to bring me into this world?"

"Yes," Fiffy whispered in triumph with a punch in the air.

18

THE EGYPTIAN CALLED Habiba on the phone from the conference room and the two reached an agreement. According to the agreement, Deji-Vita would stay in the mansion for the rest of the day and travel to the Royal Albert Hall with Habiba and the girls to listen to the Mejai. Then Habiba would accompany Deji-Vita to the Royal Gardens hotel in Kensington, where all of Deji-Vita's belongings would be waiting.

It would then be up to the Mejai to decide whether he would like to see Deji-Vita at all.

Deji-Vita rushed out of the conference room and hurried into the living room to see the girls.

He stood before them and gave a speech of thanks. Then he asked for one last favour, which he jokingly christened, 'The Last Favour'.

"There's an abridged story in *The Mejai* called *Where No Human Can Be Defiled*," he told the girls. "It deals with how to tackle crime fairly, cheaply and effectively for poor people's sake. I'll like to trade everything you bought me from Bond Street, apart from the gold watch, for one hundred copies of that book.

They are the only things I would like to take back to my country."

"Why?" Holly asked.

"I have no choice but to use the gold watch to bribe customs, or else the books will be confiscated at the airport."

"I mean why do you need one hundred copies of one book?" Holly said.

"Oh. Stories about prison conditions in my country are heartrending. Rulers in the region where I was born embraced evil before the birth of Christ; now evil will not let them get out of the embrace. They suffer victims of crime and perpetrators of crime in equal measure.

"Our National Union of Students is the only institution that is not terrified of them. They are threatened, harassed, beaten, tear-gassed and shot at. Still, they go back for more, come every year, always trying to get justice for the people who hardly get protection from crime.

"I therefore want to help our National Union of Students with fifty copies of the book. It will open their eyes to a new way of tackling crime effectively without burdening the taxpayer. I trust they will publicise contents of the book throughout Africa through their contacts in the press. Crime needs to go down for poor people's sake."

"Hear, hear," Anoushka said.

"What do you intend to do with the remaining fifty copies of the book?" Holly asked.

"I want to keep two copies for myself, just in case I lose one. I want to keep lending five copies to the few educated people in my neighbourhood, like I'm a local library. I want to give five copies to the only library in a city of ten million people..."

"I'm sorry," Anoushka interrupted. "Did you say you have only one library in a city of ten million people?"

"That's how bad things are for humans where I come from. Rulers there think people just woke up in Europe, America and elsewhere and started making trains, cars and aircrafts. They don't realise human inventions only emerge where resources are spread widely for hard workers to reach them."

"Wow. One library in a city of ten million people," Anoushka sighed.

"To rulers in the region, people are considered barriers to their intention to loot more than wonderful assets that need to be armed with education," Deji-Vita replied. "So I want to send the remaining copies of the book to teachers in the few schools in remote areas of the country; hopefully it will do some good."

"We can get you more than a million copies of the book," Anoushka said. "But the book will not be in bookshops until next month."

"What?" he gasped. "Why?"

"There are only two copies of the book in print at present," Anoushka explained, "both were read before publication. One was read by Dad; the other was read by Professor Huddleston, who wrote *The Mejai*. With the Mejai's permission, Professor Huddleston put extracts of *Where No Human Can Be Defiled* in his book to generate publicity in advance; this was because of the relentless rise in global terrorism, which is destroying our civilisation faster and furiously than our fathers could have imagined. You saw how London was bombed yesterday…"

"Please don't remind me of the disgrace," he said.

"Dad," Anoushka continued, "regards his copy of the book as priceless and won't allow it to be taken outside this house. Fortunately, boats of Dad's shipping company sail around the world. If you can leave your address with us, we will flood Africa with millions of copies of the book."

"Governments in the region will confiscate them. They hate anything that helps their people…"

"Just leave your address with us. A senior sailor will visit you in disguise. Then you'll see masters and craftsmen at their best."

"Happy?" Fiffy said to Deji-Vita.

"Yes…" he replied.

"Now it's your turn to do us a favour," Fiffy told him.

"I'd be more than delighted to be of help," he said.

"Good. Vow before your God that you will give us whatever is in your gift to give."

"I vow before God that I will give you whatever is in my gift to give."

"Good. We want to inherit the right to your wager with Dr Majid…"

"I beg your pardon?"

"We want to be the ones to make Dr Majid dance for ten years in every city on Earth, if he loses the wager with you. And I know he will lose."

"How did you know what Dr Majid and I discussed in the privacy of the conference room?"

"I eavesdropped."

"Fiffy…"

"You promised," Fiffy snarled.

"Okay," he said.

"Okay is not enough," Fiffy replied. "Please do it the right way."

"Okay," he said. "I hereby before God transfer *all* my rights over Dr Majid to Holly, Fiffy and Anoushka, if Dr Majid loses the wager with me."

"Excellent," Fiffy said

"Brilliantly done," Holly added.

"Have some chocolate," Anoushka said.

Moments later, they went their separate ways to start getting ready for the journey to the Royal Albert Hall.

PART TWO

19

THE BEJAVE MOVEMENT could have filled ten of the biggest stadiums on Earth ten times over. But the Mejai insisted his only two performances in public were not allowed to be treated like a show.

What his God wanted, said the Mejai, was for him to stand before a few thousand people in a public place and deliver a message to the whole world in their presence. The message was allowed to be broadcasted on the radio and videoed for those who would like to have copies for keeps. Yet hundreds of millions of members of the movement wanted to see the Mejai in the flesh.

So, to be fair to everybody, a raffle approach was adopted in countries around the world. And some members of the movement won tickets for either the first or second day's event. Only twenty-four people, Habiba, Deji-Vita and the Egyptian included, got tickets for both evenings' event.

By six o'clock in the evening, the Royal Albert Hall was almost filled to capacity. Habiba, Deji-Vita and the girls arrived in a chauffeured limousine about an hour later. Deji-Vita and Habiba were ushered to the same seats on the third tier that they occupied on the previous night. The girls were ushered to seats in the VIP area, the closest to where the Mejai was to stand and answer questions.

At nine in the evening, Professor Huddleston appeared on the stage and announced how the evening was to proceed. Moments later, the Mejai appeared to a deafening standing ovation.

He bowed his head and mouthed a little prayer, after the crowd had quietened down. Then it fell to a guest of the movement, a woman from Syria, to ask the first question.

"Mejai" she said, after rising to her feet, "I'm a mother of nine children from a blessed family in Damascus. All my pregnancies lasted nine months or more. Only my last-born posed a threat to my life during childbirth. It was as if the child did not want to be born. He was always sick in the beginning. Excellent medical care at the hands of first class doctors saved his life at considerable expense.

"We paid whatever we had to pay for the good of his health. We spared no expense to give him the best education. He passed all his exams and was admitted to university here, in England. During his first year at college, an Islamic cleric from the Middle East gave one sermon at his campus and that was that. My son became so radicalised he killed himself and hundreds of others in a suicide bombing operation with other radicals.

"It took me nine months to carry the child in pregnancy. I lost a lot of blood and almost died in childbearing because of him. I spent days in hospital throughout his infancy. I spent eighteen years of my life on constant care of his life. My husband, may his soul rest in peace, spent tens of thousands of pounds to give the child first class education. Yet it took one sermon, just one sermon of a cleric, to render all our years of hard work to total waste.

"The cleric who radicalised my son and his fellow suicide bombers, we later discovered, never went to university, never sent a child to college, never paid a penny in school fees in his life, and never raised a child who contributed a thing to civilisation. Yet the cleric travels in aircrafts, which children who went to college used their skills to design and build. He rides in nice cars, which children who went to college used their skills to design and build. He travels on nice trains and takes medications that college education was used to invent.

"He receives hospital treatment at the hands of college-trained doctors, whose parents had laboured to raise well. He uses electricity that college education takes everywhere on Earth. He uses everything that college education provides without fail. Yet he contributes nothing but death.

"I pray to God daily. I fast in Ramadan. I do not disturb my neighbours. I do everything my peaceful religion requires of me. Yet my son's father was murdered by people of another sect in our religion, who regard us as heretics. His uncle was murdered by the same people, who regard us as heretics.

"So I ask you, Mejai. God knows everything and sees everything before it can happen. Why did God not kill the cleric before the cleric got the chance to turn my son and other children into suicide bombers?"

The hall became dead silent.

Then the Mejai said, "What's your name?"

"My name is Mariam," she replied.

"Mariam, Jews, Moses and Judaism, which of the three came first?"

"Jews came first," she replied.

"Christianity, Jesus and Europeans, which of the three came first?"

"Europeans came first," she replied.

"Arabs, Mohammed and Islam, which of the three came first?"

"Arabs came first," she replied.

"Mariam, God does not destroy what can turn a new leaf.

127

The wisdom in this character of God can be found in what resulted from His treatment of forebears of Jews, Christians and Muslims. Forebears of Jews were atheists and idol worshippers, who killed people, before Abraham's days. God did not kill them when they were killing people as atheists and idol worshipers.

"Forebears of Christians in Europe and across the world were atheists and idol worshippers who killed people before Jesus came. God did not kill them before Jesus came. Forebears of Arabs and Muslims in the Middle East and the whole world were atheists and idol worshippers, who killed people before the coming of Mohammed and Islam. God did not kill them either.

"Had God killed forebears of Jews, Christians and Arabs and Muslims when they were killing people as atheists and idol worshippers, would there be one Jew, Christian or Muslim on this earth today?'

"No," the crowd roared.

Then he said, "God's character is not to destroy what can turn a new leaf. The presence of you Jews, Christians and Muslim of today give proof of the wisdom in this character of God. Had God killed your fathers when they were killing people as atheists and idol worshippers, you would not have been born to become the Jews, Christians or Muslims of today.

"*A tree is known by its fruit.* Every preacher or cleric who does not follow the character of God is not a servant of God. God did not send such people to you. God's character can be found in how God treated forebears of those who became the Jews, Christians and Muslims of today. God's servants follow God's character.

"The so-called Islamic cleric, who turned Mariam's son into a suicide bomber, is not a servant of God. That so-called Islamic cleric and his ilk are spiritual captives. Spiritual captives are humans captured in spirit, bound in spirit, and blinded in spirit by Satan's demons. The devil's demons control their minds. Demons speak through their tongues. Demons that speak through their tongues have powers of hex. Their powers of hex enable them to turn humans into killers. A preacher who has demons can hex you with his tongue while preaching in your presence.

"Once hexed by demons through the tongue of a cleric harboured by demons, you will become blind in mind and weak in spirit. Demons will control your tongue, thoughts and actions, until you rush to your grave or find yourself in a place of confinement.

"Mariam's son was not turned into a killer by a sermon. Mariam's son was hexed through the tongue of an Islamic cleric harboured by demons. Mariam's son rushed to his death and wasted all the talents that God gave him through suicide bombing, and he wasted precious talents of others in the process. Mariam, where is Mariam?"

"I'm here," she said, after rising back to her feet.

"There once lived a man who became harboured by demons. His demons sent him into a tomb to start cutting his own skin with stones. When his demons saw Jesus, they begged Jesus through his tongue not to destroy them. They knew Jesus had power to cast them out and destroy them, so they asked Jesus to send them into thousands of pigs that were feeding next to a lake instead. When Jesus sent them into the pigs, all the thousands of pigs rushed into the lake and drowned. That's what is happening to suicide bombers. As soon as they become hexed and harboured by demons, they want death; they want to rush to their deaths and leave this world, no matter how they get to die."

"What is the solution, Mejai?" Mariam asked.

"*By their fruits ye shall know them,*" the Mejai quoted Scripture in reply. "Distance yourselves and your loved ones from any cleric who has caused others to kill or cause anyone to kill himself. Stay well away from such clerics to avoid being hexed by their demons. They are nothing but spiritual captives that demons use to hex people, waste talents, and starve mankind of talents. Their demons send them into synagogues, churches and mosques to stain the image of God and undo works of His prophets."

The whole hall rose as one and applauded long and hard.

Then Mariam said, "The cleric in question was trained in Saudi Arabia."

"Beware of language worshippers, who like to boast about where they were trained," the Mejai replied. "Focus on the fruits not where the tree was planted. It matters little whether a man was trained in Latin in Rome or in Arabic in Arabia or in Hebrew in Jerusalem. *By their fruits* ye shall know whether they have demons.

"There once lived a priest who went on a lecture tour. He rented a cheap villa on the edge of one of the poorest places on Earth. And he drove in a hired car to wherever he was to teach. Being the first white man to set foot in a town inhabited only by black people, his presence aroused interest instantly. Curious children climbed walls to take peeps at him. And they soon discovered he was a heavy drinker of something in a flask. Whether he was resting or working on papers in his front garden, he would pour something from a flask by his side into a cup and drink it time and time again.

"One day, ten peeping children became divided over what must be in the flask, some said he was a drunk. Others said he could not be because they've never seen him stagger. One of them said content of the flask must be what makes white people invent trains, cars, ships and aircrafts, for there can be no other reason why he cannot stop drinking it so much.

"It was the priest's penultimate day in the villa. And he was busy working on his last sermon in his front garden. The children soon ended the debate and ventured into his front garden. Then they asked to know what was in his flask. He leapt to his feet and brought cups to give them a taste. But the leader of the children asked him not to pour what was in the flask yet.

"A fierce debate ensued in the children's local language, after which they asked the priest to give them a moment and they took to their heels.

"Minutes later, the priest caught sight of a long line of children heading his way. He was so shocked by what he saw he became tongue-tied.

"The children came and their leader stepped forward. 'You are the first white man to set foot here,' he began. 'We are children of a people still suffering from a bruising past. If ten of us drink what's in your flask and get special powers from it, it could lead to jealousy and tear our community apart. The last time our community was torn apart by jealousy, it led to a civil war and the civil war led to the great evil of slavery. Prisoners of war were either used as slaves or sold into slavery elsewhere. Little did the culprits on all sides realise, their actions would turn into a curse that would cause suffering to their people for centuries to come. Children after children paid a heavy price before us. And we are poor because we are paying part of that price. Our people are tired in mind from suffering and have very little patience. With consequences of our bitter history in mind, we, the ten that first approached you, ran to our elders and informed that you've kindly offered us something to drink but we don't know if it has special powers. We asked for advice and our elders left the matter for all children of our community to decide. We, the children, took a vote, after a quick debate. And the majority decision was "*all to taste or none to taste*". That's why we are all here.'

"The priest looked at him and said, 'How many of you are here now?' 'Three hundred and thirty-two,' their leader replied.

"'*Out of the mouths of babes,*' the priest quoted Scripture. Then he ran into his kitchen to count the number of teabags that he had left. He had only forty teabags left, he discovered. His stove and teakettle were nowhere near what was required, so with the help of a few of the children, he went to town and borrowed buckets and a barrel for collecting rainwater.

"They used gathered stones to make an emergency cooker that could hold the barrel. They put woods between the stones to make fire. They placed the barrel on the stones and filled it with water. Then they lit the fire and started what turned out to be a long wait.

"The barrel of water boiled eventually, and he threw all the forty teabags that he had left in it. He stirred the boiling barrel of water containing forty teabags and the time came to serve. With the cups and buckets at hand, he served the ten and taught them to serve those in the queue behind them. Those served in the queue then became servers themselves. Once the mission was accomplished, the priest waved the children goodbye and jumped into his rented car to go and deliver his last sermon.

"Later that day, he found himself unable to sleep. He turned in bed all night, until he decided to go and see the children the next morning.

"The next day, hours before he would fly back to his country, he went and looked for the children and gathered them together. Then he asked them to describe what the drink he gave them *tasted* like. Not one of the children were able to give him a good enough description of what tea tastes like. Forty teabags in a barrel of boiled water, he discovered, does absolutely nothing for the mind, body and spirit.

"So he went back home and returned with his three sons, three daughters and his wife. They came well armed with tonnes of tea, hundreds of teacups, many electric kettles, and a power generator.

"This time, the children's faces told a picture. Every single one of them became full of energy, after tasting real tea. Every one of them felt different in mind, body and spirit. Tea, as it should be made, gave them energy that they couldn't imagine. They were so reinvigorated they wanted to do something for the priest and his family in return. But he gave them what he used to serve them and asked them to go and serve the whole town.

"Through the children, the priest came to realise what has happened to the priesthood in Judaism, Christianity and Islam. The priesthood in all three faiths in the House of Abraham have been turned into forty teabags in a barrel of boiled water, which do absolutely nothing for the mind, body and spirit of God's children.

"The biggest mistake ever made in the House of Abraham was to seek quantity than quality in the priesthood. It gave the devil his chance to infiltrate Judaism, Christianity and Islam and the devil sent demon-filled men into the priesthood, who then became paedophile priests, hate preachers, breeders of murderers and suicide bombers and evil perverters of the law…"

The audience swept to their feet and cheered.

Then he looked at them and said, "Go anywhere near clerics over powered by demons and you will be hexed. Get hexed and you will become a murderer filled with hate or a suicide bomber or both. Jesus warned when he said, *'No one can destroy a house, until he conquers the strongest man of the house.'* A cleric is supposed to be the strongest man in the house of God, be it a synagogue, church or a mosque, so the devil targets them first.

"Ye came to have breeders of murderers and creators of suicide bombers not because of Islam. Ye came to have breeders of murderers and suicide bombers in the name of Islam because of demons in clerics that the devil sent into mosques. The weaker the cleric is in spirit, the greater the number of demons that will enter him to stain the image of Islam.

"Your fathers' failures as Jews, Christians and Muslims gave the devil a chance to fill the priesthood with demons and the devil took it. Then demon-filled Islamic clerics started telling children that other Children of Abraham and any human created by God that is not a Muslim is a pig. *By their fruit ye shall know them.* Hell is the only destination of such demon-filled clerics.

"He who has ears, let him hear. The future belongs to those who can use their talents to swell the flock, by lightening the burden of all of God's creations on Earth. One true cleric of God is enough to serve a city the size of London."

With that, the Mejai finished answering Mariam's question.

20

A MUSLIM OF Moroccan descent rose to her feet and introduced herself as Sophia from Marseille. Her family was scattered all over the world due to lack of meaningful jobs in North Africa.

"Mejai," she said, "I hear what you say about the character of God and how we children of Abraham, Jews, Christians and Muslims, became great beneficiaries of it. Thank you for that. Thank you also for opening our eyes to demon-filled clerics who hex our children, brothers and sisters through the power of their demons. Thank you for letting us know that it is only through hexing that we get murderers and suicide bombers, who the devil uses to stain the image of God by throwing this world into chaos, to make us suffer.

"The problem is we are now a people at a standstill because of demon-filled clerics. Europe came from behind and went ahead of us in how to create meaningful jobs for their people. America did the same. Japan, South Korea, China, India, all came from behind and went ahead of us in how to create meaningful jobs for people through technological advance. All we get are sermons, chaos and no jobs.

"Our Achilles heel is glaringly none other than the Sunni/Shite divide and their offshoots. Tonight, I've come to see how demons in demon-filled clerics took full advantage of it to stain our image throughout the world.

"Since, because of the character of God, God will not kill them before they hex people to use them as murderers and suicide bombers around the world. Why can't God, at least, intervene and rescue us, our image and our talents from their demons?"

"Sofia of Marseille," the Mejai replied, "God entertained two options at the time of creating mankind: either to intervene in the life of man at every turn; or wait and judge each after death.

"The first option does not require free will but will leave humans in no doubt about the existence of God. The second option requires endowing humans with free will but will leave room for doubt in the existence of God on the part of man. God had to choose one of the two options, because it falls into the realm of senselessness and injustice to interfere in the life of man at every turn and then judge him after death.

"Owing to the objective behind His creation of mankind, God chose the second option and endowed mankind with free will at the point of creation.

"Free will comes with diversity in talent.
Diversity in talent comes with responsibility.
Responsibility comes with accountability.
Accountability is the only reason for Judgment Day.

"To intervene at every turn, God will have to strip humans of free will and diversity in talent because the two come hand in hand. If God strips of humans of free will and diversity in talent, humans will become like animals and cannot be judged in this life or in the next.

"Having chosen to grant humans free will, which leaves room for doubt in His existence, God has to wait for each to die before judging him or her. Hence God did not kill Cain, after Cain killed his brother, Abel. Hence God did not kill forebears of Jews, Christians and Muslims when they were killing people as atheists and idol worshippers.

"Same applies to the demon-filled clerics of today. God will say nothing to them until Judgment Day. What you need to write on your hearts is this part of the law that governs Judgment Day: diversity in talent and free will were granted unto man to make decisions until death. Decisions of man are therefore his responsibility and his alone.

"It is therefore the responsibility absolute of man, be he a Jew, Christian or Muslim, to ensure that his land, synagogue, church or mosque is not hijacked by demons in demon-filled clerics to throw this world into chaos or waste its talents and resources for nothing.

"If you stand idly by and allow them to take over your synagogue or church or mosque and throw the world into chaos, you will answer to God for it. If you stand idly by and allow them to take your lands and waste the resources and human talents in them, you will answer to God for it. If you stand idly by and allow them to use your lands to throw the whole world into chaos and to stain the image of God because of their demons, you will answer to God for it. God will not intervene because of the second option.

"God chose the second option because it serves the objective behind the creation of man better. The time for God to show man without doubt that He exists is Judgment Day. The time for man to see for definite that God entertains not a speck of partiality the son of injustice is Judgment Day."

With that, the Mejai finished answering the question of Sophia of Marseille.

Then the crowd rose yet again and started cheering to the rafters.

21

A JOURNALIST FROM South Africa in the audience was unhappy. His name was Desmond and he hailed from Johannesburg. He suffered at the hands of a paedophile priest in childhood and had never been at peace since, but he'd never discussed the matter with anyone.

"Mejai," he said, after rising to his feet, "where I come from in South Africa, once you say a person is harboured by demons, he or she is no longer responsible for his or her actions!"

"Desmond," said the Mejai, "can a beaten pugilist pass the blame on anyone else, if the only reason why he lost a fight was his failure to train?"

"No," Desmond said.

"Can a defeated athlete absolve himself of responsibility, if the only reason he lost a race was his refusal to train as required?"

"No," Desmond said.

"Same applies to humans who become harboured by demons. It is the absolute responsibility of each and every human to avoid defeat at the hands of demons. For man is required to train like a pugilist determined to win a fight and an athlete that cannot afford to lose a race. You have a home and you have a heart. Which of those two can you not live without?"

"My heart," Desmond said.

"If your heart is crucial to your being, which of the two is your seat of power, your heart or your home?"

"My heart," Desmond said.

"Whose responsibility it is to lock the door to your house to prevent thieves from walking in as they please?"

"It is my responsibility." Desmond replied.

"Why then expect someone else to protect the heart that is *your* seat of power for you, mankind? Locking doors to demons that want to take the seat of power that is your heart is your absolute responsibility, mankind. The responsibility of man lies in what he failed to do *before* demons fought their way into him, not *after* demons became able to use him to disturb and destroy lives of others.

"Suffer defeat at the hands of demons and you will pay for every harm and destruction that *your* demons used you to do. Allow demon-filled clerics to use your synagogue, church or mosque to propagate harm to others and you will share in the total cost of all the crimes that their demons used them to commit.

"Maggots get life from unattended meat. Demons get life from unattended hearts. You put petrol into cars in order to drive them. Demons want to use you as their cars."

With that, the Mejai finished answering Desmond's questions. And the hall responded with yet another long applause on their feet.

22

"THE HEART OF man is a seat of power," the Mejai told the crowd to help mankind. "He who takes control of the heart of man shall take control of the earth. Every seat of power has conduits. Conduits attract would-be occupiers. The devil wants to take the seat of power that is your heart, but he cannot do so until he has succeeded in despatching his demons into you.

"Demons are squatters, which give insatiable appetite and addictions to humans. Demons give addiction to drugs, alcohol, gambling, as well as insatiable appetite for sexual activities. They cause individuals to engage in excessive consumptions, until they are destroyed beyond all recognition. Therefore, strive to know by heart how demons find their way into the souls of men; and learn how to stop them from taking over your lives.

"Jealousy, envy, hatred, bitterness and spiritual carelessness are all conduits of demons. Ambitions beyond talents at one's disposal are conduits of demons. Occupying jobs and positions that are bigger than your talents are conduits of demons. Men become bigots, racists and religious extremists when demons harbour them.

"Men acquire supremacist thoughts that are harmful to

others because of demons. Demon-filled clerics get supremacist thoughts to say whosoever does not belong to their religion is going to the fire of hell. God did not put mankind on Earth because of any religion."

With that, the Mejai ended the small help to man. And the crowd rose and started applauding.

The hall soon became silent and a foreign newspaper correspondent from the Middle East rose to his feet and introduced himself as Salim.

"Mejai," he said, "first of all, how can occupying a job or position that is bigger than your talents pave way for demons to enter you?"

"If you take on a job or occupy a position that is bigger than your talents, difficulties in the job will soon give you a troubled heart. Demons rise from troubled hearts like maggots rise from unattended meat. Many tyrants came to have many demons through jobs that they had no talents for or positions that were bigger than their talents."

"Why then can't we see demons to know that they exist?" said Salim.

"Owing to the objective behind the creation of man, Salim, God did not give man eyes for seeing everything. Humans know air exists but they have no eyes for seeing it. Air is known about through *touch* and when the wind blows things around you away. The same applies to demons.

"When demons are blowing from the life of a human you will feel it through damaging things that come out of his mouth. Look at hate preachers and you'll see what I mean. When demons blow humans away, you will see it through the destructions that they leave behind. Look at murderers and suicide bombers and you will see what I mean.

"Thirdly," said Salim, "how can demons enter a cleric, a man of God?"

"A cleric is a shepherd or he is nothing. There once lived a man, who fell in love with the robe and status of clerics but did not have the minimum strength required to be a priest. What attracted him to the priesthood was the respect that people accorded clerics, not what he was determined to give as a shepherd. Demons very first attack on him in the job floored him completely and he came to have insatiable appetite for abusing children. Nothing the Church tried was able to help him. His demons used him to engage in baffling behaviours, until they scattered the flock and people's doubt in God's existence increased dramatically. The damage he did to many children, and its subsequent effect on generation of humans to come in wasted talents, will fill ten books where they are carefully studied.

"You have to be human before you can become a priest. Conduits of demons are therefore the same for clerics and congregants alike. If you take on the job of a priest without the talent, you will end up a paedophile priest or a hate preacher or a leader of gangs and thugs who cause harm in the name of religion because of their demons. Demons will use you to tear society apart and spread sectarian violence. How did the devil get his demons, Salim?"

"I have no idea," Salim said, after rising back to his feet.

"The devil got his demons from taking on a job that he had no talents for. He took on the task of fighting God, which nothing in existence has talents for, and demons rose from his bitter heart faster than maggots rise from rotten meat. Men without talents of shepherds have been conquered by demons in the priesthood to breed murderers and suicide bombers through hexing.

"The more you stand in the rain, the more you'll get wet. Hexing takes less than a minute, not one sermon. Take your children before breeders of murderers and suicide bombers through hexing and your days in hell before you are *extinguished* to be no more shall be as long as from the days of Noah to the day you died on Earth.

"Yes, demons will shout God's name through tongues of murderers and suicide bombers before and after they kill. The right time to deal with that is Judgment Day. Judgment Day is the reason behind God's silence.

"No human can stay calm, if he sees gallons of maggots in the head of a preacher or the man leading him at prayer. Yet clerics filled with demons like gallons of maggots stand before worshippers in synagogues, churches and mosques to lead them at prayer everyday. Objective is the ruler king. The objective behind the creation of mankind is the reason why everything has to wait until Judgment Day. God will expose them for all to see on Judgment Day."

"Finally, Mejai," said Salim, "how do you close doors to demons?"

"Do not fall madly in love with the body that is your flesh. Love nothing too much. Fall not madly in love with your race, religion, sect, tribe or land. Don't worship a religion. Don't worship any language, custom, culture, tradition or society. They are all conduits of demons, which blind people from right and wrong.

"Demons use language worshipers to destroy trades, religions, countries and man. Quench ambitions for jobs that are bigger than your talents. Steer clear of positions that you have no talents for. Never worship religion, let religion serve you. These truths will come to you naturally, if you love your fellow humans. Serve mankind with all the love that you have for God and demons will find you a nightmare."

With that, the Mejai left the stage to thunderous applause for the longest break of the night.

23

MINUTES INTO THE longest break, an announcement was made and lights in the Royal Albert Hall were dimmed. Then a film called *The Generous Host: the last story that the Mejai told his pupils*, started showing.

Deji-Vita squinted long and hard but he could not see a thing on the screen, so he settled down and started taking notes from the dialogue.

At the beginning of the film, the generous host invited guests from four corners of the earth to a feast in his place, which had four entrances that required directions through different maps.

To those coming from the east, the Generous Host gave a map to the Eastern Gate. To those coming from the west, he gave a map to the Western Gate. To those coming from north and south, he gave maps to the Northern and Southern Gates respectively. He armed each party with caravans loaded with food and drinks according to the length of their journey. Then he gave every person in each party a donkey to take him on the journey, and asked them to treat their donkeys well.

"The Western Route was the longest route so he gave

travellers from the west more food and drink. The Eastern Route was shorter, compared to the Western Route, so he gave travellers from the east less food and drink. Those coming from the Northern and Southern Routes had the shortest journey to make of all, so he gave travellers from the north and south the least amount of food and drink.

The feast had a time on which it had to start and all entrances had to be closed, so the Generous Host asked each group to focus firmly on the respective maps of their given routes and keep strictly to their respective timetables, or else they would get lost or come too late, or run out of food and drink and not got to the feast at all.

He implored each group to take nothing with them, apart from what he had given them for their respective journeys. He told each group about hazards on their given route. He warned each group their food and drinks were calculated according to hazards on their given route. And he told them not to allow anything to distract and delay them.

Invitations to the feast of the Generous Host made many feel so special some started regarding themselves as the Chosen Ones.

Days into their respective journeys to the feast, travellers from the east and the west caught sight of one another but from a distance and temptations soon set in. Unaware that they were all heading to the same place but from different given routes, some in the eastern group wanted to go and boast to the westerners that they'd been invited to the palace of the Generous Host and were therefore the special ones, some in the western group wanted to go and boast to the easterners that they are the special ones for the same reason.

Despite all the warnings of the Generous Host, despite all appeals and protestations of their fellow travellers, distracted travellers from the east, who could not resist temptation, left their given routes to go and boast to the Westerners. Distracted travellers from the West that could not resist temptations left their given routes to go and boast to the Easterners.

The two groups of distracted travellers from the east and the west met in a no man's land that was full of danger, and a boasting contest that was centred on nothing but maps ensued. All the distracted travellers from the East claimed they were the special ones because of their map. All the distracted travellers from the West claimed they were the special ones because their map looked more special. The sky roared while they were busy boasting and arguing about their maps, and one month's rain of Biblical proportion fell on them in less than a day. None of them were able to go forward or backward because the ground became so muddy it caused them to sink up to the waist. None of them could move an inch, let alone hasten back to their respective given routes to the feast.

They were left trapped in mud to stare at each other, yet they could not tolerate the sight of one another. They could not stand the sight of one another because each saw themselves as the special ones *and thought the other was beneath them, so, trapped deep in mud to their waists, they kept hurling abuse at each other, like the insane. One group w*ould shout and point at their map. Then the other group would shout louder and point at their map.

The Easterners would throw their mud at the Westerners. Then the Westerners would throw their mud at the Easterners. Darkness fell and they had no light to see. Still, they kept shouting at each other in the dark.

What they did not realise was that demons were rising in them when they started having urges to go and boast. Their demons multiplied when they started hating each other. They barked at each other as demons grew in them. And the more they barked at each other, the more they looked insane.

The devil soon appeared in his truck. And the devil ordered his cohorts to load them into different trucks and take them to his feast, where the blood of those who were considered losers were drunk by the devil and his guests, and their flesh was eaten by the devil and those whom he called his winners.

The more the guests ate the devil's foods and drank his drinks, the wilder they became. The wilder they became, the more they looked for something to attack and destroy. Once the devil was sure they were ready, the devil took them to a place called Satan's Junction and stationed them there.

Their jobs at Satan's Junction were to seize passers-by and send them to the devil's feast. All travellers and passers-by came under attack at their hands. Those that they could seize they sent to the devil's party. Those that they could not seize, they killed or wanted to kill. They were subjected to severe punishments whenever they failed to send people to the devil's party, so they roamed about in disguise looking for people to seize or kill.

It turned out that was how distracted Jews, distracted Christians and distracted Muslims came to start throwing this world into chaos.

Starting with the distracted Christians, the voice of Jesus was heard in the film saying to them, "Take nothing with you on your journey; take no stick, no beggar's bag, no food, no money, not even extra shirt. Wherever you are welcomed, stay until you leave. Where they will not receive you or listen to you, shake the dust off your feet and leave."

Yet, in a bid to make others feel bad about themselves through their boast, distracted Christians, who failed to keep travelling on the backs of their talents to the Kingdom of Heaven, ended up at the devil's party. Ruled by demons and fuelled by the devil's food and drink, the distracted Christians started marching toward Jerusalem to kill in the name of an idol called Crusade, which could not be found anywhere in the teachings of Jesus.

The voice of Jesus was heard in the film saying to them repeatedly, *"I am the bread of life which came down from Heaven."*

Then the voice of Christian leaders were heard in the film saying to them, "The bread of life from Heaven has no need for Holy Land, not even Jerusalem, for nothing *on Earth* is holier than him." It all fell on deaf ears.

Ruled by demons and fuelled by the devil's food and drink, the distracted Christians kept marching toward Jerusalem to kill for the idol, Crusade, which could not be found anywhere in the teachings of Jesus.

Even when they were nearing Jerusalem, the voice of Jesus was heard saying to them in the film, *'Not only those who call me Lord shall enter the Kingdom of Heaven.'* It all fell on deaf ears yet again. Demons in the distracted Christians kept saying only those who become Christians will go to Heaven and all they need to go to Heaven is to become Christians.

So the film showed Nazis from Christian homes slaughtering six millions Jews.

Then a voice in the film said unto them, "Behold, who in his right mind can say Nazis are going to Heaven simply because they came from Christian homes? Who in his right mind will say Nazis will go to Heaven after death because they were Christians who killed Jews? *Jesus who gave Christians their faith came as a Jew.*"

The film moved on to show distracted Muslims marching from Satan's Junction to Rome. Once in Rome, they started slaughtering Christians in their thousands. Those who refused to convert to Islam by force were murdered.

Demons in distracted Muslims kept telling them that every human on Earth was meant to convert to Islam. Demons kept telling them it was right and proper to kill any human that was not a Muslim. The same demons in the distracted Muslims kept telling them that all non-Muslims are destined for hell.

So the voice in the film said to them, "Behold, Abraham was not a Muslim. Ishmael was not a Muslim. Ishmael's mother,

Hagar, was not a Muslim. Can a Muslim in his right mind say Abraham, Hagar, Ishmael and his wife and children are in hell because they were not Muslims? Woe betide th*ose* used by demons. Heaven is filled with the willing, not the compelled."

The voice went on, "God is not a landlord looking for tenants. The Kingdom of Heaven needs not the compelled. The route of force has no place to Heaven. The ruled by demons shall not set foot in Paradise. Abraham will look at them with disdain for slaughtering his children before they are burnt."

The film moved on to show distracted Muslims saying the Islamic flag will fly on Downing Street, the White House and on all offices on Earth.

So the voice said to them, *"Hear, all ye that are nothing but only sons and daughters of men. Flags are rags. God is most Holy. Associate the Lord our God with any of your dirty rags and yours shall be the sin against the Holy Ghost. All sins are forgivable, except sins against the Holy Ghost."*

The voice went on, "Hear all you Muslims that are not conquered by demons. Demons in distracted Muslims want to use them to start a LOFWAR, the acronym for Lucifer's Own Favourite War, which the rest of mankind will come to know as the Third World War. Demons in distracted Jews and distracted Christians are trying to use them to reach the same end. None can win the LOFWAR that men will call Third World War. Human talents will only be wasted through the LOFWAR. Generations of humans will suffer terribly as a result. Then you, you who stood idly by and let talents be wasted, will weep bitter tears in the fire of hell.

"God did not promise Abraham how to make people suffer. God did not promise Abraham how to waste talents. God did not promise Abraham chaos. God did not promise Abraham failure. God promised to make children of Abraham flourish throughout the face of the Earth."

Lastly, the film showed distracted Jews at Satan's Junction

149

saying gentiles are beneath them; claiming superiority over gentiles; boasting about being the chosen ones; claiming in their madness that being children of Abraham was more important than the second of the Ten Commandments.

The distracted Jews were also seen in the film throwing Jesus out of a Synagogue, shouting at Jesus all the way to the crucifixion, throwing stones at early Christians, and sending early Christians to their deaths in Israel.

So the voice said to them, "Behold, it says in the Jewish Torah, *'The Lord said to my Lord, sit Thou at my right hand until I make thine enemies thy footstool.'* Who do you think was the Lord that the Lord asked to sit at his right side?"

Distracted Jews were also shown calling the Prophet Mohammed an impostor, according him no respect whatsoever in their conversations.

So the voice said to them, "Behold it says in the Jewish Torah, 'Abraham said to God, 'Why not let Ishmael be my heir?' God said to Abraham among others, *'I have heard your request about Ishmael; I will bless him and give him many children and many descendants. He will be the father of twelve princes, and I will make a great nation of his descendants.'*

"Where then did you, distracted Jew, think Mohammed and Islam came from, if not from the promise that God made to Abraham? Who did you expect to help Mohammed bring the Koran into being, if not God? Did you expect God to promise Abraham that He will bless Ishmael and not fulfil it? Can you claim to love God but cannot respect His wisdom and His prophet?"

The voice went on, "It says in the Scriptures, *'the Earth is fixed'*, meaning bad behaviour is imbued with a curse, good behaviour is imbued with a reward. All human actions and inactions have fixed consequences and rewards. Curse is imbued in every human attempt to fight against promises of God, the promise that God made to Abraham included. God promised

Abraham He will bless Isaac in one way and bless Ishmael in another.

"Moses came to honour the blessing on Isaac that God promised Abraham, and then distracted Jews, ruled by demons, started saying they are the best. Jesus came to honour further the blessing on Isaac that God promised Abraham then distracted Christians ruled by demons started saying they are the best. Mohammed came to honour the blessing on Ishmael that God promised Abraham, and then distracted Muslims, ruled by demons, started saying they are the best. None of them are the best.

"If any of them are the best, demons can never conquer a soul in their midst. Each of them have cruel rulers, corrupt lawmakers, crooked officials, drug addicts, drug dealers, murderers, wasters of talents and blasphemers of their own, which shows that demons conquer people in their midst so none of them are the best."

The voice concluded, "All God gave Jews, Christians and Muslims to honour His promise to Abraham were different paths to the Kingdom of Heaven through different prophets, not means of judging people on Earth by clerics. The time to judge who made it to the feast in the Kingdom of Heaven and who did not is Judgment Day. And God alone will be the judge of that."

With that, the film ended.

Then the whole hall rose and started clapping.

24

PEOPLE STARTED CHATTING about what they'd learnt from the film.

So Habiba turned to Deji-Vita and said, "What's the most important thing that you learnt tonight?"

"Every country on Earth today is facing serious danger because of demons, as we saw with the bombing of London yesterday," Deji-Vita replied.

"I don't understand," Habiba said to test him.

"Okay," he sighed. "If I fail to bathe for a year and wear the same unwashed clothes for a year, can you sit next to me and chat happily?"

"No."

"Why is that?"

"The smell will force me to stay away from you. It will be too much."

"Yet if I sit close to you with a heart that is not cleansed for a decade, you will not smell a thing, until I start beheading people, shooting people or bombing people."

"That's very true."

"That's why every nation on Earth today is facing serious

danger because of demons. Decades ago, you need a nation and thousands of soldiers to make millions of people in a city live in fear. Today you only need ten people harboured by powerful demons to do that."

"Why?"

"As we learnt from the film, religion is not what makes people want to kill people. Demons make people want to kill people, not religion. Bomb making is now easy, so ten people harboured by powerful demons can make bombs and kill people in their thousands and hold cities to ransom in the name of religion. The solution to the problem we face can therefore not be found in religion. Experts in Judaism, Christianity or Islamic Studies cannot help us solve the problem of religious terrorism. They will only make matters worse by feeding demons in religious terrorists."

"Why is that?"

"Experts in Christianity or Islamic Studies don't have the power of Jesus to cast out demons. Nothing they say can make demons in terrorists go away. What we need to solve the problem is a thorough understanding of the religion/spirituality divide, and how to factor it into decision-making in all countries. Until then, we cannot tackle terrorism in this age. That's what the Mejai wants us to understand."

"What's the religion/spirituality divide?" Habiba asked, looking very surprised.

"One is a requirement of nature so everybody needs it; the other is not a requirement of nature so not everybody needs it," he replied. "Worship, to call religion by its other name, is not a requirement of nature so not everybody needs it. Inner self-cleansing, to call spirituality by its other name, is a requirement of nature so everybody needs it.

"If I were teaching religion/spirituality divide at university, I would say, there are no universal problems that arise when all or some humans don't engage in worship, so religion is not a requirement of nature. There is, however, a universal problem that rises in humans when they fail to engage in inner self-cleansing, so spirituality is a requirement of nature. The problem that arises when humans fail to engage in inner self-cleansing is the inevitable rise of demons in their hearts, which gives them urges to want to kill or harm other creatures or terrorise people in the name of religion or something else. Spirituality is the practice of hygienic needs of the human heart. We need it to hold on to civility and progress."

Habiba smiled and her eyes glowed.

Then she said, "If you were talking to me like someone from the street, how would you put the same concept to me?"

"If I were to be talking to someone in the street, I would say, if you don't worship anything, demons cannot rise in you and make you want to kill people or become cruel to animals. But if you don't engage in inner self-cleansing, like you need a daily bath, demons can rise in you and make you want to kill or harm people."

"So we don't need religious experts to fight religious terrorism."

"No. They don't have the power for casting out demons like Jesus did, so the Mejai is trying to open our eyes to what we need to keep demons at bay, and how to factor them into our decision-making…"

"For instance, steering clear of positions that you have no talent for, which, as he said, caused some people to become breeders of suicide bombers and paedophile priests in the priesthood."

"Yes. We cannot treat the problem of demons as some joke to do with religion and defeat terrorism. That's nigh impossible. You don't take medicine for stomach-ache when what you've got is a headache. That's stupid."

25

THE MEJAI RETURNED to the podium to yet more thunderous applause, which went on for almost a minute before the hall quietened down again.

Turning to the crowd, after he had bowed his head and mouthed a little prayer, he said, "You can be spiritually strong without being religious. You can be highly religious yet highly evil and immoral. You can be highly religious yet extremely weak spiritually.

"Religion is about worship. Worship includes idol worshipping. Idol worshipping is about the worship of anything that was created by humans.

"Humans have, since Babel, worshipped idols that have led them into wrongdoings and highly immoral activities, especially when they become Beelzebub warriors. Beelzebub warriors are humans harboured by powerful demons, which causes them to create sects in religion, kill for their religious sects, and start worshipping them instead of worshipping God.

"Among the religious sects that humans created from their minds and killed people for are the Catholic/Protestant divide in Christianity and the Sunni/Shiite divide in Islam.

"A Christian's hate of Jews and Muslims is idol worshipping, as it is a worship of Christianity and not the worship of God. A Muslim's hate of Jews and Christians and other non-Muslims is idol worshipping, as it is a worship of Islam and not the worship of God. A Jew's hate of gentiles is idol worshipping, as it is a worship of Judaism and not the worship of God.

"A Catholic's hate of Protestants and vice versa is idol worshipping, as it is worship of a branch of the Christian faith that was created by humans with their hands and not the worship of God. A Sunni's hatred of Shiites and vice versa is idol worshipping, as it is worship of a branch of Islam that was created with humans' hands and not the worship of God. All who hate others on religious grounds are Beelzebub warriors.

"Upon creating mankind, God said unto him, *'Be fruitful and multiply'*. Life and liberty are thus God's first and foremost gifts to every human. He who takes life or liberty from any human thus engages in a theft war and will not be allowed to go scot-free. He who asks you to take liberty from the grasp of another human invites you to a theft war.

> *"He who invites you to murder calls you to a theft war.*
> *He who wants you to make others live in fear is engaged in a theft war.*
> *He who denies others freedom of worship is engaged in a theft war.*
> *He who compels is a theft war-monger.*
> *He who stands in the way of liberty is a theft war-monger.*
>
> *We warn you now that sectarian killing is a theft war.*
> *We warn you that sectarian killers are Beelzebub warriors.*
> *We warn you now that not one murderer shall set foot in Paradise.*
> *We warn you now that what your demons use you to do you did."*

With that, the Mejai ended the brief lesson on Beelzebub warriors to help mankind. Then the whole hall rose and applauded the helping hand.

26

A RICH RANCHER from Brazil in the crowd had spent millions of his hard-earned money to build churches in Rio to thank God for his blessings. He had also housed the poor and fed the hungry because of the teachings of Christ. For years he had been hearing rumours about paedophile priests but he could not bring himself to believe a word of it.

Even when victims were taking the Church to court left, right and centre, he told his wife, Elena, that the victims were lying.

"How would you know?" his wife said, looking horrified.

"Elena, Jesus served little children and taught his followers about their importance in the Kingdom of God," he replied. "I cannot see how a priest, who calls the name of Jesus daily, can harm little children anywhere on Earth, let alone harm them so cruelly in the House of God."

The Mejai's teachings on the powers of demons changed all that.

With that, he rose to his feet and said, "Mejai... tonight is the night that everything changed. Tonight is the night that I finally came to believe paedophile priests can exist and harm little children in the House of God."

"What changed your mind?" the Mejai said.

"Your teachings about how demons can enter priests, as well as laymen, and cause them to do horrifying things changed my mind. What helped me the most, however, was when you said demons can rise in any human who takes on jobs that he has no talents for or takes on jobs that are bigger than talents at his disposal. My brother took on a job in public office that he clearly had no talent for. He hanged himself while our part of the world was asleep at night. I now believe he killed himself because he could no longer live with the demons that entered him in office."

"But you had Judas Iscariot," the Mejai said.

"I don't understand, Mejai," said the rich Brazilian rancher.

"You had Judas Iscariot to make you see beyond doubt that demons can enter any priest or Pope."

"I still don't understand, Mejai," said the rich Brazilian rancher.

"Judas Iscariot was one of the twelve disciples of Jesus, which makes his position in this life greater than that of all Popes and priests that have come and gone and will ever be. For Judas sat with Jesus. Judas conversed with Jesus. Judas dined with Jesus. Judas was taught by Jesus. Judas saw Jesus cast demons out. Yet demons were able to conquer Judas and use him to betray Jesus. Judas only killed himself after the devil subjected him to mockery by opening his eyes to what his demons had used him to do."

"So the life of Judas was meant to teach us about powers of demons?"

"Yes. The life of Judas was meant to open eyes of mankind to the magnitude of evil that demons can use humans to do. Jesus performed miracles. Jesus had the power to escape Judas and death on the cross in a miraculous manner for all to see. But he allowed the betrayal of Judas to be his last teachings to people of this world. He wanted people to see that, if demons can conquer one of his Disciples to betray him, any human – Pope, priest, ruler, lawmaker or judge – can be conquered by demons."

"In that case, sir," said the rich Brazilian rancher, "I have a question about we the people's rights."

"Go ahead."

"We, the people, have the right to enter church and all Houses of God without fearing paedophile priests or breeders of suicide bombers that could be lurking in there, so I want to wage a holy war against hate preachers, paedophile priests and breeders of suicide bombers and drive them out of every House of God. What do you say to that, Mejai?"

"And how do you intend to fund your holy war?"

"God blessed me with money. I will spend a billion US dollars if I have to."

"But we cannot finance holy war with money."

"Why can't we, Mejai? The Arabs do. The Muslims do. The crusaders did. The Muslims call it Jihad. We call it crusade."

"Crusaders and Jihadists delude no one but themselves. No human can fight a holy war with money, not even an inch of it."

"I would be most grateful, if you can show me why, sir."

"Can you raise money to fight against yourself?"

"No."

"A holy war is a fight to prevent demons from entering your soul. Holy war is a war to prevent demons from turning you into a criminal through twisting of your thoughts. Holy war means inner self-cleansing: a war to keep demons away from the human heart. It is deemed holy because it requires no weapon that can harm anything or another person. It is regarded as a war because it involves a lifetime struggle to stop demons from wasting your talents and that of your fellow humans."

"Thank you for that illumination," said the rich Brazilian. "Thank you so much. But we want all paedophile priests, hate preachers and breeders of suicide bombers out of the House of God. How can we do it?"

"Who said this to you: 'Give unto Caesar what belongs to Caesar and give unto God what belongs to God'?"

"Jesus. Jesus said that."

"Who do you pray to and who collects your taxes?"

"I pray to God and the government collects my taxes."

"How to keep demons at bay belongs to teachings from God. How to protect taxpayers from crime belongs to government."

"Mejai, this is a very, very serious matter because of little children, so please lay bare all the ammunition required. There are more believers than there are nonbelievers. I want to call believers to arms. And I want to fund strategy. We want all paedophile priests and breeders of suicide bombers out of the House of God. And we want to be armed to the teeth before we go to war with those responsible.

"So I have to ask you, sir. Whose job it is to keep demon-filled clerics out of the House of God? Is it the job of congregants, like me, or heads of the Church, like the Pope and the Archbishop of Canterbury?"

The Mejai allowed silence to hold for a moment.

Then he said, "In the division of labour for the protection of man, God and government have different roles on Earth. God is the Church. Caesar is the law. Caesar makes the law. Taxpayers fund the law. Caesar follows taxpayers everywhere to collect taxes. Yet Caesar failed to go to church to protect taxpayers from those who can cause them harm there. Protection of taxpayers does not stop at the gate of any house that taxpayers set foot, the House of God included, so Caesar should have gone to church.

"It is Caesar's full responsibility as a tax collector to protect guests and citizens alike from paedophile priests, hate-preachers and breeders of suicide bombers in every building or inhabitable space imaginable."

"What about the Pope?" the rich Brazilian rancher said.

"Demons cause humans to become hate-preachers, breeders of suicide bombers and paedophile priests. But it is not the role of Popes or priests of any religion to keep demons out of the souls of men who harm children and adults alike. That role belongs to God. And God fulfilled this obligation when he taught men how to fight holy war as individuals.

"Again, without demons, humans will not commit crime, so, to help you protect yourselves from becoming constant perpetrators of crime due to demons, God taught you how to fight a holy war through the prophets.

"Holy war was given to help you avoid breaking the law of Caesar. If you lose your Holy War and break the law of Caesar, it is for Caesar to punish you, not God. God punishes on Judgment Day. God will punish both Caesar – any lawmaker and judge – and citizens alike, if He finds them to have caused His creations to suffer during their days on Earth."

"In that case," said the rich Brazilian rancher, "we must go to war with Caesar. Because Caesar failed victims of paedophilia in the priesthood, Caesar failed victims of suicide bombings by not going to church to protect taxpayers there with laws, and Caesar is still failing us all on both counts."

"Yes, Caesar failed and is still failing. But why is Caesar still failing?"

"Please tell us, Mejai," said the rich Brazilian rancher.

"Caesar is still failing because many men and women are in politics as lawmakers without the right talents for the job. Many more took on Caesar's tasks that were bigger than the talents at their disposal. Lawmakers are supposed to be shepherds. True shepherds never fail mankind, someone will come after me. Through him you will discover how badly Caesar failed because many men took on jobs in politics that they had no talents for. It is easy to protect taxpayers in church without interfering with the Church."

"Someone will come after you?"

"Yes."

"Thank God for that, but what should we do until then?" said the rich Brazilian rancher, who was itching for a fight.

"Until then, protect yourself from demons."

"How do I that again?"

"Leave meats unattended and maggots will rise from them. Leave your hearts uncleansed and demons will rise in you and give you thirsts and addictions that will ruin your life and shock all onlookers no end."

"What about churches and mosques?"

"You have hate preachers, breeders of suicide bombers and paedophile priests not because of Judaism, Christianity or Islam. You have hate preachers, breeders of suicide bombers and paedophile priests because Caesar failed to determine how taxpayers and their offspring are to be protected in every place habitable, including church. The devil saw an opportunity in Caesar's failure and took it. Hence you have many killers of the True Holy War, who twist words of prophets to maim and kill to cause chaos. Caesar has to change; not buildings and Scriptures."

A thunderous applause swept through the hall for almost two minutes.

Then, with the plight of the whole world on his mind, the Mejai raised his voice and said, "*Killers of the True Holy War, who demons use to hex the weak. You failed to heed calls of the prophets to cleanse your hearts and demons got the chance to take complete hold of your senses. Demons use you to kill, after killing the true meaning of holy war and Jihad in your minds and in the minds of those that they use you to hex.*

"*Demons in you are like maggots but far tinier and by far more powerful than maggots. Demons twist words of prophets through your tongue. Demons use you as cars to killing fields. Demons maim and kill through you. Demons use you to throw this world into chaos through waste of humans' talents.*

"Demons turned you into idol worshippers who worship religion, language and sects.

"You worship what was fashioned by damaged minds. You kill in the name of Jihad to blaspheme because you are not in control of your mind to realise it as idol worshipping. You worship religion instead of God because you no longer know the difference between God and religion. You worship language and religious sects instead of God because demons blind you from knowing the difference between God and language and religious sects.

"Come Judgment Day, God will expose your shame. Weaknesses and foolishness that caused demons to enter you will be exposed. Every generation of humans that were affected by the consequences of what demons used you to destroy will witness your shame.

"That day, you will at first feel like you've been woken from only a few hours sleep. Then God will open your mind to your past and you'll realise you've been fast asleep in death for over two hundred years.

"That day, you will know why God had to wait for all the generations that were affected by your evil to die before waking you from the dead with them to judge both you and them together.

"That day, you will see all the men, women and children that your demons caused you to suffer. Then you will realise you were nothing on Earth but one of Satan's tools.

"Demons cannot set foot where God wakes souls from the dead to judge them, so you will become free of demons for your mind to become as clear as daylight. Then you will see.

"Then you will see that, contrary to what your demons were telling you on Earth, no one goes to heaven for murdering people and wasting talents that God gave them to serve others.

"Then you will also see that no one goes to heaven from earth before Judgment Day, except those who were sent down from heaven in the first place.

"You will see. You will see. That day, you will see Paradise from afar and know straightaway that you will never set a foot in Paradise. For, upon waking you from the dead, God will make you stand where those who go to hell are made to stand.

"All the people that you murdered, tormented and did not allow to have peace on Earth will laugh at you from a better standing place. Buckets of tears will not save you. Nothing you do will change God's mind. Then, totally free of your demons, you will realise the only weapons humans need to fight a holy war on Earth are good thoughts."

The Mejai continued, *"To those of you whom demons have failed to conquer to date, hear this if you have ears to hear: good thoughts keep demons at bay. Good thoughts are the only reason why we need prayers. Good thoughts are the only reason why we need to fast at times. Good thoughts are the only reason why we need meditations. Good thoughts are the only reason why we need to recite Psalms in the Bible.*

"Good thoughts are the only reason why we need to recite verses in the Koran. Good thoughts are the only reason why we need to give alms. Good thoughts are the only reason why God sent the prophets. Good thoughts bring out good things in us. Good thoughts are the only reason why God gave Moses the Second Commandment.

"The most potent weapon in a holy war is the Second Commandment, which says 'Thou shall love thy neighbour as thyself'.

"Adherence to the Second Commandment cleanses man in spirit like nothing else can. It is irrelevant to the Second Commandment whether a neighbour has faith or has no faith or belongs to another religion or religious sect.

"Fail to love your neighbour as yourself and you'll lose Holy Wars more than you drink water. Demons will then rise in you and control your thoughts to fill you with what wastes talents of humans on a large scale. No man, whose days started on Earth,

has ever won Holy War for another human. Each man was meant to win his own holy war because God judges each on his own.

"All the prophets needed to do to help each of you win his own holy War are already done.

"The sole purpose of holy war is to help each of you avoid becoming a constant crime perpetrator who wastes talents. Every time you fail your neighbour, you lose a holy war. Every time you fail your profession, you lose a Holy War. Every time you fail your community, you lose a holy war. Every time you fail your country, you lose a holy war. Every time you fail the rest of mankind, you lose a holy war.

"Every time you lose a holy war, get up and try again. Always get up in spirit and try and try again. God will give you chance after chance, until the day you die. Then there will be nothing more but Judgment Day."

The longest applause of the night swept through the hall when the Mejai finished.

Then the rich rancher from Brazil rose back to his feet and said. "Mejai, is it possible for me to love everybody on Earth?"

"Love is not always required, until you have to make a decision," the Mejai replied. "Love is not always required, until your fellow human is in need. Love is not always required, until you are provoked. Love is not always required, until your neighbour comes under threat or attack. Love is not always required, until you have to make decisions in a profession. Love is not always required, until you have to make decisions that will affect everyone that you have responsibility for. Love is not always required, until you have to make decisions that will affect all peoples under your care as a leader.

"Nothing is more powerful in holy war than the Second Commandment. Get the Second Commandment badly wrong in any matter and it will harm you in spirit like nothing else can. The Second Commandment is the most potent weapon in a holy war."

A lady from Japan rose to her feet, after raising her hand.

Then she said, "Mejai, it seems like you are saying a holy war is not about religion."

"I am," the Mejai replied. "Holy war is not about religion. Holy war is needed by anyone who works for humans or lives among humans, because even the mildest of demons can blind you and make you breach laws that were meant to protect peace and prosperity of others. Even the tiniest amount of demons can make you harass and attack innocent people in streets, homes, neighbourhoods, workplaces and even countries.

"Some will tell you all you need is religion. They are wrong. You can go to church, mosque or synagogue ten times a day, pray hard and read the Scriptures as often as possible, give generous alms, and visit holy cites weekly. None of that can stop demons from rising in you, if you harbour jealousy or evil intentions toward your neighbour or fellow human. The holy cannot be gained by the unholy. Jealousy is an unholy act. Stay away from killers of the True Holy War and you will be fine."

The crowd rose to their feet and showed their appreciation of his help through a thunderous applause.

Then the lady from Japan said, "Is there another way in which demons can enter us, apart from failure to cleanse our hearts?"

"Yes," the Mejai said. "There are demons that rise in humans. And there are demons that are despatched into humans by the devil. The devil's demons are far more powerful and far more aggressive; they always shout God's name through tongues of their captives before and after they kill.

"But, whether demons in you rose in you because of your failures or the devil despatched his demons into you because your failures gave him the chance to do so, you will be absolutely responsible for everything your demons used you to waste or destroy.

"Hence God made means of fighting a holy war to depend not on money. Hence God made means of fighting a holy war to depend on no one but on you as an individual. No one can blame his defeat in a holy war on another person, priest, group or religion. Each man's holy war is his own. Those who have ears let them hear."

With that the Mejai finished answering questions about holy war.

Then the crowd rose to their feet again and started cheering.

27

FOR AN ENGLISHMAN in the crowd, the night had been a disaster. He was a university lecturer with a doctorate degree in biology. He had no belief in the existence of God whatsoever because of a book called, *The Origin of Species*. Jihadists and crusaders affirmed his belief that God cannot exist. Paedophile priests made matters even worse. For months, he had been preparing to take the Mejai to task on the question of God's existence. He wanted to take the opportunity to show that there can be no life after death, so people better enjoy this world the best they can.

Then, bang, the bombing of London changed everything, for the hall was informed at the beginning that no other question would be entertained until no one had any questions to ask about terrorism in the name of religion. The Englishman feared he might not get the chance to ask any question at all, so he started his question on the point of God and war.

"Mejai," he said, after rising to his feet, "if God exists, what is stopping him from halting religious wars that are being fought in His name left, right and centre?"

"There's not a single war fought in this world that can be called a religious war," the Mejai replied.

"Why?"

"There are only five sources of war in this world. Every war that has been fought since this world began can be traced down to one or more of those five sources. Religion is only used as a cover in order to gain wider support. A visiting angel was the first creation of God to trace the five sources of war on this earth. He disliked them so much he put them on a list and called them only by their number."

"All right, what's source number one on the list?" the Englishman said.

"Source number one on the list is jealousy. The best known example of source number one can be found in Cain and Abel. Both Cain and Abel made religious offerings to God. God had praised Abel for making the best offering to Him but did not praise Cain to the same degree. Cain became jealous of the praise that God showered on his brother and he killed him. Most Jealousy Wars are disguised as religious wars. Many nations and peoples have started Jealousy Wars by disguising them as religious wars in order to gain wider support from people of their faith."

"What is source number two?"

"Source number two on the list is theft. One of the oldest examples of theft war can be found in the history of the seven kings. Seven kings joined hands in Biblical times and went from country to country to steal things and people that never belonged to them. Abraham gave chase after them when they took Lot captive. And Abraham rescued Lot from captivity at their hands, after defeating them in battle.

"Humans have always lusted after other people's properties: lands, mineral resources, holy sites, holy relics, historic sites, historic relics and works of art, labour and liberty included. What humans often do is to use religion as a disguise to engage in theft wars, knowing it will gain them wider support from people of their faith.

"The cruellest form of source number two, theft war, is slavery: theft of a man's life, liberty, his labour and his happiness. Many rulers have started theft wars and camouflaged them as religious wars in order to gain wider support in their communities and countries. Many claim to be fighting for God when thieving. Yet the visiting angel said this of God to men in his message:

"Of His splendour, nothing on Earth can add value.
Of His majesty, nothing in Heaven or Earth can make greater.

Kindness is greater in His sight than all holy sites on Earth put together.
Children well raised are worth more to Him than all temples combined.
Holy sites can aid worshipers.
But no holy site can make God holier or greater than He already is.
God lacks nothing.
Once His spirit departs a place, its holiness becomes null and void."

The crowd rose and applauded long and hard, after which the Englishman said, "What is source number three?"

"Source number three on the list is greed, the best example of which can be found in the life of Saul, King of Israel. In the beginning, Israel existed but had no king. God saved Israel from the hands of Pharaoh, who was engaged in a theft war by enslaving Israelites. God took Israel to safety through prophets. God ruled Israel through the Prophet Samuel.

"One day, the elders of Israel went to the Prophet Samuel

and demanded for themselves an earthly monarch. As a true prophet, Samuel asked the elders of Israel to give him a moment; then he ran to God and told Him what the elders of Israel were after. God warned Israel what an earthly monarch would cost. Still, the elders of Israel said, 'Give us our own king.' They had seen kings and queens of other nations and lusted after their pomp and ceremony, not realising how fortunate they were to be ruled by God through a prophet, so God asked the Prophet Samuel to make Saul first king of Israel.

"Saul was a man from the least tribe of Israel. Yet, upon tasting power, Saul became disobedient to God. God decided to replace Saul with King David because God made Saul king so God was responsible for whatever evil Saul uses the throne to do. Sadly, Saul chose not to go quietly.

"Saul chose to fight decisions of God Himself by killing David. He raised an army and gave chase after David, determined to kill David and stop him from becoming king. Saul lost the war, lost his crown and lost his life, which paved the way for David to become the next king of Israel.

"Now, Samuel was a prophet but he did not try to keep power when Israel demanded for herself an earthly monarch. God saved Israel from Pharaoh's hands and used Moses to serve Israel. Still God did not declare war, let alone a so-called holy war, against Israel for rejecting Him, their God. Saul, who was not even a prophet and was from the smallest of the tribes of Israel, was the only one who did not relinquish power gracefully. Instead of saying, 'Thank you, God, for making a king out of nothing', he fought to the bitter end because of greed

"Yes, both Saul and David were made king of Israel by God, but the war that Saul fought against David had nothing to do with religion and cannot be called a religious war.

"Human history is littered with greed wars disguised as religious wars. The vast majority of today's developing countries are littered with greed wars disguised as Jihad or crusade or a religious war by another name. Most greed wars are disguised as tribal wars or racial conflicts or a fight between east and west. Election rigging is a greed war.

"Unlike God and His prophet Samuel, people of less talent always try to rig elections to stay in power when they are rejected by the people. Hundreds of millions of children's talents are wasted on Earth yearly because of greed wars. Most unemployment and poverty on Earth today are due to greed wars disguised as something else."

The crowd rose and applauded long and hard.

Then the Englishman said, "What is source number four?"

"Source number four is lazy men," the Mejai replied. "There once lived a man called Lazy, who owned three horses called Race, Tribe and Religion. Lazy hankered after power but had neither the energy nor the talents needed to go with it. Jesus fasted for forty days and forty nights to help him serve all of mankind for life; Lazy could not fast for a day and night to help him serve his people for a week. He hated all sacrifices that could help leaders lead people to green pastures. Yet, upon tasting power, he enjoyed it so much he decided to keep it, until he died.

"What Lazy had in abundance was an insatiable appetite for parties, accompanied by extreme love of munificent coverage of himself in the media.

"He therefore brought the state media under his control. Then he started spreading untruths and propaganda to help him keep power for life. He threw parties and lavished presents on those who sang his praises. He hardly worked more than three hours in a day in office. His excuses for not working hard could fill the length of the Bible.

"He soon wrecked the economy and unemployment went through the roof throughout the land. Schools failed to open due to lack of funds. Parents failed to feed their children because they had no jobs. Hospitals failed to treat patients due to lack of funds to buy medications and equipment and pay doctors and nurses. Everything failed to function because of Lazy and Lazy alone. Waters of the land became badly polluted due to poor sanitation. Men, women and their children died in their thousands of starvation and disease.

"God, in His mercy, had given unto the people a major weapon, the power to *decide* who is to occupy their seat of power through elections, so that, come Judgment Day, the people cannot say they had no hands in the choice of leadership that ruined their lives and wasted their talents.

"Election took place and the people voted to get their seat of power back from Lazy. Lazy called some of the people to his office and asked to know why they wanted him out. The people told him that they just wanted to try their luck with someone else. Lazy thought about things for a moment. Then he asked the people to go home and wait for a broadcast to the nation.

"Moments after the people's backs were turned, Lazy ran to his stable and checked the state of health of his three horses, Race, Tribe and religion. He jumped on Tribe and found it had serious limitations for the task at hand. He jumped on Race and found it was sick. He jumped on Religion and found it could take him the farthest, so, late at night, while the people were fast asleep, Lazy jumped on religion and rode fast to people of his faith.

"'Rise, people,' Lazy told the few gathered at his invitation. 'Infidels have come to me demanding the seat of power of this nation. I have more than enough money to lead a fight against the sacrilege and desecration of our faith by infidels. Let's use it to save our faith and our honour from infidels.'

"'Get Tribe,' one of the gathered shouted.

"'Tribe has serious limitations; we won't get far,' Lazy shouted back.

"'Get Race,' another man shouted.

"'Race is sick; the whole world will turn against us for riding on a sick horse,' Lazy shouted back.

"A long argument about the risks involved ensued, after which corrupt members of Lazy's religion took Lazy's looted money and went and hid it where Lazy could never get it back. Then they hurried back to Lazy and said, 'Use what you've got or forget about the seat of power.'

"Lazy looked at them and said, 'What have I got?'

"The bravest amongst the looters stepped forward. Then he said, 'Unemployment has hit the roof. Starvation and disease have killed people in their millions since you took the seat of power. People's talents turned to dust in countless number. Everybody knows you have no talent for the job, Lazy, so we say, yes, Tribe has serious limitations; yes, Race is sick; and, yes, religion has faults. But they are still all you've got to keep power, Lazy, so use them, if you really want to keep power. Give us all three horses that you've got and we will do the rest.'

"Lazy gave them all the three horses and they jumped on Race, Tribe and Religion and charged forward. People of different race, tribe and religion came under severe attack within days. They were subjected to attacks after attacks in a bid to subdue and silence them, until they were left with no choice but to jump on their own horses of religion, race and tribe to fight back.

"A nation of two hundred million people soon became *the land of two hundred million slaves of two hundred millions horses*: one slave for every horse. Every human in the land became slave of a horse. Why?

"Horses are three times bigger than humans. Horses occupy more space in fields, streets, villages, towns and cities than humans. Horses have by far bigger stomachs than humans. Horses need more feeding fields than humans. Horses drink more water than humans, so water, food and space became scarce in no time at all. Two hundred million horses were in constant need of food, drink and spaces to stand, sleep, rest, urinate and excrete.

"The two hundred million people came to find themselves in

a quandary. Get off their horses and they risked being crushed to death by those still on their horses. Stay on their horses and they faced long waits on horseback to get their horses food and drink. They faced thirst, starvation and bad air because of horse urine and excrements. Streets became congested with horses. Smell of horses' excrement made people's lives a living hell. Roads leading to riversides were always blocked by horses dying for a drink.

"Two hundred million humans were left with no choice but to house, feed and quench the thirsts of horses first before anyone else. Horses called Race, Tribe and Religion drank all their water, ate all their food, occupied all their spaces, urinated everywhere they needed to sit, dropped their excrement everywhere they needed to relax, and started eating every plant and flower when there was nothing left for them to eat.

"Two hundred million humans lived in fear as the slaves of horses and became so mentally unstable it was difficult to classify them as humans, for they could not organise anything, let alone be creative. They lost their minds due to malnutrition and unhealthy environments unfit for animals, let alone humans. What they foolishly thought would guarantee their safety and security turned them into slaves, paupers and the biggest laughingstock on Earth.

"Farmers could not get off their horses and farm. Teachers could not get off their horses and teach. Physicians could not get off their horses and heal. Engineers, traders and people of every profession imaginable could not get off their horses and work, so farming died; justice died; education died; electricity died. Jobs died. Everything died.

"Eventually, Tribe lost. Race lost. Religion lost. Everybody lost because the horses, Religion, Race and Tribe, could no longer be fed by people who could not get off their horses and work. All their horses became weak and useless. Behaviours that are preserves of beasts of the wild took hold, and the people started behaving like beasts born without talent. They created nothing and invented nothing. God, meanwhile, was waiting to throw all of them in the fire of hell for wasting all the talents that He gave them.

"Through one lazy man's war, two hundred million humans faced hell on Earth. Children suffered from birth to the grave. Children who could flee the madness ended up abroad. But those fit to be kings and queens of industries at home became cleaners and ignored nonentities abroad..."

The audience interrupted the Mejai with applause.

Then he said, "Cast a gaze at any developing countries on Earth today and you will find the horses – Tribe, Race and Religion – in the way of human talents; enslaving humans to leave them with nothing but chaos, abject poverty, starvation, total waste of talents and overwhelming stench of excrements of beasts. Money needed for job creation, education and training to make talents flourish throughout the lands is being used to accommodate, feed and quench thirsts of the horses Tribe, Race and Religion, which makes lazy men's war the most expensive war on Earth today.

"Yet lazy men's wars are disguised as Jihad, holy war or a battle between east and west. They deceive no one but themselves. Come Judgement Day, they will have no one to blame but themselves."

The audience leapt to their feet and cheered.

Then the Englishman said, "And source number five?"

"Source number five on the visiting angel's list is the LOFWAR, which is an acronym for Lucifer's Own Favourite War. The LOFWAR is the only reason why humans need holy war, namely, constant cleansing of the heart.

"The devil's demons chase after humans in the following order: they want clerics first and most; then rulers; then lawmakers; then decision makers; then judges. All humans in positions of authority are under constant attacks at the hands of demons despatched by the devil, who wants to control all things on Earth through bad rulers and corrupt judges.

"Whosoever fails to constantly engage in the cleansing of his heart in a position of authority will sooner or later fall in spirit to the devil's demons. Then he or she will start having supremacist thoughts. Demons give humans supremacist thoughts to start LOFWARs (Lucifer's Own Favourite War) because it is the quickest way to waste human talents in their droves.

"The most wasteful LOFWAR ever fought on Earth to date through supremacists thoughts was the one waged by the Nazis, who wasted human talents to an extent that will affect this world for many centuries to come. LOFWARs are always disguised as something else in other to gain wider support in a country or countries or within religious communities.

"No war ever fought on this earth can be accurately described as a religious war, where the characters involved are carefully examined. Religion is only used as a cover to fight a jealousy war, theft war, greed war, lazy men's war or a LOFWAR, or two or more of them combined."

The Englishman was not satisfied, far from it. "What about the battle that Moses fought with Pharaoh?" he asked. "Where is it on the list?"

"Who started that war, Moses or Pharaoh?" the Mejai replied.

"Well, it can be said that Pharaoh started it," the Englishman replied.

"And what did Pharaoh want from it?"

"Pharaoh wanted to keep the Jews as slaves in Egypt to work for him."

"That makes the war that Moses fought with Pharaoh in Egypt a greed war preceded by theft war. Slavery is a theft war. Pharaoh took Jewish life, liberty, labour and happiness for free in slavery. Then he became greedy and would not let Israel go when God asked him to let Israel go. Everybody, did Moses use a sword to free Israel from the hands of Pharaoh in Egypt?"

"No," the crowd roared in unison.

"Therein lays another character of God that exposes all Crusaders and Jihadists as liars," the Mejai said. "God needs not swords and guns to get anything that He wants on this Earth. God used spiritual powers through Moses to free the Jews from slavery. God changed waters of the Nile into blood and caused fish of the Nile to die. God caused the Nile to stink and Egypt did not have any water to drink. God made blood to be everywhere in Egypt and plagued Egypt with frogs which clambered over Pharaoh and his people. God turned Aaron's staff into maggots which filled the land of Egypt and were everywhere on man and on beast. God infested Pharaoh's palace and the houses of his courtiers with swarms of flies which threatened Egypt with ruin. God killed all the livestock of Egypt with pestilence and caused all of Egypt's horses, donkeys, camels, cattle and sheep to die.

"If God can defeat Pharaoh's Egypt without a sword, and turn the River Nile into blood and cause fish in it to die, will God need so-called Jihadists and terrorists to get anything for Him on this Earth?"

"No," the crowd roared, and started cheering on their feet.

Then he said, "How God crushed Pharaoh in Egypt with spiritual powers exposes all crusaders and Jihadists as lying captives of demons.

"Every man and woman was endowed by God to provide talents to serve mankind on Earth for over 1,500 years but through their children and their children's children. He who kills a man will therefore owe five hundred years of life, which is the cost of talents that the murdered man's bloodline would have gifted this world. He who kills a woman before she gives birth to any children owes a thousand years of life.

"They know not what they do because they know not why

God created humans. Demons control their thoughts day and night, so they bomb cities, town and villages around the world in the name of Islam when what they are actually engaged in is a LOFWAR(Lucifer's Own Favourite War).

"Killing in the name of religion is a LOFWAR. Killing in the name of a religious sect is a LOFWAR. The bombing of London yesterday was a LOFWAR, preceded by jealousy war.

"LOFWAR-mongers with jealous hearts call themselves Islamic. Come Judgment Day, they will know what is Islamic. God will judge them as individuals not as a group of Islamic clerics. Then Muslims who failed to do everything to protect the peaceful heritage of Islam for generations of humans to inherit and walk the earth with honour will know that God is God, so He does not engage in injustice of any kind."

With that, the Mejai waved and left the stage for a ten minute break.

Then the crowd leapt to their feet and engaged in the longest cheering of the night.

28

DURING HIS YOUNGER days on Earth, the Mejai used to travel quite often in disguise to carry out field research by himself. During the course of one of his travels, he came across a man, who introduced himself Hindu Guard.

They met on a day when the Mejai was fasting. Christians are not allowed to say it when they are fasting. When fasting, Jesus told his followers, they should let it be a matter between them and God, who alone can reward them, so the Mejai could not tell Hindu Guard that he was fasting.

Hindu Guard offered the Mejai an orange and the Mejai took the orange to eat it later. Hindu Guard wanted to know why the Mejai would not eat the orange there and then, like he was eating his, but the Mejai could not tell him that he was fasting.

It turned out Hindu Guard carried pocketsize copies of the Bible and the Koran with him at all times because of "the brothers", as he liked to call Jews, Christians and Muslims, whom he liked to argue with no matter where he found them.

Upon realising that the Mejai was a Christian, Hindu Guarded wielded his Bible and Koran and said, "You Jews, Christians and Muslims think God belongs to you alone."

"No," the Mejai replied.

"You claim God uses only your prophets."

"No. Pharaoh was not a Jew, Christian or a Muslim. Yet God used Pharaoh through a dream to save mankind from of a great famine that lasted seven years. Yes, Joseph, a Jew, interpreted Pharaoh's dream. But it was Pharaoh's dream that saved mankind."

"So you believe God made Pharaoh dream?"

"It was God who gave humans the ability to foresee things through dreams. Every human can dream, if he does not with his own hands block what makes humans see things in dreams before they can happen."

"Do you believe a Hindu can be used by God in this way?"

"Yes. God endowed us all abilities to serve His creations."

"Then why do you Christians say only you are worthy of Paradise? Why do Muslims say those who do not convert to Islam will not go to Paradise?"

The Mejai took the Bible from Hindu Guard and he read from the chapter and verses that said, '*Many will come from the east and the west and sit down with Abraham, Isaac, and Jacob at the feast in the Kingdom of Heaven. But the sons of the kingdom will be cast into the outer darkness, where there will be weeping and gnashing of teeth*'

The Mejai closed the Bible and gave it back to Hindu Guard.

Then he said, "All humans are God's children. Children of Abraham are just a specific group of God's children tasked with different duties, like salt, tomatoes and pepper have different duties in a soup.

"As you've just heard from the Bible, many boastful Jews, Christians and Muslims, who think they are worthy of Paradise, will be greatly disappointed come Judgment Day. Just being a Jew, Christian or a Muslim is not enough. You have to perform your duties in the soup that is this world, so that all who come to taste it can realise how much God loves them."

"Okay," Hindu Guard said. "Now answer the huge question."

"What is the huge question?"

"Jews, Christians and Muslims bark at each other, like dogs, as soon as they meet in a street. Why is that?"

"Is that the huge question?"

"Yes. Dogs bark and growl at each other as soon as they meet in the street. Jews, Christians and Muslim do the same. They bark and growl at each other in every street on Earth, until their owners – the difficulties of life – drags them away. Okay, Jews and Christians don't bark at each other so much when they meet. But when Jews and Muslims meet or Christians and Muslims meet, oh my God, they bark and growl and bark and growl at each other, until the difficulties of life drag them away. Is that a curse or what?"

The Mejai chuckled.

Then he said, "There are Jews, Christians and Muslims. And there are distracted Jews, distracted Christians and distracted Muslims."

"What's the difference?" Hindu Guard asked, looking curious.

"Distracted Jews, Christians and Muslims are individuals who are harboured by demons. Demons in distracted Jews and demons in distracted Muslims bark at each other as soon as they meet in the street. Demons in distracted Muslims and demons in distracted Christians bark at each other as soon as they meet. Same thing happens whenever demons in distracted Jews meet demons in distracted Christians. They're no longer in control of their minds. Demons speak through them. I trust you know about King David."

"Yes."

"David, king of Israel, said of their ilk in the Scriptures: '*they make a noise like a dog and go round about the city. Behold, they belch out with their mouth; swords are in their lips... the Lord shall laugh at them. God will have them in derision.*'"

"What?" Hindu Guard gasped. "The greatest king of Israel agreed with me that Jews, Christians and Muslims bark like dogs?"

"Yes, King David spoke about their barking. But barking things are not humans in control of their faculties. Demons make barking noises through their tongues. That's why you hear a lot of barking in the streets."

"Okay," Hindu Guard said, "which one of them has the more powerful demons in their bodies, the barking dogs?"

"*By their fruits ye shall know them*," the Mejai replied.

"Please don't joke with this now," Hindu Guard snarled. "Barking dogs with the most powerful demons will set this world on fire, I tell you."

"What made you think that?"

"Muslims want world domination. Christians want world domination. Jews want the same. They are fighting each other for world domination. The winner will become the most powerful beast on Earth. The winner will then set their sights on India and China. Then the whole world will go down in flames. Do you know what I call them because of this?"

"No."

"I call them armpit rovers?"

"Why?"

"They go around the world looking for people to put under their armpits. Yet the armpit rovers don't want to be under anyone's armpit themselves, which makes them the biggest hypocrites on Earth. What do you think?"

"God owns the Earth, not demons barking through tongues of men."

"What does that mean?"

"It says in the Bible, 'The Earth is fixed.'"

"Yes, I saw it. What does it mean?"

"It means God imbued fixed rewards and fixed consequences in every aspect of nature and in every act and inactions of man.

Curse is imbued in every attempt to fight against the instituted by God, which includes the promise that God made to Abraham. Lands that any of the three children of Abraham call their own will face devastating consequences, if they go against God's promise to Abraham…"

"What was God's promise to Abraham again?"

"God promised Abraham that He would bless Isaac in one way and bless Ishmael in another. Jews and Christians got their blessings through Isaac. Muslims got their blessings through Ishmael. Any Jews, Christians or Muslims that fight against this promise that God made to Abraham will face chaos, severe pestilence, droughts, floods, and all manner of natural disasters in their lands. Then, come Judgment Day, they will be sent into the fire of hell for fighting against God's promise to Abraham.

"The more distracted Jews or distracted Christians try to harm or humiliate Muslims, the more angels of God will go and help Muslims win that particular battle because of God's promise to Abraham. The more distracted Muslims gang up against Jews, the more angels of God will go and help Jews win that particular battle because of God's promise to Abraham. The more distracted Muslims try to kill Christians or push Christians around to impose Islamic norms and laws on them in their own lands, the more angels of God will go and help Christians win that battle because of God's promise to Abraham. Not one of them can conquer the other because of God's promise to Abraham. If God has to kill ninety per cent of them He will, for God's promise to Abraham is far more important than any of them."

"What about the rest of us?" Hindu Guard asked

"God will never let them conquer you," the Mejai replied.

"Why are you so sure?"

"Their fortunes are tied to God's promise to Abraham. Their resources will diminish in value for them to suffer like never before if they try to conquer what God did not promise

Abraham. The curse is imbued in attempts to fight what God instituted. Nothing can overcome God's promise to Abraham."

Hindu Guard took a huge sigh of relief.

Then he said, "May the God of Abraham keep it that way."

"Fear not," the Mejai said. "Jews do not refuse wealth that came from products of Hindus. Muslims do not refuse to board aircrafts that were built by non-Muslims. Christians do not stop bowing before Jesus because he came as a Jew. Jews, Muslims and Christians flee to each other's lands when they face ruin. How humans live reveals the true depths of their faith. As for God, did He deny Hindus any talents that can be found in Jews, Christians and Muslims?"

"No."

"That is God. God gives to all equally. How each organises themselves is what makes the difference. Whether a man has faith or has no faith, God gives him talents to serve the rest of mankind. Turn your back on anything that God gave to serve you and you will have only yourself to blame in this world and in the next."

"The God of Abraham is wise," Hindu Guard said.

The Mejai replied, "Not one human on Earth is an enemy of God, as demons in distracted Jews, Christians and Muslims want you to believe. God does not love any people more than the rest, as demons in distracted Christians and distracted Muslims would like you to think. God showed His equal love for all by hiding something from every people and every faith."

"Are there things that Jews don't know?" Hindu Guard asked, looking greatly surprised.

"Yes," the Mejai said. "God did not have to tell Jews everything, and God did not tell Jews everything, so Jews don't know everything there is to know about God. God did not have to tell Christians everything, and God did not tell Christians everything, so Christians don't know everything there is to know about God. God did not have to tell Muslims everything, and God did not tell Muslims everything, so Muslims don't know everything there is to know about God.

"God hid Himself from humans of all faiths, without exception. Yet pointless ignorant aggressive persons harboured by demons will come to you and say, 'You must worship God the way we do. You must. You must. You must.'

"Ask the same pointless ignorant aggressive persons to tell you what God looks like and they'll become so lost in their thoughts that they will make you feel so sorry for them. Who has earned the right to force anyone to worship what he has not seen and does not know himself?"

"Nobody," Hindu Guard replied.

"No people and no faith know everything there is to know about God, so none has right to compel," the Mejai said.

"Did God hide something from Abraham, the father of faith?"

"Yes."

"What did God hide from Abraham, the father of faith?"

"When God said to Abraham, *Abraham, take your only son, Isaac, whom you love and go to the land of Moriah and offer him as a sacrifice to me,* Abraham did not know God was testing him. God hid what He was trying to do from Abraham. As it was with Abraham, so it is with every human. God is testing everybody. The test of every individual is different. Tests of people of different faiths are also different. God is testing you as a Hindu."

"How is God testing me as a Hindu?" Hindu Guard frowned.

"God did not reveal everything there is to know in one religion. What you know in your religion is your blessing. What you do not know in your religion is your test. What you can understand in your faith is part of your blessing. What you cannot understand in your faith is part of your test. "

"What about non-believers, did God leave them out of things?"

"No. What non-believers can't understand about believers is part of their test. What believers can't understand about non-believers is part of believers' test. Fail to concentrate on your test and you'll fail. Allow tests set for others to distract your attention from tests set for you and you'll fail. Foolish is the believer who concentrates on tests set for others than his own.

"All believers who kill non-believers simply because they are non-believers are distracted and will fail."

Hindu Guard embraced the Mejai with great joy. Then he said repeatedly, "God's servant; God servant; God's servant."

29

HINDU GUARD WAS in the audience at the Royal Albert Hall as a special guest of the Mejai. He had been calm and attentive and happy all night.

Then a young man rose to his feet to ask about the last prophet and Hindu Guard started shifting in his seat, knowing what was coming next.

The young man was a British Asian, who had just left university.

"Mejai," he said, "Islamic scholars have it that Mohamed is the last prophet. They are all in agreement that God sent prophets to Jews before Jesus came and Christianity started. Then God sent Mohamed as the Last Prophet to convert all humans to Islam. Why are Jews and Christians refusing to yield to the message of God's last messenger?"

"This is the root cause of all the bombings," Hindu Guard mumbled.

The Mejai, meanwhile, waited until the hall had become dead silent.

Then, turning to the young British Asian, he said, "Did the Islamic scholars tell you that they read everything in the Torah before they started reading the Koran?"

"No."

"Did the Islamic scholars tell you that they read everything that Jesus said in the New Testament before they started reading the Koran?"

"No."

"Are you conversant with contents of the Torah, the New Testament and the Koran?"

"I know a lot about what's in the Koran but not what's in the Jewish Torah and the Christian Bible," the young British Asian replied.

"From what you've learnt in the Koran, when Moses came to the Jews did God ask Arabs, Indians, Chinese, Africans and Europeans and the rest of mankind to become Jews and practice Judaism?"

"No."

"From what you know in the Koran, when Jesus came did God ask all Jews, Arabs, Asians, Africans, Americans, Europeans and all humans on Earth to become Christians?"

"No."

"Did you come across gradual global religious progression in the Koran?"

"I don't know what that is."

"Gradual global religious progression is where one form of worship is imposed on all humans by God each and every time a new prophet comes along."

"I don't think I came across something like that in the Koran, no."

"Then know it now. God has never imposed one religion on all of mankind. Do you know why?"

"No."

"The objective behind the creation of man is the reason why God has never and will never impose one religion on all mankind. God compels not because of Judgment Day. It will be insane, unjust and unfair to compel man to do anything, and then turn round to say you want to judge him on Judgment Day. How can you judge the compelled? How can you force a person to sit in one place and then turn round to judge him for sitting in one place? What will you judge him on... for sitting exactly where you forced him to sit until the day he died?"

"Okay," the young British Asian said. "Why then would Islamic clerics and scholars teach concept of the last prophet?"

"Mohammed is God's prophet," the Mejai replied. "Mohammed came to fulfil God's promise to Abraham that He will bless Ishmael and give him twelve princes. Go and check pre-Islamic history of Arabs and Muslim countries in Asia and beyond before the coming of Mohammed, you will find Mohammed made them by far better than what they were with his message from God through the Koran, which God gave to Mohammed in a miraculous manner of its own.

"Concept of the last prophet, which distracted Muslims take to mean 'one sent by God to annihilate all the faiths that existed before his arrival', is not a message from Mohammed. It is a bogus human invention devised through tongues of distracted Muslims harboured by demons. Concept of the last prophet was born out of supremacist thoughts. Supremacist thoughts are given to humans by demons. Demons teach supremacist thoughts through tongues of men to cause chaos. Demons got distracted Muslims to teach gradual global religious progression, which has no basis whatsoever in God's behaviour toward mankind throughout history.

"Satan's demons speak through the tongues of those who teach global religious domination. They will enjoy brief fame among humans on Earth, but come Judgment Day, they will grind their teeth on the way to hell to pay for every chaos, confusion, waste and destructions that their demons used them to cause."

Hindu Guard beamed with joy and blew the Mejai a kiss.

"Strong desire for global religious domination is a lust for power fuelled by total insanity," the Mejai continued. "Total insanity is brought about by the devil's powerful demons in humans. Demons give them insatiable thirst for throwing this world into chaos. But the Holy Koran is clear.

"It says in Heifer section 8: 62 of the Holy Koran, *'Those who believe (in the Koran) and those who follow the Jewish (scriptures) and the Christians and the Sabians – any who believe in Allah and the last day, and work righteousness, shall have their reward with their Lord; on them shall be no fear, nor shall they grieve.'*

"If the Prophet Mohammed came to annihilate all religions before him and turn all humans into Muslims, what is the Heifer section 8: 62 doing in the Koran?

"Beware of distracted Muslims parading themselves as scholars and clerics whose teachings part from the Koran. Through them demons throw this world into chaos to waste your children's talent. Through them hatred, pain and suffering multiplies throughout the face of the earth for doubt in God's existence to increase.

"God has made His decision and He made it loud and clear: He decided to bless Isaac in one way and bless Ishmael in another. From the blessings that God chose to bestow on Isaac came Jews and Christians. And from the blessings that God chose to bestow on Ishmael came Muslims. That's how it will remain until the end of the world."

Hindu Guard leapt to his feet to his feet in a bid to start cheering before anyone else. Then the whole hall followed suit and cheered to the rafters.

30

AMONG THE THOUSANDS of people in the crowd, was a lady from Sydney in Australia. Born in Chicago in America, both of her parents were doctors. Her mother opted for research work in medicine that took her to Australia and the whole family followed her to the country.

She passed all her high school exams in Australia and she was admitted to university to study medicine in Sydney. During her first week at medical school, she met a bright Aboriginal girl and they became firm friends. Both were keen swimmers and they swam together regularly.

One day, on their way back from swimming, they were attacked by two labourers who wanted to rape them and the bright Aboriginal girl died of heart failure in the process. The Chicago-born American girl in Australia failed to recover fully from the incident. She left medical school and ended up a journalist in a bid to expose failures in government and deficiencies in law enforcement. She lost her faith completely and stayed away from preachers and their churches, until she read about the Mejai, whom she had since wanted to interview.

"Mejai..." she said, after rising to her feet. "What is the point of prayer, if someone who prays to God daily and goes to church or mosque weakly is among those murdered by terrorists in the bombing of London yesterday? And, if God exists, why could He not prevent those who pray to Him from being murdered by terrorists yesterday?"

Silence fell throughout the hall.

Then the Mejai looked at her and said, "Of all the things in this hall, what is the one thing that you cannot do without?"

"People," she said.

"What about air?"

"Yes, I cannot do without air," she replied.

"Can you see air?"

"No."

"Can you feel air?"

"Yes."

"In that case, let's deal with the existence of God first through what happened to your good friend, the murdered bright Aboriginal girl…"

"How did you know about that?" she interrupted, looking greatly shocked.

"Jesus did not perform miracles for nothing," the Mejai said. "He performed miracles to give men something to think about."

"You knew about what happened to me thirty years ago without anyone telling you?"

"I can tell many people in this room what happened to their parents before their parents got married, but that is not why I'm in this world."

"Why are you able to do that?"

"Why were you able to win a lot of dancing competitions, until a bad foot injury changed the direction of your life?'

"You know about that, too?"

"Please answer the question."

"I had a gift for it."

"And I have a gift for what I do, so let's not waste time and use the life of the lost bright Aboriginal to look into another character of God. Air cannot be seen yet it is what men cannot do without. Air cannot be caught or held yet men feel its existence daily. Men cannot see their own breath yet breath is the one thing they cannot do without.

"*Sweet breeze causes mouths to utter praise.*
Gale-force wind causes wailing and gnashing of teeth.
There are days when the wind blows not.
Then men forget they live covered by air from floor to roof of the skies.
There are days when the wind blows wildly.
Then men realise they live in a pool of air that can end their days.

Fish of the ocean are covered by water from surface to bottom of the sea.
Men on land are covered by air from the soil to roof of the sky.
Yet fish can't hold water in their fins, men can't hold air in their hands.
That's evidence that what matters is not proof of what gives life.
What matters is how to seize the great chance to be through thought.

Fortunes of all creatures on Earth depend on abilities and capacities.
If you cannot prove existence of air by holding it to show it to people, don't waste your time trying to seek proof of the existence of God.
It is sure proof that you don't have the ability to prove God's existence.

To say what men cannot prove cannot exist is a sign of
brain defect.
Seek of proof of the existence of God is a sign of disability
in thought.

Existence of air is established through the contact known
as feel.
Feel establishes faith so those who have no faith are not in
the wrong.
And those who have faith have nothing to prove.

When wind blows not in the direction of man he cannot
ask it to do so.
When the wind blows in man's direction he cannot tell it
what to do.
All man can do is to act according to what he feels or
cannot feel.
Hence sweet breezes cause mouths to utter praise.
And gale-force wind causes wailing and gnashing of teeth.
Hence those who have no faith are not in the wrong.
And those who have faith have nothing to prove.
What touches man steers his utterances and behaviour."

A thunderous applause swept through the hall.

Then the Mejai said, "The manner of the bright Aboriginal girl's death caused wailing and gnashing of teeth. Had she lived to pass all her exams to become a doctor, mouths would have done the reverse to utter praise. But can the manner of her death really call the existence of God into question?

"Upon deciding to create mankind and upon deciding not to let mankind have concrete proof of His existence until Judgment Day, God imbued mankind with spiritual antennae at the point of creation. Spiritual antennae enables mankind to foresee things before they can happen. Spiritual antennae gives warning-signals through instincts, intuitions and dreams. A human's spiritual antenna is supposed to protect him or her on all travels, as well as when he or she is contemplating ventures of any kind.

"Ensuring provision of spiritual antennae to each and every human at the point of creation is the surest way to give mankind spiritual protection on his travels without constant interference on the part of God.

"God made animals to be food that other animals must depend on to be. Yet God endowed animals, too, with spiritual antennae of their own, which enables them to enjoy the game of life before they are eaten.

"There is, however, one huge difference between humans' spiritual antennae and animals' spiritual antennae. Humans' spiritual antennae can be diluted and damaged. Animals' spiritual antenna can neither be diluted nor damaged. The only reason for this is free will. Animals have no free will, so animals cannot damage their spiritual antennae with bad behaviour. Humans have free will so humans can damage their spiritual antennae with behaviours that are not conducive to the spiritual aspect of their nature. Unfair and unjust use of free will damages spiritual antennae of individuals to leave them in harm's way or put them in harm's way.

"Hence animals can escape war zones and would-be natural disasters before bombs are dropped, whilst many humans are totally oblivious to what is about to happen until they are killed in large numbers.

"Every use of free will enhances or damages a human's spiritual antenna. Every decision of a human will strengthen or weaken his or her spiritual antenna one way or another, especially when dealing with interests of another human. It's the best way for God to fix things on Earth and avoid interference at every turn.

"Once you use your free will to damage or dilute your

spiritual antennae badly at one point or another, it cannot offer you the strongest protection possible. Then you can hardly know things in advance through dreams or intuition. Hence many people die at the hands of natural disasters and man made disasters.

"Most humans' spiritual antennae are damaged early in this age, mainly through one or a combination of the following: corrupt child rearing, corporate corrupt child rearing involving bad laws of a state, parental ignorance, and, finally, self-misdirection.

"Community or countrywide total ignorance of the spiritual needs of man, encouraged by brute human determination to engage in excessive enjoyment of certain aspects of life, regardless of their spiritual consequences, is the first source of danger to an individual's spiritual antenna.

"The second source of danger to an individual's spiritual antenna is religion taken the wrong way through self-misdirection in sectarianism, which causes humans to constantly engage in behaviours that are extremely harmful to spiritual antennae.

"Corrupt child rearing, the self-misdirection of harming nonbelievers and innocent people, and discrimination on a variety of unfair grounds in matters relating to religion, sect, race and gender, all dilute and destroy an individual's spiritual antennae."

A thunderous swept through the whole hall at this juncture.

Then the Mejai continued, "No one can tell why the spiritual antenna of the bright Aboriginal girl failed to alert her to lurking danger before she was murdered. No one can tell why her best friend's spiritual antenna failed to alert her of lurking danger on the day they were subjected to the brutal attack. But remember that it is possible for a human to dream and not remember the dream, let alone what warnings it contains, until it has become too late to make good use of it.

"Remember that Pharaoh could not interpret his own

dream. And, until Joseph was called upon from a prison yard to interpret the dream, Pharaoh's dream had no value to anybody. Remember also that all sorts of evil forces were at work to kill or destroy Joseph. Thankfully, and thanks also to Joseph's enormous spiritual strength, some of which was displayed when Joseph refused to sleep with Potiphar's wife, Joseph survived every lurking danger to live and interpret Pharaoh's dream and lead Egypt to prosperity as second-in-command only to Pharaoh.

"Nothing is for nothing in this world. Everything we do has a consequences or reward. But we have so much to do in a day to remember everything to the last detail. Hence it is always better to leave matters of this nature for Judgment Day, when every minutia of our days on Earth will be laid bare for us and all to see before we are judged.

"I am not here to judge why anybody's spiritual antenna failed or why anybody's prayers did not yield result. That is a matter for Judgment Day. I am here to enlighten. I am here to warn. I am here to tell mankind that every act and inaction will be accounted for. Every evil will be paid for, and every payment shall be real.

"As for those who attack vulnerable people to take advantage of them, here is what happened to their ilk.

"There lives a creator who creates things out of love. One day, he decided to create containers out of love with sands. He filled some of the containers with air and sealed them up. Then he filled some of the containers with water and sealed them up.

"He left the containers filled with air on land to see how far air can take each of them. And he rolled the containers filled with water into the sea to see how far the ocean can take each of them. Then he sat back to watch his created containers on land and sea.

"A few fools came along and frowned at the sealed containers but failed to see what was in them, and failed to understand ey were where they were, so they drew their swords and _,ued to pierce every container on land and sea opened. What they could not pierce with their swords they open with their guns .

"Then they realised they had a problem. For, as soon as they pierce a container on land open, air from the container will disappear into the larger pool of air around them. Each time they shoot a container on sea open, water from the destroyed container will escape straight into the larger pool of water that was the sea. Every air in every busted container and water from every busted container escaped their grasped, until they became exhausted and fell into a deep sleep.

"One day, after rousing from a deep sleep, they found themselves staring at something that made no sense to them, for their eyes could not tell where it begins and where it ends.

"Then, suddenly, a voice said unto them, '*You destroyed my handiworks. You pierced my containers. You caused my air and my water to escape from containers in which I had kept them. Bring back my air. And bring back my water. And put each and every one of them back in the exact container in which they were before you caused them to escape. Then seal the containers and give them back to me in the exact conditions that you found them. Else I will punish you and I will annihilate you. I will make you pay seven times seventy-seven times the number of your years; then I will annihilate you with fire to be no more.*'

"Tongues that were once sharp as blades froze. Legs that once strode the Earth became worse than jelly. Hands that were once quick to draw swords and guns could not stop trembling. Minds that once churn out boasts became empty. Awe shot down their senses down completely.

"It was not in their gifts to see where water from a particular container now lives in a larger pool of water, let alone go there and get it. Neither did they have talents for spotting where air from a particular container now lives in the larger pool of air, so they lost. They were punished, as was promised. And they were later extinguished, as was promised."

The audience rose and clapped long and hard.

Then he said to them, "What were you cheering, the story or the punishment?"

"Both," they roared.

Then he said, "Man lives on the Earth's floor, like some sea creatures live on the ocean's floor. There are more things on Earth than God gave humans eyes to see, for the vision cap of man and the mental cap of man imposed by God was meant to make man's days on Earth worth living.

"The vision capacity of every creation of God is tailored to match its mental capacity. Its mental capacity is tailored to match the objective behind its creation. The reason for both is as follows: if a creation sees what its mind cannot cope with, its life will become unbearable; then the objective behind its creation will be defeated. God gave man eyes to match his mental cap. Man is not to see what can defeat the objective behind his creation.

"There are things wandering above your heads right now that God gave you eyes not to see, because watching their activities will take control of your senses and interfere with the objective behind the creation of man."

A table and a glass of water were brought to the stage at this juncture.

The Mejai dipped his index finger in the water. Then he pointed his index finger downwards for the water to drop for all to see.

After the water dropped from his finger, he turned to the crowd and said, "The soul in man is lighter than a drop of water from his index finger. The soul of man is so tiny it can be contained in a drop of water. God alone can identify the soul of a man once it departs his body.

"Throw a cup of water into a lake and it will be lost to your eyes for good because the vision cap imposed on man was tailored to match the mental cap required to meet the objective of his being.

"Throw water from your cup into the sea and God can get that cup of water back from the sea, and show you why it is the water that once lived in your cup. Same applies to the soul of man. All souls depart the bodies of men on Earth to end up in the vast pool of souls from whence God gave man soul.

"God has no need to interfere just to prove anything to those living on Earth. The bright Aboriginal girl is lost to man but not to God. God sees her daily because God can. I've already told you why God does not interfere in what individuals choose to do to others on Earth, be it murder or robbery.

"The day will come when God will raise the bright Aboriginal girl from the dead to stand beside you and all who shared her life. Then you will see Justice at its very best. Death is hard on the living but not on the dead.

"Souls of the dead return to the pool of souls, until the Day of Judgment. We humans speak and behave selfishly when it comes to life and death; we want our loved ones to be with us for life, yet we cannot grant them eternal life, let alone make it worth their while. We cannot make a human live strong for life and not suffer from old age. Yet none of us want our loved ones to die. None of us want those that we consider good to depart because mankind lacks good understanding of why God granted him free will and consciousness.

"Grant your shoes free will and you'll never be able to wear them at will ever again. Grant your beds free will and you'll seldom find them where you need them at night. Grant your chairs free will and they will never be available when you want to sit on them. Grant your clothes free will and they'll never be in your wardrobe when you need them.

"Free will is granted to be used. Free will comes with rights. Once free will is granted to a creation, its creator has no right to interfere with how it decides use it. Interfere with free will as a creator and you'll be unjust for breaking laws that govern free will. Man is too small to argue with God and win, far too small."

The audience rose and cheered to the rafters yet again.

Then he said, "To the small mind of man, only those who use swords and guns and violence to kill are murderers. No. Bad laws kill. Corruption in courtrooms kills. Unfairness kills. All bad laws, unfairness and corruptions kill humans but slowly, which is, arguably, the worst form of death.

"We have researched thoroughly. And we know that most of your leaders, lawmakers and judges are murderers who kill people but slowly, so, if God is to kill murderers and kill would-be murderers before they kill, you will have no one to lead you or act as judges in your courtrooms, for God will have to kill most of your leaders, lawmakers and judges, who kill people as well but slowly. Come Judgment Day, you will see how many of your rulers, lawmakers and judges killed millions of people daily but very slowly, which is the worst form of murder."

The crowd swept to their feet yet again.

When the hall quietened down again, the Chicago born American girl from Australia rose back to her feet and said, "Mejai, where did God keep my friend? Where does God keep souls that have left this world until Judgment Day in heaven?"

"Good question," the Mejai said. "There's life with awareness and life without awareness. Death is life without awareness. Living is life with awareness. You may lose awareness for over a hundred years before God wakes you up from the dead. Yet when God gives you awareness back to be judged, it will feel like a normal four or eight hours sleep. Hence death is hard on the living but not on the dead. The reason for this is the behaviour of souls.

"Souls are effectively trapped in the body of the living. They can live nowhere on Earth, except in the human body. Hence the soul escapes through the last breath of man to head straight back to the Pool of Souls, which it can smell from the bottom of the ocean to the roof of the skies.

"The Soul flies faster than anything man will ever see. The soul never stops and nothing can stop it, until it nestles back in the pool of souls. To those who read the Bible, do you remember God saying to Cain after he killed Abel, *'The voice of thy brother's blood crieth out to me'*?"

"Yes," the crowd roared.

"It is because God hears cries of souls on their way back to Him from this world. The pool of souls is like the bosom of God. God hears the propelling wings of souls that are about to leave the Earth. God hears them when they are on their way. God knows the jubilation sounds of souls. God alone understands the jubilation sounds of souls.

"On its way back to the bosom of God, the soul becomes life without awareness. Once back in the pool of souls, the soul loses individuality – it can no longer say I or we. Come when you are to be judged, God will grant awareness back to your soul. Once granted self-awareness back, the soul will rise in an identifiable body to become an individual again; then it will get all its memories back intact.

"Now, if you die today and your son dies fifty years later, your son will be woken from the dead at the same time as you because humans are judged by generations that their lives and talents were meant to serve, as well as all the generations that their use of talent or waste of talent affected. Humans don't go straight to heaven or hell when they die, except those who came from heaven in the first place, like John the Baptist, who had a life before this life and God made him aware of it from the beginning to the end."

The crowd leapt to their feet, yet again, and applauded long and hard.

Then a young Spaniard from Hoxton in Hackney in the East End of London rose to her feet.

"Mejai," she said, "Jewish, Christian and Islamic scholars speak as though the gates of Heaven became open to humans only after their faiths came into existence. Did all humans go to hell, until Abraham, Judaism, Christianity and Islam came to be? If people went to Heaven before Abraham was born, how did they gain entrance to Heaven without Judaism, Christianity or Islam?"

"Good question," the Mejai said. "Foolish faith paves paths to Heaven with religion. Wise faith relies on God's justice. Humans were being sent to heaven long before Abraham was born to give rise to the birth of Judaism, Christianity and Islam. Jesus told stories about people that were sent to Heaven long before the Christian faith and later the Islamic faith came into being. Religion takes not a soul to the Kingdom of Heaven. Good use of talent is a ladder that goes straight to Paradise.

"It is through use of talent that men come to see God. It is through use of talent that man comes to experience love, kindness, fairness, helpfulness and generosity. God's mercy and generosity are seen through talents that God gave unto you to help one another. He who is consisted in good use of talent will keep climbing the ladder to Paradise, until he finds himself in the Kingdom of God."

With that, the Mejai brought the questions and answers to an end.

Then the crowd leapt to their feet and started singing and cheering.

31

THE TIME CAME for him to depart and he chose to give them a parting gift, so he left the podium for the first time and stood where he could pace up and down.

Then, while going from one side of the stage to the other, he said, "Man will have no choice, if God wants all men to love Him. It is God's wish that some should have faith and others to have doubt: believers to love Him and nonbelievers to wonder why.

> *"Believers are like the many in love with one.*
> *Nonbelievers are like the few that cannot see why.*
> *That is God's ardent wish.*
> *Kill one nonbeliever therefore and you'll face the wrath*
> *of God.*
> *Heaven is filled with the willing, not the compelled.*

"Man is born into debt because of free will and his talents that comes with it. Kill a human in a world that is fixed to rely on talents that are fixed and you'll inherit debts of the murdered one. Your fathers failed to understand what the Scriptures meant by '*the Earth is fixed*', and they started talking nonsense after nonsense. Steer clear of demon-filled clerics, whose spiritual antennae are so badly damaged whoever they touch shall end up ruined.

"Two pillars of God stand to help you identify them: God's promise to bless Ishmael one way and bless Isaac in another is the first pillar of God. The second pillar of God is the gifted saying, '*By their fruits ye shall know them*.'

"When faced with provocations, think first and foremost about damages that your response can do to your spiritual antenna. For in every provocation lies the devil's attempt to get you to damage your spiritual antenna with your response. You need your spiritual antenna like you need your breath. Decisive victories come from good fortune that is greater than that of your every foe, not the amount of fire power at your disposal.

"Firm but fair must therefore by your abiding guide in every course of action. Then chaos cannot reign over you and talents shall not flee your abode. The biggest serpent of all lies in the bottom of the ocean as I speak. If God allows you to see it, you will find it has eyes that are bigger than anything you'll ever encounter. God, in His mercy, shepherds you out of the way whenever it ventures out of its hiding place, knowing your lives will never be the same again, if you ever set sight on its highly disturbing presence.

"We say '*Blessed, blessed day of Pentecost*' whenever we remember what God alone enabled us to see and still stand to deliver.

"Cain made his offering to God with less love and little care, it earned him less praise that led to a jealous heart. Abel gave his best to God and got the highest praise from the Most High. The best offerings that a human can give to God in any age are his best service to man in time, talents and tolerance, which makes you the Abelites of your age, meaning you are following Abel's approach to sacrifice. To respect and tolerate people of every race, tribe, religion, sect, and gender is to hold the Second Commandment dear. I began my work here with a prayer of peace. With that peace I wish you safe journey back to God. Thank God. Thank you. Farewell."

With that, the Mejai waved and the crowd went wild with joy.

Then soon he was gone.

32

OUTSIDE, PEOPLE WERE lining both sides of the street in their thousands; virtually all of them were members of the BEJAVE Movement without tickets for the two-day event. They've travelled thousands of miles from all over the world to London just to catch a glimpse of the Mejai, knowing it was the only opportunity they would ever get to see what he looks like with their own eyes.

Habiba, meanwhile, was nervous about losing Deji-Vita in the vast crowd. The boy did not know London at all so it would be an absolute disaster to lose him in the vast crowd. She therefore asked him to hold her tightly. Then they made their way forward slowly but surely pass Kensington Palace nearby to the Royal Gardens Hotel in Kensington, where they found Holly, Fiffy and Anoushka chatting in the lobby about a fellow celebrity.

Habiba shepherded them into a lift and they soon ended up in a penthouse suite. There, to the girls' great astonishment, Habiba announced that none of them was going back home to Primrose House, until the Mejai had seen Deji-Vita.

"Is the Mejai staying in this hotel?" Anoushka asked.

"No, he's returning to the hotel near Heathrow airport. But he wants to see Deji-Vita by eight in the morning before flying to America. He wants to see you girls, too."

"What?" the girls exclaimed in unison.

The girls had promised to be at a friend's birthday party for at least an hour before the night ended, so they jumped on the phone, one after the other, to apologise for not being able to attend and wish the birthday girl happy birthday.

While they were on the phone, Habiba called room service and ordered some snacks and soft drinks.

Moments after she finished eating, Holly sipped her drink and said, "I'm so glad to be part of history tonight. But I had a slight issue with the Mejai about rape and spiritual antennae."

"Why?" Habiba asked.

"He said our spiritual antennae are supposed to alert us to danger on our travels. Yet he did not leave his hotel room before terrorists bombed the area last night."

"I believe in what he said about animals' spiritual antennae," Fiffy said. "I saw a television documentary that showed all the fish in the sea disappeared before tsunami killed thousands of people in South East Asia."

"We watched that documentary together, Fiffy, and I was amazed by it," Holly replied. "My question is why did the Mejai himself not foresee what was about to happen and leave the area before it was bombed by terrorists and the police sealed off the place?"

"Deji-Vita, what do you think?" Habiba said.

"Two things happen to holy men on days like that," said Deji-Vita. "One is known as foreseen calamitous event allowed to lead. The other is known as foreseen calamitous event allowed to serve. Holy men use the first to expose secrets of a foe, and they use the second to keep serving long after their deaths. Jesus, for instance, knew beforehand that the devil will take him to the top of a mountain and subject him to some tempting offers.

Yet Jesus allowed the temptation to go ahead, and he used it to expose how the devil goes about getting the weak and greedy to work for him to the detriment of us all. That's an example of a foreseen calamitous event allowed to lead.

"Jesus, also, foresaw how he would die and he told his followers long before it happened. Jesus could have used his spiritual powers to avoid being nailed to the cross; he did not do so because he knew in advance that nailing him to the cross will come to serve the most important message of the Christian faith without need of a sermon for thousands of years to come…"

"Which is what?" Holly interrupted.

"Which is… 'the greatest amongst you shall be the servant' – my most favourite saying of all. Jesus allowing himself to be nailed on the cross is the highest example of foreseen calamitous event allowed to serve. The cross brings the message of Christ to mind without need of a sermon. Yet Jesus died over a thousand years ago."

"So what the Mejai did yesterday was a foreseen calamitous event allowed to serve?" Habiba said

"Yes. He must have known through his spiritual antenna that where he was in the Heathrow area was about to be bombed. Yet he chose not to leave because the drama that will precede his very first public appearance will serve his message to the world for life. Every time people talk about the day he gave the world the materials needed for answering the questions 'Who are we?' and 'Why are we here?', they will talk about the bombing of London by religious extremists that preceded it. People will therefore constantly see the difference between true holy men and tools of demons, which are used by the devil's demons to stain the image of faith via bombing of innocent people."

Habiba reached for Deji-Vita's soft drink and took a sip from it.

"What on Earth did you that for?" Anoushka asked Habiba.

"To remind me of the first humans to hear about foreseen

calamitous event allowed to lead and foresee calamitous event allowed to serve. We are the very first people to hear this teaching on Earth," Habiba replied.

"Is that true, Deji-Vita?" Anoushka asked.

"It is true," Deji-Vita replied.

"In that case, I'll have to follow suit," said Fiffy.

"So do I," Anoushka said.

"And so do I," Holly said

So it was that they all sipped Deji-Vita's drink, one after the other.

Hours later, while everyone was fast asleep, Habiba sneaked out of the hotel room and left them a note, asking them to be ready to be picked up at six in the morning.

At five in the morning, the phone in the hotel room rang and roused them from slumber to find Habiba's note.

An hour later, they trooped out of the hotel room and jumped into a waiting car in front of the hotel.

33

HALF WAY INTO the car journey to Heathrow, Deji-Vita started thinking about how he would present his case to the Mejai.

"I am Deji-Vita," he resolved to tell the Mejai, after he had quietly rehearsed in his head how he would present his case. "I had no idea why I was given the name but I am Deji-Vita. The other boy is an imposter. But then, a day after my arrival in London, the Egyptian came and said he had a dream that suggested the other boy is Deji-Vita, which is nigh impossible. I believe the devil himself is hiding in that boy. A seer warned me about him. But it has always been my ardent wish to meet the devil face to face. I've been begging God to let me meet the coward since my eyes fell on the monumental problems of this world and I'm still waiting for God's reply. I therefore implore you, I implore you, Mejai, to question the devil hiding in that boy and I at the same time and see something for yourself."

The car journey ended in front of a huge hotel near Heathrow Airport, and they were welcomed and ushered into one of the hotel's restaurant by a lady dressed in a blue suit, who turned out to be the hotel manager.

She made sure the girls were served tea and coffee and croissants. Then she took Deji-Vita away and ushered him into a lift. They came out at the penthouse to find a tall, handsome man dressed in a white shirt and navy blue slacks had been waiting.

To the hotel manager's obvious surprise, the man rushed forward and fell on Deji-Vita's neck and kissed him five times on the cheek.

"Who is this man?" Deji-Vita wondered.

The man thanked the hotel manager and she disappeared.

Then the man ushered Deji-Vita into the penthouse, closed the door behind them and said, "I'm your brother."

"What?"

"I'm your brother."

"Good try, Lucifer," Deji-Vita snarled, after a brief silence.

"What?" the man gasped.

"Seers told me."

"Seers told you what?"

"Seers told me there's a treasure that you want to steal. And you will turn yourself into whatever you want to steal it…"

"Why then would I bring you here…?"

"You tell me," Deji-Vita snarled.

"You want to kill the devil against God's wish, don't you?"

"Yes, I want to kill you…"

"I'm your brother."

"You are my brother; turn around," Deji-Vita yelled.

Three times Deji-Vita asked the man to turn around. Three times the man did as he was told. Deji-Vita's grandfather had asked him to look for two marks when he meets his only brother but he did not want the man to know.

Suddenly, he looked at the man and said, "Why is the Mejai not here to prove who the impostor is?"

"It was revealed unto him last night that you are my brother, the *real* Deji-Vita, so he decided not to waste your time."

"Then how come the Egyptian did not tell me that?"

"Dr Farouk Al El Majid, you mean?"

"Yes."

"He's scared."

"Why?"

"He said the two of you had a wager and he lost."

"He told you that?"

"Yes. He said you will make him dance and he doesn't want to dance so he has run away."

Deji-Vita studied the man for a moment.

Then he said, "You smell like a king. Why?"

"Blessed be thy name O' Lord our God," the man said.

"*Thou shall not call the name of the Lord thy God in vain,*" Deji-Vita snarled.

"I said that because it was revealed you will say those words to me."

"What words?"

"'You smell like a king. Why?'"

Silence fell between them at this juncture.

Then Deji-Vita glared at him and said, "How did you get the mark on the left side of your face?"

"I was born with it," the man replied.

"What about the mark on the right side of your face?"

"I was an only child. My mother started miscarrying since I was two. For some reason, she became determined to have a second child but she miscarried at every turn. She kept saying I need a brother but I had no idea why. At the age of twelve, I came to believe it was my fault…"

"Why?"

"I've been fighting spiritual battles and spying on demons since shortly after I learnt how to walk, so the devil wanted to see harm come to those who brought me into this world. I decided not to stop what I was doing because I knew God will reward my mother more than a thousand times over. I started leaving home to fight long spiritual battles from when I was fourteen.

215

"One day, after the toughest spiritual battle of my life, it was revealed unto me in a vision that my mother would, at long last, give birth to a baby. And it would be a boy. But she and my father would die on the day the baby would be born. The next morning, a missile hit me on the head while I was thinking about the baby and blood started pouring down my face like never before. That's how I got the mark on the right side of my face."

"And how did you respond to the difficult revelation?"

"I returned home to wait for my brother's birth and my parents' death."

"Did you tell them about the revelation?"

"I was not allowed to share revelations with any human in those days."

"You laughed and dined with them knowing they were about to die?"

"It was not that simple. I cried a lot in hiding."

"Then what happened?"

"My father went on a short journey to buy a ram to be sacrificed for my would-be baby brother. He died in a lorry crash on the way back with the ram. Upon hearing about her husband's demise, my heavily pregnant mother collapsed and fell into a difficult labour and never recovered. She lost so much blood she died seconds after she gave birth to you. I buried both of them within twenty-four hours and turned all my attention to your care."

"Yet you abandoned me and never wrote to me once."

"It was a punishment from God…"

"I beg your pardon."

"I fell so madly in love with you at first sight I took you everywhere with me. Whatever you liked, I liked. You loved smelling flowers a lot so I took you to West Africa College at least three times a day just to smell flowers. One day, it was revealed unto me that it was time I left you to continue with what I was doing and I became upset. Our grandfather, the only member of our family left alive, was getting old, so I asked to be given a little more time with you and the Lord got angry with me..."

"What did He say?"

"According to His messenger, before your birth, I obeyed all of God's commands without fail. I did whatever was asked of me without even the slightest hint of a murmur. Then God gave me a brother and I changed, so much so I dared to tell God what was wise and unwise for a child and it infuriated Him. His angels were working well with me on a plan to rescue countless children from suffering and my love for you got in the way.

"I became a bit lazy and argumentative, after you became a part of me. You came first in everything instead of my mission. I virtually looked at everything through your eyes. Yet it was God who gave you to me in the first place. It was God who made me know what it feels like to have a little brother. Instead of thanking Him by working harder, I wanted to delay things so that I can be with you. I wept bitterly when I was asked to leave you and return to the battlefield for all children's sake. I cared little that all the work that I did prior to your birth could go to waste. Yet it was for the sake of countless suffering children that God brought me into this world, so God subjected me to four punishments.

"Firstly, for crying for you without putting the suffering of countless children first, God decided I must not be allowed to see you again until the day that I was to hand over a treasure to you, for it was only because of the treasure that God decided I must have a little brother. God gave you a life because of a treasure that will terrify the devil to death."

"Carry on."

"Secondly, for putting you above everything I was given life for in this world, I was not allowed to be in the same country as you for more than twenty-four hours until I die. I was, thirdly, not allowed to carry a picture of you with me. Fourthly, if I dare dream of writing to you, I will die before I finish writing the first line of that letter. God will change His plans for rescuing the people that we were given life to rescue from hardship. Then I will be subjected to severe punishment in the next life.

"To make God change plans is a sin that scared me to death, so I gave you *Journeys Back* and left in tears. During my travels, I realised God was right. My love for you was getting in the way. Billions of children are suffering terribly in this world. And there are far too few people who care."

"So we must part before this day is over or you'll be punished?"

"Yes."

"Where would you go?"

"I'm not allowed to say until we're about to part."

"Have you been living in luxury like this since you left me?"

"No."

"Then how come you are here living like a king?"

"That will become clear after I've handed over the treasure."

"Where's the treasure?"

"I cannot hand over the treasure, until you've told me about the dream."

"What dream?"

"You had the same dream on three successive nights in Germany."

"How did you know that?"

"God reveals things about you to me from time to time."

Deji-Vita broke down at this juncture and started crying, as the dream that he had years ago about the crying child flashed through his mind. For years he was very angry with his brother for not contacting him. Now he realised the dream about the crying child was a sign from God that his older brother was among demons, learning things that are extremely hard.

34

THE BROTHERS HAD less than twenty-four hours to do what they had to do for the sake of suffering children of this world, and time was running out.

So Deji-Vita dried his tears and went straight to the point.

"I saw myself and a man called Sir in the middle of a plantation full of dead coconut trees," he began. "The man called Sir was feared by everybody. Around us on the plantation, were many idle workers and countless malnourished men, women and children.

"Suddenly, a stern-looking man appeared from nowhere, glared at us, and whisked Sir and me before a revolving door, above which the inscription, 'The Smoky Casino', was written in the colour of blood. He forced us through the revolving door into the Smoky Casino and we started choking and coughing badly. The place stank and was so full of smoke all we wanted was to get out of there, but we could not find the way out.

"We kept looking for the way out, until, suddenly, our eyes fell on a host of people, some were chain-smoking, some were drinking, some were gambling, some were shouting at each other, some were fighting. Wherever we looked we saw nothing but bad things that disturbed our senses. Most of the people we found there, however, found our reactions hilarious.

"We coughed less and less in the Smoky Casino as time went by. Then we stopped coughing altogether. We, gradually, started talking to people around and many stopped laughing at us. Sir became so comfortable in the place he started drinking, smoking, gambling and fighting with people.

"Just as we started feeling at home in the Smoky Casino, the stern-looking man came and dragged us back into fresh air, where life felt fantastic.

"While we were standing in fresh air, the stern-looking man asked us to sniff the back of our skins and clothes and I went mad with rage. The stench of tobacco that made us choke and cough in the Smoky Casino had permeated our skins and clothes and we stank terribly. I hated the smell on my body so much I wanted to ask for soap, water and sponge to wash myself clean but I was scared of the stern-looking man.

"The stern looking man whisked us back to the plantation of dead coconut trees and hardened the look on his face. Then glaring at Sir, while pointing at the dead coconut trees and the idle and malnourished men, women and children, he said, 'What happened to them?'

"In reply to the question, Sir pointed at the idle labourers; then he pointed at some garments hanging on a rope; then he pointed at some ornaments around. Just as he was about to point at something else, some terrifying creatures appeared and carried him shoulder high. They took him away while he was kicking, screaming and begging for mercy. The stern-looking man turned to look at me at this point and I woke from the dream, sweating like water had been poured all over me. I dreamt this dream in three different German cities on three successive nights. And on all three occasions I awoke at the same point to find myself sweating."

Tea, coffee, chocolates and biscuits were already on a table.

The brother sprang to his feet and poured hot tea for the both of them.

Then he sat next to Deji-Vita and said, "Our conversation is being recorded by two recorders. You can listen to them whenever you want."

"That's very good," Deji-Vita said.

"The plantation in the dream," the brother began, after sipping his tea, "represents talents of a people. Idle labourers on the plantation represent unemployed humans afflicted by depression due to lack of creative people. Garments on the rope symbolise culture. Ornaments in the dream symbolise customs and traditions. The dead coconut trees symbolized sorrow and lamentations. The chokes and coughs that you had when you first entered the Smoky Casino symbolise what happens to humans when their minds first become open to the hazards of this world. Attempts on your part to get out of the Smoky Casino symbolise what all children want to do when their minds first become open to the problems of this world.

"Return to fresh air from the Smoky Casino in the dream symbolized Life after Death. The stench that you discovered in your body upon sniffing your skin in fresh air symbolises what happens to all humans when God wakes them from the dead to pass judgment. All humans discover they stink of evil deeds from this world when God wakes them to judge them.

"There was no sign of creative people in the dream, but there were ornaments, garments, idle workers and malnourished men, women and children; a clear sign that customs, culture and traditions stood in the way of creative people, whose gifts create jobs to make humans' lives on Earth worth the while through gainful employment.

"The middle of the plantation symbolises the heart of a nation or community. You and Sir were in the middle of the plantation so you were responsible for enabling creative people to emerge. It was your job to remove impediments in the way

221

of creative people by providing leadership. Failure to provide leadership led to waste and lamentations on the plantation of dead coconut trees. Everything went to waste on the plantation because Sir failed to provide leadership.

"Now, do you remember how God used Pharaoh to reveal seven years of harvest and seven years of famine through a dream?"

"Yes."

"The same God turned against Pharaoh and humiliated Pharaoh, until Pharaoh had to let Israel go. Do you remember how God asked the Prophet Samuel to make Saul the first king of Israel?"

"Yes."

"The same God replaced King Saul with King David when King Saul preferred sacrifice to obedience. The dream that you had on three successive nights in three different cities represents a warning in the strongest terms."

"God is warning me?"

"Yes."

"Continue."

"Forewarned is forearmed so listen to me carefully. God has put everything you need to succeed in a treasure so He will not tolerate any excuse at your hands. The full interpretation of your dream is already typed. It is one hundred pages long..."

"What?"

"I told you God reveals things about you to me from time to time. What you dreamt about and how you reacted were all revealed to me days ago. I typed the interpretation of your dream by myself to let you know this is serious..."

"I'm not like you; I always listen to God," Deji-Vita interrupted.

"Good. In the Kingdom of Heaven culture, customs and tradition does not excuse leaders from providing leadership on Earth. Leaders are responsible for removing every junk of culture, custom or tradition that stands in the way of humans' talents. Fail to get junks out of talents way as a leader and you'll be shown no mercy..."

"Why is that?"

"Humans are born with five to twenty talents; every one of which is needed if unnecessary human suffering is to be avoided. Every lost talent affects different generations of humans, so no talent is allowed to go to waste. Even the hairs on humans' heads are counted by God, as Jesus told his followers. Since lost talents of a generation affect many generations of humans to come to accelerate avoidable human suffering, wasted talents through senseless custom, culture and tradition are paid for by leaders, whose responsibility it is to get all junks out of the way of talents."

"I see," Deji-Vita sighed.

"Waste one million people's talents as a leader and the number of generations of humans that will be affected by it will surely cause you to end up in the fire of Hell. "

"I see," Deji-Vita sighed yet again.

"Everything starts with children because children are the true humans."

"Why are children the true humans?

"You are required to discover that by yourself when reading the full interpretation of your dream. You will also discover what happens to children when they first set foot in this world. I will therefore only discuss aspects of the Smoky Casino that could raise important questions on your part, so I that can answer them for you before we part."

"Go ahead."

"Every human community is like a Smoky Casino: a dangerous health hazard to all newborn souls. Jewish, Christian, Islamic, Hindu, Buddhist, Sikh and all religious communities contain behaviours that are hazardous to the souls of all newborns, who are the true humans. Tribal, racial, political and trade communities pose the same threat to all new souls.

They all shock and surprise new souls at the beginning of their lives on Earth. The reason for it is what children bring into this world."

"What do children bring into this world?"

"What children bring into this world is known as prior knowledge of the soul. You'll read more about it in the full interpretation of your dream. Prior knowledge of the soul causes children to cry or blush or become angry or feel ashamed when they first encounter bad or evil behaviour in society. But, like your senses adjusted to health hazards in the Smoky Casino with time, the longer children live in on Earth, the more their senses adjust to embrace Lower Forms of Behaviours in societies that are hazardous to their souls."

"So children are subdued by time and compelled by circumstances to embrace lower forms of existence to their prior knowledge?"

"Well done, brother. All children do and can do subconsciously, after embracing lower forms of existence in society, is to make the best of what they are left with in this life. By then the overwhelming majority of them can no longer remember their first day of thought, let alone recall the high morals that they came into this world with."

"What is first day of thought?"

"First day of thought is the day a human started thinking in this world. The human mind has jump-starters. Every human experienced his or her First Day of Thought through one of the mind-jump-starters…"

"Can we discuss those mind-jump-starters now?"

"No, we don't have the time. You will learn that from reading the full interpretation of your dream."

"Okay."

"Now, God does not intervene in matters on Earth, until the objective behind the Creation of Mankind is threatened…"

"Why?"

"There'll be no point in keeping humans on Earth once the objective behind their creation is defeated."

"I see."

"Remember Noah and how God destroyed things on Earth with a flood in Noah's time for a handful of humans to start all over again?"

"Yes?

"It was because the objective behind the Creation of Mankind was threatened at that time. This age has become a Smoky Casino of hazardous religious, racial and tribal communities that is threatening the objective behind the creation of man, so the main purpose of the dream is to get you out there and warn. The problem is there are all sorts of dangers in your way..."

"Why?"

"When people first take office or enter professions anew, existing bad practices in the profession or institution afflict their senses, like heavy smoke and bad smell made you to choke and start coughing when you first entered the Smoky Casino. The longer you stay in office or an institution without tackling existing corruption or causes of ails and ills that you inherited or found in them, the more your senses will adjust to embrace the hazardous lower forms existence that once made you sick."

"So I'm going to come across characters along the way that will prove a health hazard to prior knowledge of my soul."

"Well done, again. They will spare no trick and expense to help you get your hands dirtied, so that you can embrace their lower form of existence and become one of them, some are highly religious but extremely weak spiritually; they are the most dangerous humans in any society. Like the gamblers and chain-smokers in the Smoky Casino, they have no idea what has happened to them. They will have no idea about how the stench of corruption has permeated and destroyed their minds, bodies and spirit, until God's wakes them from the dead to judge them.

"Human senses detect hazards faster when in good health. Humans make better judgments when their vision are neither blurred nor impaired, so deal with ails and ills you found in office before they deal with you. Axe evil before it permeates your mind, body and spirit to blur your vision."

"Thanks for that," Deji-Vita said. Then he quoted Scripture: *"Those who have little, even the very little they have will be taken away from them."*

"Well done, again," his brother said, looking well pleased. "Life proves the Scripture that you've just quoted right. Bad health robs you of work. Lack of work robs you of income. Lack of income robs you of enjoyment of life. Lack of enjoyment of life can make you dull or bitter. The more dull or bitter you become, the more people stay away from you to become vulnerable. The more vulnerable you become the more badly people treat you, so deal with ails and ills before they end up dealing with you. Thank you for quoting that Scripture. It makes my job a lot easier."

"You're welcome."

"Now, hazard makers – the chain-smokers and drunks and noise makers that you found in the Smoky Casino – are talent wasters. Africa has them in huge number at present, so, apart from the main job that God wants you to use the treasure to do, God wants you to give Africa a helping hand, which was why you saw the man called Sir in the dream."

"What sort of help?"

"Rulers in Africa like to blame custom, culture and tradition for their failures. They also like to blame the very people that their failure to provide leadership made poor for everything. God therefore wants you to help Africa back to fresh air."

"Show me what needs to be done and I'll give it everything I've got."

"Good. Step one: to help Africa back into fresh air, you have to tackle junks of customs, culture and tradition head on without fear or favour. You are to warn the people as a whole in no uncertain terms that humans do not come into this world with custom, culture and tradition. Customs, culture and traditions, you are to warn, are mere human creations borne out of fortunate and unfortunate circumstances. All who cause talents to go to waste on a vast scale through customs, culture and traditions are never shown mercy by God on Judgment Day. No leaders facing huge debts in wasted talents accrued by junks of the people known as custom, culture and tradition, escapes the fire of hell."

"I will warn them without fear or favour," Deji-Vita said.

"Good. Step two of helping Africa back to fresh air: the devil tricks men into treating laziness, cruelty, and thuggery as customs, culture and tradition. We found evidence of this even in places where prophets have laboured to educate people extensively. Men, especially, call what were born out of ignorance, laziness, cruelty and thuggery their custom, culture and tradition. Men in many countries see sinful and unfair advantage over their women as their custom, culture and traditions, unaware that unfair advantages are traps of the devil. The devil uses unfair advantages to waste human talents exceedingly, knowing wasted talents increases human suffering for doubts in the existence of God to increase."

"I see," Deji-Vita sighed.

"Increase in doubt in the existence of God causes increase in human wickedness, which, in turn, leads to more wasting of human talents."

"I see," Deji-Vita sighed yet again

"You are therefore to warn, in no uncertain terms, that every unfair advantage has the devil's fangs in its core. All who fall into the devil's trap by way of unfair advantages gained through custom, culture or tradition will therefore not be shown God's mercy. They will be burnt in hell before they are extinguished to be no more."

"I will make sure they get the message without fear or favour."

"Good. Step three of helping Africa back into fresh air: talent is a command of God. Why talent is a command of God is explained in full in the written full interpretation of your dream. You are to let the people know that, because talent is a command of God, it is the overriding duty of man to obey talent, confer honour on talent, and place talent above all else."

"I will do that."

"You are to show how love of God and obedience to God are known through talent and honour conferred on talent. You are to make them see how every talent was meant to serve no less than thirty generations of humans. Every wasted talent therefore adversely affects no less than thirty generations of innocent people. No amount of prayers can therefore save leaders who cause generations of humans to suffer through disobedience to the command of God."

"I will. But have customs, culture and traditions no place in our lives at all?"

"Talent is bigger than a king, country, custom, culture and tradition because talent is a command of God. The place of mere human creations, like custom culture and tradition, is therefore to serve talent, obey talent, and confer honour on talent. God imbued talents in humans to match the needs and wants of man, for it was His responsibility to ensure that His creations do not suffer unnecessarily on Earth. Those who waste talents are thus interfering with His work and will be punished."

"I see. What if a ruler or lawmaker has no faith, and does not believe talent is a command of God?"

"Rulers and lawmakers are judged by the number of talents that they helped to flourish or hindered, not by their faith or their lack of faith. However, if lack of prayers, or failure to strengthen his self in spirit, caused a leader to hinder than helped talents to flourish he will have no one to blame but himself. The purpose of prayer in decision-making is to help us make right decisions."

"Okay. If they ask how the price of talent is measured, what do I say?"

"The value of a man's talents cannot be accurately measured until the Day of Judgment, when the number of humans that his talents were meant to serve shall be laid bare before him. The more he failed to help, the more he will have to pay. Then men shall see for themselves how their laziness and foolishness robbed children of enjoyment of childhood and what it led to. Such culprits shall be punished as though they offered children's life to idols on the altar of pain."

"Thank God for that," Deji-Vita said.

"The man called Sir in your dream was given more than enough in talent to prevent hundreds of millions of children from suffering. He bowed to custom, culture, and traditions and turned children's enjoyment of childhood to dust, which, in turn, wasted children's talents like sand. Yet he had the gore to blame custom, culture and traditions and the very people that made terribly poor for his failures."

"Who was the stern-looking man in the dream?"

"That was the lord of all leaders."

"What?"

"Every trade, vocation and profession on Earth has a lord in one of God's angels, who can appear unto men in human form. The lord of all leaders has more wisdom than all leaders of the world that has come and gone put together."

"Why did he take us from the plantation to the Smoky Casino and then back again to the plantation?"

"Good question. He took you and Sir from the plantation to the Smoky Casino and back for only one reason: to show that what is bad for the rich and powerful is bad for the poor and downtrodden as well. There were two of you but only Sir had power. Yet health hazards in the Smoky Casino had the same effect on you both. Nothing destroys the rich and powerful more than what they allow to harm the poor and the downtrodden.

"A lawmaker cannot get good things for himself and his loved ones regardless of custom, culture and tradition, and then let people suffer and waste their talents because of the same. All humans stink of bad behaviour when God wakes them from the dead to judge them. But bad leaders and cruel rulers stink much, much more. Good and strong leadership is built on obedience to talents. That ends all that I must tell you about your dream. The typed full interpretation of your dream will tell you much, much more."

35

THE BROTHER CALLED room service and they dined together for the first time since Deji-Vita was a four year old. During the course of conversation, Deji-Vita told his brother about his dream about the crying child. Then he asked his brother to tell him about his experience amongst demons.

"It was sickening, terrifying, horrifying and extremely dangerous but highly revealing," his brother replied.

"Why was it necessary to send you in their midst?"

"The devil was despatching demons into weak people in their millions, getting ready to send them around the world to undo works of prophets, by killing, maiming and terrorising innocent people in the name of religion."

"Why did God make it possible for the devil to harbour humans with demons anyway?"

"God did not do that."

"Why then is it happening?"

"God did everything to perfection. Then humans used their free will to destroy it all in the Garden of Eden."

"Have we got time to talk about that?"

"Yes."

"What happened?"

"What happened in the Garden of Eden is known as the first defeat, because it was the very first spiritual battle that humans fought and they lost. Before the first defeat, demons could not rise in humans. God made humans so strong in spirit they could command demons, like Jesus did. The devil tried and tried to despatch demons into humans and failed. Then the devil came to suspect why.

"God had said to Adam, *'Eat of every tree, except the tree of the knowledge of good and evil, for the day you eat of it you will surely die.'* The devil suspected if humans eat from the tree of knowledge that God warned about they will become weak in spirit and he started plotting.

"You know the rest of the story. The devil tricked Eve into eating from the tree and Eve got Adam to do the same. What people don't know is that humans lost what made it impossible for demons to enter them from then onwards, and the devil gained the upper hand. What the devil wanted badly was to destroy all of humans' talents. Man became a sitting duck after the first defeat and the devil started despatching demons into humans to destroy their talents."

"Why was the devil after humans' talents so badly?"

"To show them love, teach them love and make them love, God made humans to thrive by working together in very large groups consisting of various talents that need each other. You therefore cannot overcome humans, until you can destroy or waste their talents on a vast scale. To destroy human talents on a vast scale, you need to harbour them or some of them with demons, especially those in strategic positions, who make decisions that affect families, communities and countries. The devil therefore focuses on despatching demons into humans in strategic positions like mad. "

"Okay. If God did nothing about it during Adam and Eve's time, why did He try to do something about it now by sending you among demons?"

"God did something about it in Adam and Eve's time."

"What did God do about it?"

"There will be no need to keep humans on Earth if the objective behind the creation of man is defeated. The first thing therefore was how to avoid defeat of the objective behind the creation of man, so God put Eve to sleep. Then, while Eve was asleep, God opened her womb to alter how He originally intended babies to acquire talents before leaving the womb.

"The objective behind the alterations in Eve's womb was to make it extremely difficult for the devil to destroy talents of humans before they could walk. God came up with two means of meeting this objective, which were to make it possible for each baby to collect more talents in the womb than originally intended, and to give every baby a bigger capacity for hiding talents deep in the mind, body and spirit before leaving the womb.

"God met both objectives: every baby became able to collect more talents while forming in the womb than God originally intended, and every baby inherited more capacity for hiding talents deep in the mind, body and spirit subconsciously before birth than God originally intended.

"After God finished the alterations in Eve's womb, He turned to Adam and said, *'In the sweat of thy face shall thou eat bread, till thou return unto the ground...'*"

"I thought that was a curse," Deji-Vita interrupted.

"No. That was partly a punishment but mainly a statement referring to how humans will sweat to retrieve talents from their minds, bodies and spirit to enjoy life than God originally intended."

"I take it the alterations that God performed in Eve's womb caused babies to be born way bigger than God originally intended."

"Well done. The womb was reprogrammed for would-be babies to become bigger in the womb than God originally

233

intended. Babies start work subconsciously to earn their talents before leaving the womb than God intended, which is why God does not forgive those who waste talents.

"Above all, the deeper you have to hide talents in your mind, body and spirit subconsciously before leaving the womb, the more work you will need to do after birth to retrieve those talents. Hence God said to Adam, *'In the sweat of thy face shall thou eat bread, till thou return unto the ground.'* God was talking about mankind as a whole when He said that to Adam, knowing how hard it will be from then onwards to retrieve talents from the mind, body and spirit."

"Okay. Why did God say to Eve, *'I will increase your trouble in pregnancy and your pain in giving birth'*?"

"Babies needed to work more in the womb than God originally intended, so God had to make the womb bigger than originally intended during the alteration. The womb had to become bigger. Babies had to become bigger. Babies had to collect, at least, five talents and hide them deep in the mind, body and spirit subconsciously before leaving the womb. Big babies work in the womb for months to collect talents that will increase trouble for women during pregnancy. Getting big babies out of the womb will bring more pain at childbirth. The price that women have to pay to protect their children's talents from the devil became huge. That was why God said to Eve, *'I will increase your trouble in pregnancy and your pain in giving birth.'*"

"And why do babies need to collect at least five talents in the womb?"

"The more talents you put in each individual, the harder it will become for the devil to stop human progress by destroying individuals."

"That's shrewd."

"Yes. The devil came to know about all the new help that God was giving humans and he went berserk, claiming God was being unfair in a fight because God was always doing something to help humans. That was not all. Humans, too, became angry with God and started moaning."

"What?"

"The talent retrieving process proved so complicated and extremely difficult for most humans it drove them mad; so you had two mad creatures screaming at God from different directions for different reasons: humans could not retrieve talents from their minds, bodies and spirit fast enough to enjoy life; the devil could not destroy humans' talents quickly enough to stop them from enjoying anything. Both became angry with God and started moaning."

Deji-Vita laughed for the very first time since their reunion.

Then his brother said. "Do you know what it will take to get all humans to retrieve every talent in their minds, bodies and spirit?"

"No," Deji-Vita said, while supressing laughter.

"Owing to free will and humans' problems with demons, talent retrieving requires the biggest and most complex organising on the face of the earth. Organising a community of humans with different tastes, different strengths and weaknesses, different visions, different start-points, to mention but a few, proved so complicated and so difficult it caused so many humans to go mad and start questioning the existence of God, so many humans became so mad they actually believed God gave them no talent at all, which would take God into the realms of injustice."

Deji-Vita laughed for the second time and said, "They don't know God."

"I know," his brother said. "A lot of humans are mad because difficulties involved in the talent retrieving process made them mad. Organising people to make sure everybody gets a good start is difficult enough because of humans' problems with demons. Then the devil came to discover new means of making talent retrieving even more difficult and made matters worse."

"What new means did the devil discover?"

"Money and taxes..."

"What?"

"Talent retrieving from the mind, body and spirit require kindergartens, schools, colleges and training schools after training schools; all of which have to be paid for through money and taxes. You then need good food, clean water, facilities for exercising and suitable homes and environments, if humans are to learn well – all of which, also, have to be paid for through money and taxes, so the devil came to realise that, if he can despatch demons into people in strategic positions to either steal or waste money and taxes on a huge scale, he can make it next to impossible for the overwhelming majority of humans on Earth to retrieve talents from their minds, bodies and spirit."

Deji-Vita chuckled.

Then his brother continued, "So the devil started despatching demons into individuals in government and strategic places, and they started stealing and wasting money and taxes through bribery and corruption. Consequently, billions of humans in this age came to be left behind in the talent retrieving process, which exacerbated and accelerated the problem of human suffering. Poverty, crime and chaos multiplied; and war spread everywhere."

"So, despite all of God's help, the devil defeated man yet again."

"Yes. The devil will despatch his demons into people in strategic places to make them steal and waste money and taxes, so that many humans can be left behind in the talent retrieving process. Then he will go after those left behind, gather them together with some crazy ideas, turned them into his troops, use them to kill people, and keep shouting God's name as they kill..."

Deji-Vita found the devil's strategy so funny he laughed, yet again.

"Bad start," his brother continued, "make it is easier to dispatch demons into most humans and use them to disrupt or retard progress. Even if you get a good start and become careless or vulnerable, the devil can inhabit you with demons and use you to disrupt progress, which is where most religious terrorists are coming from. The overwhelming majority of them either had terribly starts or were born into chaos. The Talent Retrieving Process drives them mad so easily they want to rely on religion to rescue them…"

Deji-Vita interrupted his brother with laughter yet again.

Then his brother said, "They develop intense hatred for evil rulers, which paves the way for more demons to enter them. The evil rulers, in turn, cannot stop thieving and wasting money and taxes because of their own demons, so they use stolen money to buy guns to kill those who hate them."

"That's a win-win situation for the devil," Deji-Vita interrupted.

"Of course, that's what the devil wanted in the first place. This is why spiritual wellbeing of leaders is crucial to progress. The devil's top generals are rulers, lawmakers and top judges that are conquered by demons. Leaders of terrorist organisations and their cohorts are just the devil's lieutenants. The devil uses them both from different ends to make the talent retrieving process impossible to fund successfully through taxation."

"Why then is the devil not taking credit for his achievement?" Deji-Vita asked. "Why doesn't the devil ask his forces to sing his praises, instead of shouting God's name when they maim and kill and waste talents?"

"Good question. The more demons in terrorists shout God's name before and after they kill, the more people will have doubts in God's existence and the afterlife. The more people doubt God's existence and the afterlife, the more they will do cruel things to each other. The more people do cruel things to each other, the more they will waste talents. The more people waste talents, the more so many humans will keep suffering for the devil to gain more recruits, so the devil is winning. The worst part of it, however, is this: the devil can cause babies to have bad starts in the womb."

"What? What about the alterations that God did in the womb to help?"

"Babies have three needs when forming in the womb. The first is blood of both parents, which babies need to gather talents subconsciously in the womb. The second is the need to gather no less than five talents before leaving the womb. The third is the need to hide talents subconsciously deep in three vaults in the mind, body and spirit before leaving the womb, or else the devil and his demons will destroy all children's talents before they could walk.

"Now, here is why the devil can give babies bad start in the womb. God guaranteed the second and third needs of babies in the womb. The only thing that God did not guarantee is the quality and degree of talents that a child can gather before leaving the womb. That fell in parents' hands."

"So, thanks to the two guarantees of God, every child is guaranteed no less than five talents before birth?"

"Yes."

"Why did God leave the third need of babies in parents' hands?"

"The third need of babies in the womb fell in parents' hands because of free will and how free will works. Every use of free will strengthens or weakens individuals spiritually and physically. Spiritual health of would-be parents comes from acts and actions that are good or evil. Physical health of would-be parents depends on consumption of what is good or not good for their health.

"Babies forming in the womb use parents' blood to shop

for talent. The degree and quantity of talents that babies gather before leaving the womb therefore depend on parents' spiritual and physical wellbeing prior to pregnancy and during pregnancy. God cannot force would-be parents to make the right choices because of Judgment Day..."

"Sometimes you sound like the Mejai," Deji-Vita interrupted.

"The Mejai is my master so that cannot be a surprise."

"Okay. At what point during pregnancy can the devil or demons cause babies to have bad starts in the womb?"

"Man is made of spirit and matter. Spirit gives life to matter. Matter gives manifestation to what's going on in spirit through human actions. The womb is humans' first shop of life; it is where we get everything we need to lead life on Earth. Badly congested shops badly affect shopping. A spiritually badly congested womb badly affects a baby's ability to shop well subconsciously before leaving the womb. The devil knows this, so the devil adopted a strategy of putting all would-be mothers' wombs in a congested state, so that babies shopping in the womb can find it difficult to shop before leaving the womb."

"How can the devil achieve that?"

"To congest wombs and disrupt the first shop of life, you have to create chaos and conflicts in communities and countries to get hate and bad thoughts. Conflicts cause humans to hate and have bad thoughts.

"The more bad thoughts would-be mothers have towards their enemies in conflict, the more their hearts and stomachs will become bitter. The bitterer they become, the more it will affect their spiritual wellbeing adversely. Adverse spiritual wellbeing results in muddles in the pit of stomachs. Muddles in the pit of stomachs create fogs in spirits and wombs.

"Fog in spirits blurs would-be babies' mental vision to shop well in the womb subconsciously. Would-be children badly affected by blurred mental vision will struggle and fight harder than necessary to end up with poor shopping before leaving the womb, which is not good for a child, not good for a community, not good for a country, and not good for mankind."

"The devil is so cruel," Deji-Vita sighed.

"The devil does not see babies. The devil only sees mankind. He says he is at war with mankind, and in war you have to do everything you can to win, so he will do whatever it takes to destroy mankind's talents before they can use their talents to defeat his goal. Sadly, the most common cause of bitterness and bad thoughts in women's world is jealousy. One woman's jealousy of another before and during pregnancy causes many children to be born paupers in talent, so the devil does everything to encourage one woman to be jealous of another where he can."

"A woman has to be strong in spirit and have a good heart to give birth to children who are rich in talent."

"Yes. Good heart is most essential for children to be rich in talent."

"Now I can see why there's war everywhere," Deji-Vita sighed.

"Well done again," his brother said. "The devil encourages war everywhere, knowing it will cause a surge in anger, hatred and bitterness to affect pregnant women, which will, in turn, result in many born paupers in talent in the long run."

"I think the devil has a very strong card here," Deji-Vita said.

"Tell me why," his brother replied.

"Humans are divided by race, religion, tribe, taste, profession and the rest of it, so the devil can exploit these differences so easily and spread anger, hate and bitterness everywhere. Look at the Middle East and Africa."

"Man can still win this fight."

"How can man win it?"

"They can set up expeditious means of settling their differences wisely. They can encourage women to engage in constant inner self-cleansing before and during pregnancy. They can educate women to see why it's in their best interests to keep jealousy and bitterness at bay. More and more children will be born rich in talent, if they do all that. Then life on Earth will be far better than what it is now for most humans. All they need is spiritual awareness and how to make one's self strong in spirit, which is what we must provide."

"How do you get rid of a jealous heart that easily?"

"You get rid of jealousy by counting your blessings. The more you look around you, the more you'll find things that are good about your life. The secret is how to detect what can make you happy."

"Okay. If I came to you and said, please show me how to detect all the things that are good about my life, where would you ask me to start?"

"Start by being grateful that you have a life at all. Being grateful will give you a cheerful spirit. A cheerful spirit will increase your awareness of things in you that will keep you happy. Happiness will increase your baby's chances of becoming rich in talent. Since your child's successes will fill you with joy to enrich your life, you are helping your would-be child to help yourself. The more people succeed at this, the more poverty will diminish for people to see less and less upsetting things around them to make them rich in spirit. Witnessing poverty is bad for children.

"Ignorance has caused so many children to be born as paupers in talent. Ignorance has caused so many people to think they were not born with any talents at all."

"Okay. Let's say you did very well in the first shop of life that is the womb; you got a good start because your mother did everything she could to help you shop well for talent before leaving her womb. The next big problem is how to overcome cruel rulers, bad lawmakers and corrupt officials waiting to help you waste all your talents."

"Yes."

"Now I'm beginning to feel sorry for children of this world."

"Feeling sorry will change nothing. Religion will change nothing. Bombs will change nothing. What will make a change is total focus on how to make the talent retrieving process fair for all throughout the world."

With that, the brother rose to his feet and called room service.

36

THE BROTHERS WERE served more tea and they continued with their conversation. Then, suddenly, the brother reached for a small chest and placed it on a table before them.

"What's that?" Deji-Vita asked.

"The blessings of Dekile," his brother replied.

"Who is Dekile?"

"You are not allowed to know anything about him, until forty days after I've left the face of the Earth."

"When do you do that?"

"That's the last thing you'll hear from my lips. I'll whisper it in your ear."

"What about the spray?"

"What spray?"

"I dreamt of a spray that can kill poverty outright when I was six..."

"There's no such a thing."

"What? O' Eli. O' God of our fathers..."

"What's the matter now? *Thou shall not call the name of the Lord thy God in vain*, remember?"

"I prayed hard and fasted every month, philosophising and

asking God everyday to help me invent or find the spray that I saw in the dream…"

"God was just testing you."

"What?"

"Glorious Pishon, mother of wealth that flows around the Havilah River of all rivers," the brother said, after reaching for a briefcase from which he soon retrieved a bulk of files.

"Read the summarised three pages only due to lack of time," he said, after handing one of the files to Deji-Vita.

"What?" Deji-Vita gasped, after reading the said pages. "Are you serious?"

"Am I serious about billions of American dollars and gold bars in banks around the world? Why would I joke with things like that when I know your temper? That's your spray."

"What do you mean by my spray?"

"People's money is their spray. Your money is your spray. How you use it is what makes it kill poverty as you spray it around. Poverty, hunger, diseases, chaos; all can be killed by it, if you spray it wisely. Hospitals can help you kill some diseases, if you spray a few their way wisely."

"I am a billionaire several times over?" Deji-Vita wondered.

Then, suddenly, he said, "From where did you get so much money and gold bars?"

His brother retrieved five stones and placed them on the table.

"What are these?" Deji-Vita said.

"Your stones," his brother replied.

"What do you mean by my stones?"

"One day, it was revealed unto me to follow you covertly and see something for myself. You were barely three years old then. I waited in hiding, until I caught you stealing yourself away from home and I followed you covertly. To my surprise, you walked deep into the forest and gathered many stones in one place near a rail track. You looked around a few times to make sure no one was watching. Then, to my great shock, you started throwing your gathered stones at intervals, brimming with anger with every throw, while challenging the devil to come and meet you face to face.

"Every demand that came out of your mouth was about the poor. Every argument you made was exceptionally intelligent and fair. But your temper worried me greatly. You shook at times when speaking in anger. You fell occasionally while trying to hurl stones hard in anger. Your confidence in God was never in doubt.

"One day, while I was watching you in hiding, I broke down and sobbed. I felt you were far too young for what was happening and wanted to help. It got me into serious trouble with God and I left you with your stones, arguments and demands.

"Days later, I waited until you left where you were throwing stones in hiding to go back home. Then I left my hiding place and picked up ten of your stones. I took five with me on my travels and buried five in Africa with a message. The five stones before you now became the nearest thing to a picture of you. I looked at them from time to time. A year after I left you, it was revealed unto me to start building a war chest for you, which energised me like never before. That's how the wealth that is now yours came to be."

Silence fell between them, as Deji-Vita let his head droop.

Moments later, he looked at his brother and said, "Did God let you meet the devil face to face?"

"The blessings of Dekile will tell you everything you need to know, after I'm gone," his brother replied. "What I need to know before we part is what started your stone throwing days."

Deji-Vita became silent for a moment. Then he said, "At the very beginning of my days on Earth, something used to come to me every night before I fell asleep. Yes, I was only a baby at the time but I knew what used to come to me nightly was so special

245

and so powerful it could solve any problem for me. *Its* presence was so powerful and it helped me a lot.

"One day, my eyes fell on the poor for the very first time and I panicked badly. I was so shocked and confused by what hit me in the eye I ran helter-skelter looking for God. 'What was that?' I wanted to ask God. I fell badly among the many tobacco plants in our compound instead while running and started crying like the child that I was."

The brother laughed.

Then Deji-Vita said, "That was the day I started seeing things for real in this world. I was so disorientated by the poverty around me I did not know what to do with myself. For some reason, I was in no doubt that what used to come to me nightly could explain things to me or get me out of there. I therefore went to bed early that day because it always came at my bedtime. It did not show up that night. It did not show up the following night. It never showed up again. While waiting for it to show up, frustration got to me and I started stealing myself into hiding to throw stones and argue."

The brother smiled and then recited:

"Minds made boats. God gave men minds to do that.
Boats sail through waters. Minds sail through difficulties.
Ships blow their horns when leaving port.
Minds make noise of anguish when first setting sail.
Minds first set sail when difficulties of life first meet with the eye. Then angels step back for mind's voyage of enquiries to take place.
Else minds' days on Earth shall be rendered worthless and senseless."

The brother continued, "We leave God to come to this world to load and unload Thoughts. At some ports, we unload more than we load. At others, we load more than we unload. At a few ports, we get to neither load nor unload. Now… can you describe the powerful thing that used to visit you nightly, until you first set sight on the poor?"

"No."

"That's it. Eyes of babes can see angels; minds of adults cannot describe them."

"What used to visit me nightly was an angel?"

"Yes, a sure sign that you are a servant of God. Angels change ways of communicating as humans grow. The treasure made yours to inherit will open your eyes to more, after I'm gone. The sources of your wealth are well documented. They are in two of twelve files that I must leave in your care."

With that, the brother left Deji-Vita and made a phone call.

Moments later, a short man and a tall man joined them in the hotel room. The short man introduced himself as Deji-Vita's new lawyer. The tall man introduced himself as Deji-Vita's new accountant.

The brother signed a host of documents and got Deji-Vita to countersign them all. Then the lawyer and the accountant jumped to their feet, having signed what they had to sign and agreed respective meeting dates with their new client, Deji-Vita.

Not long after the lawyer and the accountant disappeared, the brother turned to Deji-Vita and said, "How many ears was God kind to give you?"

"Two," Deji-Vita replied.

"Use them wisely to make them feel like a thousand, for there's a level below which your wealth is not allowed to fall."

"How would I know that? And why?"

"The twelve files will tell you everything you need to know. Venture forth to no meeting until you've read them all."

"Was that why you insisted that my first meeting with the lawyer and the accountant should not be earlier than three months from now?"

"Yes. I believe by then you'll be ready. It's your wealth but God's leash."

"What does that mean?"

"It means God has tied your wealth to the fortunes of a people. If you falter and your wealth falls below a certain level, it will resonate in the lives of the people and they will experience descending spirals in their fortune, until you manage to turn things around, if you can turn them around. It's God's way of holding you in check out of love."

"There must be spiritual rules and guidance for that, I'm sure."

"There are spiritual rules and guidance for the likes of us in every step we take. Seven of the twelve files are full of rules and guidance just for you."

With that, the brother rose to his feet and asked Deji-Vita to kneel before him. Deji-Vita did as he was told, and his brother anointed him with oil.

Then, minutes later, they dined together for the very last time.

37

A BALLROOM ON the first floor of the hotel was occupying a few chosen people. Among the distinguish guests were the German priest who helped Deji-Vita in Frankfurt, the English priest who helped Deji-Vita in Cologne, the American priest who helped Deji-Vita in Wiesbaden, the stammering priest who took Deji-Vita to the white mansion in Primrose Hill, and the Egyptian Dr Farouk Al El Majid who called Deji-Vita an imposter.

Deji-Vita's mouth fell wide open upon spotting all five of them together in the ballroom.

Then, turning to his brother, he said, "What's going on here?"

A lanky man hiding behind a door moved close and said, "Nice to meet you, Deji-Vita. I am Professor Huddleston."

Deji-Vita was so star-struck that he hardly knew what to say. He read about the famous professor in a book; he could hardly believe he was meeting him for real.

Holly, Fiffy, and Anoushka walked into the ballroom at this juncture in the company of Habiba and her husband, John.

Upon catching sight of Deji-Vita in the ballroom, Anoushka turned to her father, John, and said, "What's going on here?"

"Just watch," her father replied.

Professor Huddleston got everybody to surround him and the brothers in the middle of the ballroom.

Then, while pointing at Deji-Vita, he said, "This young man here is a history man. The story of his life brings to mind the biblical story of Joseph and his rise to second-in-command only to Pharaoh in Egypt. Joseph, as you all know, was sold into slavery in Egypt by his own brothers. While in slavery, he refused to sleep with his master, Potiphar's wife and Potiphar's wife falsely accused him of attempted rape. He was therefore thrown in jail on false charges. While in jail, he met Pharaoh's chief cupbearer and chief baker, both of whom were serving time in jail for crimes committed against Pharaoh.

"The chief cupbearer dreamt in jail. And so did the chief baker. As a result of their respective dreams, Joseph told them that Pharaoh will restore the chief cupbearer back to his position in three days, and the chief baker will be hanged in three days. Joseph's interpretations of their respective dreams were proved right, so when Pharaoh himself had two dreams that no one in all Egypt was able to interpret, the chief cupbearer told Pharaoh about Joseph and Joseph was taken from jail to the royal palace.

"Upon hearing Pharaoh's dream, Joseph said, 'Seven great years of plenty throughout Egypt will be followed by seven years of famine, so find a wise man to lead Egypt in storing food during the seven plentiful years.'

"Pharaoh said in reply to Joseph, 'Since God has shown you all this, there can be no wise man other than you.'

"Pharaoh then took his signet ring from his hand and put it on Joseph's hand, clothed him in garments of fine linen and put a gold chain about his neck. Egypt became very rich, thanks to Joseph's gifts, and the world was saved from a famine that would have killed humans in their droves.

"Joseph's rise to prominence in Egypt began with a dream of his own: he saw his brothers bowing before him in a dream and he told them so. It made his brothers so angry they plotted to kill him. They later changed their minds and sold him into slavery in Egypt instead. Then they went home and lied to their father that Joseph had been killed by a lion. His brothers came to bow before him in Egypt, as his dream had foretold.

"What people don't realise in the story of Joseph is that the devil tried to kill two birds with one stone. No one could interpret Pharaoh's dream, except Joseph, so, if you were to kill Joseph or keep Joseph out of Pharaoh's path, you would kill two birds with one stone. Then seven years of famine would have killed humans in their droves. Thankfully, the devil did not succeed. Joseph ended up in the only place where a Jewish boy could be taken to meet the Pharaoh.

"Centuries after Joseph, the devil tried again to kill two birds with one stone. This time, an Egyptian had a dream that troubled him deeply and he called me. Dr Majid, here, was my pupil at Kings College, London, where I taught medicine. As soon as he finished telling me about his dream, I called the Mejai in New York and told him about it. Through the Mejai's interpretation of Majid's dream, a nasty surprise that the devil had in store became revealed.

"God sent two brothers on a mission. The older brother was asked to gather a rare treasure for his little brother to inherit. The little brother was required to use the treasure to save hundreds of millions of people that were suffering terribly. The devil came to know about the mission and decided to stop the mission one way or another

"Both brothers disliked the devil badly, because the devil's injustices caused God to send them down on Earth to help. Both brothers wanted to meet the devil face to face. Each brother begged God to let him meet the devil. God had a problem with their respective requests.

"In the Divine Game of Life, God grants means of defence, retreat, and attack to every creature that is likely to be attacked by another. Where a creature was meant to be living food for another creature, God only grants it ability to escape and live for another day, until it is, finally, eaten. God felt it was only just to treat even living food that way.

"We humans must be capable of fighting the devil in spirit, so God granted us means of fighting the devil in spirit. But, if God goes a step further and grant us eyes for seeing the devil, God will have to arm us with weapons that can help us kill the devil as well, or else it will not be a fair fight.

"So God looked at the two brothers and thought, *'If I grant the little one the eyes needed for seeing the devil and the weapons that has to go with it as well, he will do nothing with his life but look for the devil everywhere. If he finds the devil, he will never stop fighting, until one of them ends up dead, knowing he will end up back with me and I will raise him from the dead.*

"*If the little one kills the devil, he will hurry back to me and say, 'I have killed your enemy for you.' He will not be aware that he achieved next to nothing, for if killing the devil will solve the problems on Earth fairly, I would have killed the devil myself. I will therefore not arm the little one beyond spirit. He will waste his life. I will grant the older brother alone the eyes needed for seeing the devil and all the weapons that has to go with it, because he is very patient. He will be as civil as possible even with the devil.'*

"Not long after God made His decision and battle commenced, the little one became frustrated and started throwing stones while in hiding, asking the devil to come out and meet him face to face if he calls himself a man."

Everybody laughed.

Then tears started falling down Fiffy's cheeks. Deji-Vita saw that and his head drooped.

"The little one did very well in spirit," the professor

continued. "The devil tried everything to despatch demons into him and failed. The devil tried to give him an addiction but failed. Eventually, the devil despatched demons into a few weak men and women, and they came to have thoughts about kidnapping the little one for money, which was where Dr Majid came in. Majid's dream revealed the devil's new intention to use kidnappers. If they succeed, they will kill two birds with one stone without knowing what demons have used them to do, just like Joseph's brothers.

"Armed with the Mejai's interpretation of Majid's dream, I flew on a private jet to Africa with a party of twelve, ten of whom were former soldiers. Our objective was to get Deji-Vita safely to Europe without arousing suspicions on his part. I sent a black lady to his house, and she got his grandfather to attend a secret meeting with me at my seaside hotel, where the old man and I planned everything to the last detail. Later that day, the old man stole his own grandson's flight ticket and one thousand American dollars…"

"What?" Deji-Vita gasped.

"I asked your grandfather to steal your money…" said the professor.

"May I know why, sir?" Deji-Vita replied.

"It was the only way to get you out of Africa without arousing suspicions on your part. There was a plot to kidnap you in Germany. The gang behind it were sure they only wanted you for money; but their demons had something else in mind. Once they got hold of you, their demons would cause things to go badly wrong and they'd panic. Then they'd harm you badly or kill you in a bid to stop you from talking.

"Thanks to the Mejai, we came to know that this devil's trick has been going on for centuries. The devil dispatches powerful demons into humans and gives them strong urge to commit a relatively small crime. Then he causes things to go badly wrong so that the thugs can panic and commit a bigger crime in the process. The bigger crime will then cost mankind a million times more than the original crime that they had in mind.

"Where the devil cannot get his demon-filled thugs to kill a person, he will try and get them to waste the person's talents in jail. Potiphar's wife tried to waste Joseph's life in jail without realising what demons were using her to do. Many highly talented souls, Nelson Mandela included, fell victim to this devil trick; their talents were wasted behind bars for years."

Fiffy gave Deji-Vita a stare. Again, Deji-Vita just let his head droop.

The professor continued, "Most thugs are remotely controlled by demons, which cause them to do horrible things before they know it, so we decided to take no chances. I asked your grandfather to steal your flight ticket and American dollars, and pretend he needed to borrow money to buy you a replacement. I also asked him to tell you all his borrowed money could buy was a cheap flight ticket from Port Novo to Frankfurt. It was the perfect excuse to send you to Porto Novo without arousing suspicions on your part."

"But why send me to Porto Novo?" Deji-Vita asked.

"Port Novo is in a French-speaking African country. You are a boy from an English-speaking country about to inherit untold wealth, plus a treasure that scares the devil to death, which makes you a double VIP. The demon-filled thugs waiting for you in Europe would not expect a double VIP to travel by road to Porto Novo and catch a cheap flight to Germany from there. Above all, there are no manifests to check your movements when you travel by road. All the passengers and the driver in the van that took you to Porto Novo were your bodyguards, all of them were former elite soldiers."

"Why didn't you send me straight to London?" said Deji-Vita.

"Fortunately, this is not our fight," the professor replied. "This is a fight between God and the devil. What was revealed through Majid's dream suggested God wanted your journey to start from Germany, no matter what, so we sent you to Germany, after consulting with the Mejai."

"Did God tell you why He wanted me to go to Germany first?"

"No," his brother said. "You will know that when the time is right."

"I was so looking forward to meeting the Mejai."

"Your brother is the Mejai," the professor said.

"What?" Deji-Vita gaped.

"One day, you will know why things had to be done this way," the Mejai told Deji-Vita.

Then, turning to Habiba, the Mejai said, "I believe it's your turn now."

The girls gaped, as Habiba stepped forward to give Deji-Vita his glasses back.

"You were not supposed to know your brother is the Mejai, until you've inherited the treasure," Habiba told Deji-Vita.

"From where did you get my lost glasses?" Deji-Vita asked Habiba.

"Your glasses were not lost," Habiba replied. "Professor Huddleston instructed your bodyguards to steal them at the earliest opportunity. They took them quietly while you were fast asleep on a bench at Porto Novo Airport."

"Why?"

"We knew you won't be able to see the Mejai at all from the third-tier of the Royal Albert Hall without your glasses…"

"But I wouldn't have known he is my brother."

"We knew that. But had you seen his face in the Royal Albert Hall, you would have known he's the Mejai as soon as you met him in this hotel. You were not supposed to know your brother is the Mejai, until you've inherited the treasure. It's among the instructions that God gave us through Majid's dream."

"Habiba lied to us," Anoushka told her father, John.

"I'm sorry, girls," Habiba said. "I was sworn to secrecy. We were very concerned one of you might make a genuine mistake and spoil everything, so I was asked to do everything not to let any of you know."

"And I don't have a stammer," the stammering priest said now.

"What?" Deji-Vita gasped, looking greatly astonished.

"I was told you are very dangerous with questions. To avoid mistakes on my part, I feigned a terrible stammer to stop you from asking questions and it worked. You fell terribly sorry for me at Heathrow Airport when it took me almost a minute just to say hello, which delighted me no end. The Mejai told us there's a tiny but complicated job for you to do before you can go on to do your main job. We were asked to make you suffer in preparation for that tiny job ahead. The experience will do you a lot of good, we hear. I practiced my stammer on Dr Majid a day before I picked you up at Heathrow."

Deji-Vita turned and looked at the Egyptian.

Then, smiling, the Egyptian said, "Peace, brother."

"Tell him everything, Farouk," the Mejai told the Egyptian.

"I was born in Cairo, Egypt and was taken to Knightsbridge, London before I could see," the Egyptian began. "Time was when I knew no further than Sloane's Square and Marble Arch, where I attended prep and primary school respectively. I cling to my birthplace, Egypt, because its Biblical heritage gives me an aura.

"My father's work with the United Nations took us to India and Pakistan and my life changed beyond all recognition. I became sickly and was prescribed antibiotics and other drugs so often my father feared side effects of drugs could kill me before too long. Peers referred to me as sickly, weak or too sensitive, some called me weird. Others regarded me as abnormal.

"My father left the UN for my sake and my health and exam results improved dramatically upon our return to London. But the psychological scars of my days in Asia remained. During my first year at medical school at King's College, London, I met and confided in Professor Huddleston, who lent me a book called *Slums, Demons & Spiritual Captivity*, which is commonly known as the fifth teachings of the Mejai.

"God," said the Mejai in the book, "made mankind pure, beautiful and full of mercy. True man means the uncorrupted. The uncorrupted cannot stand the sight of waste and evil, and stands not idly by where pain and suffering is prevalent. There are, however, things on Earth that can alter the true nature of true man and corrupt him. Once corrupted, man becomes insensitive and irresponsive to the pain and suffering of others.

"Whatever is capable of altering the true nature of true man is thus listed amongst the truest foes of man. On the list of the truest foes of man, said the book, are slums, stench, filth, decay, muddle, congestion, harassments, terrorism, and constant witnessing of pain and suffering – all of which defiles man and erodes what makes true man *feel* sick at the sight of evil to want to root out evil and its root cause.

"Once what makes man feel sick at the sight of evil is eroded, said the book, he will suffer a terrible drop in morals and wisdom to embrace talent-wasting activities on a scale that will send him on a descending spiral. It will place him on the list of the truest foes of man because of the pain and suffering that he will unleash on other humans through terrorism and the creation of slums, ghettos and all sorts of chaotic conditions that alters the true nature of man. Once a community or country suffers this terrible drop, which Satan, the first on the list of the truest foe of man, wants to see, man has to keep them on the list of the truest foes of man until they change for the better.

"It therefore turned out that I, who was falling sick all the time in India and Pakistan, was not weak, too sensitive, weird or abnormal. I was allergic to moulds and all the horrifying things that can only be found in slums and where human suffering is prevalent, because I had not yet become corrupted man in the terrible drop. I was true man standing, so slums will make me sick; sight of badly malnourished children will make me sick; witnessing of any form of human suffering will make me sick and want to root out evil and its root cause.

"All around me were those who no longer felt sick at the sight of human suffering and they were no longer true men. Their true nature had been altered by life in the slums and their constant witnessing of killings and various forms of human suffering. They had become corrupted men in the terrible drop. They lost what makes men feel sick of evil and want to root out evil.

"'God made man in His own image', said the book. 'Then God said, '*Let mankind have dominion over all the Earth.*' God did not say let a handful of mankind have dominion over all the Earth. That which was made in God's image was not meant to live in slums, stench, ghettoes, filth, and face starvation, lack of water, and poor sanitation – all of which defiles man and makes it difficult for man to retrieve talents from his mind, body and spirit.'

"The book continued, 'Wherever you go, look first and foremost for the first temple of God. The first temple of God on Earth is how your fellow human is being treated in a place and how he is fairing as a result. For man was meant to worship God on Earth through how well he treats his fellow human. Wherever you find men in evil conditions, know that the first temple of God had been defiled. The community or nation responsible should be placed on the list of the truest foes of man. People who escape from that terrible drop must be helped to recover and encouraged to play roles in how to help their nations come off the list of the truest foes of man, or else the devil will turn such nations into military camps and use them to attack you next.'

"Armed with teachings of the book, I travelled across continents to visit God's first temples around the world. I crumbled and cried in Africa. I wept in many parts of the Middle East. I cried in Latin America. I fumed in Eastern Europe. The first temples of God have no iota of human rights in those places, let alone *'have dominion over all the Earth'*, as God demanded. Terrifying living conditions of broken first temples broke me to tears, so I joined the BEJAVE Movement to help those trying to do something about it.

"Then I had the dream that you've just heard about and my life changed yet again. I experienced great joy when the Mejai interpreted my dream and showed me its true worth. I felt like a king when the Mejai compared the importance of my dream to that of Pharaoh.

"But then my joy was curtailed. The Mejai called me from New York himself and asked me to call you an impostor when you arrive in the UK. I told the Mejai I have no strength for it. Then the Mejai said I was chosen to reveal the devil's cruel intentions, so it was my duty to do it.

"I know how hard this world is. I know how rare it is to find true servants of God who are not just interested in fame in society. I know such rare creatures can suffer a lot, so I hated the thought of treating you badly. I begged the Mejai to find someone else to do it; he insisted it was my duty to perform so I should take acting lessons, if I must.

"I took acting lessons and practiced how to be cruel to you. I practiced and practiced how to make Holly, Fiffy and Anoushka hate me and stay well away from me, fearing I could become lightheaded and start boasting about what God had chosen me to do. I read scripts after scripts to master how to deal with all eventualities, after I've labelled you an imposter.

"I visited the white mansion thrice before you arrived in the UK. I knew I could do it when, with Habiba's covert collaboration, I got the girls to hate me so much they wanted to kill me. I meant no harm, brother. I was only a servant and a very bad actor put to work for the benefit of all mankind."

Deji-Vita fell into the Egyptian's arm and they embraced warmly, after which Deji-Vita went round and thanked the four priests that helped him on his travels, one after the other.

"Time to go," the Mejai said.

Then they trooped out of the hotel to head to the airport in various cars.

38

THE GIRLS HELD a meeting in their car on the way to the airport. Then they resolved to spring into action when opportunity presented itself.

Moments after the Mejai finished talking to an airport official, Fiffy hurried to his side and said, hurriedly, "Mejai, we girls have never asked a holy man questions before. Can we ask you a question or two before you go... please?"

The Mejai talked to Professor Huddleston and Professor Huddleston gathered all who escorted the Mejai to the airport in a corner.

Then the Mejai stood before them and said, "Girls, I'm all yours."

Fiffy gave Anoushka a nudge.

Then Anoushka said, "Mejai, my father told me that you could neither see nor hear at the very beginning of your life. How were you cured? What made you start seeing and hearing?"

The Mejai smiled.

Then he said, "The earth was given to good and then evil rose from it. Life on Earth therefore became governed by good and evil spirits, which fights for ascendancy all the time. Chaos and misfortunes rise for human suffering to accelerate and intensify when evil spirits gain the ascendency. Order replaces chaos, talents flourish and peace and prosperity reigns when good spirits regain ascendency.

"God decided I must be born where evil spirits reigned, so maximum spiritual protection became necessary. I was therefore accompanied into this world by an invisible escort, which blinded me at birth and blocked my ears for a very good reason…"

"What's an invisible escort and what do they do?" Anoushka interrupted.

"Invisible escort are angels from angels' realm. They do not leave their abode until they have to protect somebody. Humans have no eyes for seeing them. Humans cannot tell when they are around. They can come here now and not one of you can know it. They block human senses to perform their duties. And once their job is done, they depart. Their powers are stronger than that of the sun.

"My parents and all around me had no idea that I could not see them, I could not hear them, and I could not feel their touch. They were around me but did not exist in my life, which was what the invisible escort had to do. I woke in this world as a baby to see what looked like the tiniest version of the sun before me; it took over all my senses and governed all my actions.

"I behaved and looked like normal children do because my invisible escort, which was always before me, made me do everything that a normal child does. I moved where it led and followed it everywhere because it was all I could see. When the time came for me to crawl, I crawled where it led. When the time came for me to learn how to walk, I ventured where it headed.

"Then, one day, I heard the flapping of wings at the back of my ears, which caused me to make a swift turn in panic. I turned round to find my invisible escort had placed itself a little higher from where I normally see it. It was distancing itself from me but slowly. It kept climbing higher and higher and the distance between us was getting bigger and bigger, so I yelled in a language that I speak no more, 'Stop, stop.'

"It did not listen to me, so I tried to give chase and fell. I tried to give chase again and fell. After the third fall, I stood in one place and watched. Then I saw it going higher and higher, until a huge thing fell on my eyes and I lost all sense of calm.

"The huge thing that fell on my eyes turned out to be the sky, so the very first thing I heard in this world was the flapping of wings by my invisible escort, which was flapping its wings to fly back to the heavens. And the very first thing I saw in this world was the sky, which fell on my eyes as soon as my invisible escort disappeared from my gaze."

"So you started seeing things in this world from the moment you lost sight of your invisible escort?" Anoushka asked.

"Yes. Invisible escort block all your senses to give you maximum protection, until they leave."

"What happened immediately after you first saw the sky and panicked?" Anoushka asked.

"I started hearing noises, human voices, for the very first time, so I looked around in fear and looked down. It was so strange to see sands beneath my feet for the first time. Then the next thing I knew I was in tears."

"Why were you crying?" Anoushka asked.

"The poverty of this world shocked me badly. Everything around me was terribly poor. The people looked terribly poor. Everything around them was terrible to look at. Never had I seen creations of God so poor and so surrounded by many horrifying things. My heart was badly broken."

"Your turn, Holly," Fiffy said

Then Holly said, "Mejai, why did you fall three times when you tried to give chase after your invisible escort?"

"I did not know it then. But I had just learnt how to walk so my legs were not yet strong enough to run after anything."

"Why did the invisible escort leave you at all?" Holly said. "And why did it leave you when you've just learnt how to walk?"

"The invisible escort was on Earth to do two things: to protect me from being killed by evil spirits that could end my life before I could walk; and to blind me completely from the poverty of this world, until my heart had become strong enough to withstand what I was about to see. Without that protection, I would have died of shock in infancy. This world is far too poor, compared to what I already knew before my birth. My heart became ready when I could walk, so the invisible escort left me to what I was sent on Earth for."

"Why are you so sure that there's another world that is better than this one?" Holly said.

"Shock is an experience that comes with previous knowledge. Nothing can horrify you if you have no prior knowledge of a better one. If I had not live in another world that is by far better than this world, nothing on this earth would be capable of shocking me so badly. The poverty of this world broke my heart and reduced me to tears because I've lived in a far better world. There's nothing I know for sure more than the fact that there's another world that is better than this one. We shall meet again in that place, and I will come to you and say 'I told you so'"

"What's the main difference between this world and that world?"

"There are no poor people, no old people, no wrinkled faces and no deformed bodies in that world. There's no illness, no shouting, no bad buildings, no terrifying cooking pots, no poor things to look at, and no death in that world. Nothing that disturbs the senses or kills exists in that world."

"You said your parents and all around you had no inkling that you had an invisible escort. How come you were able to see the invisible escort when other humans couldn't?"

"God did not deny me the eye needed to see my invisible escort because of what I already knew, and because I needed to have a relationship with it, until its departure. I came to do a job that those who have never seen the other world can never do."

"Where exactly did your invisible escort leave you before it flew away?"

"It left me by the side of a palm tree surrounded by many tobacco plants, in the compound where my brother and I grew up."

"What was the significance of where it left you?"

"What can hinder man on Earth far outnumbers what can help him. That is what the palm tree surrounded by many tobacco plants came to teach me. Fruits of the palm tree can serve both the inner and outer strengths of man. Leaves of tobacco plants can damage man's skin and his inner strengths, drain him of energy and shorten his day on Earth, all of which will waste talents given to serve his fellow man."

"Why do we need good and evil?" Holly sighed. "Why did God not just impose good on us and that's it?"

"Good was given not imposed. Evil rose from good because of choice. Choice gives rise to temptations. Yet without choice you cannot attain Individuality. Then none can say I, except God. Man will then become like a drop of water in the ocean with no mind of its own. That which has no mind of its own cannot attain Individuality, let alone yearn for eternal life."

"Some say we come into this world as blank slates," Holly said.

"Fall to the devil's blank slate trap at your peril," the Mejai replied.

"May I ask why, sir?" Holly said.

"There are three essential qualities required to be human; not one of them can be acquired from the world of experience," said the Mejai. "The three essential qualities required to be human are: ability to engage in exhaustive enquiries; ability to make good use of the analysed, and ability to be creative with materials of this world.

265

"Every hut, building, cottage, village, town, city, country, furniture and machine on Earth owe its existence to the three essential qualities of humans, which cannot be acquired from the world of experience. Humans bring those three essential qualities into this world so humans cannot be called blank slates at birth.

"Where you got your essential qualities from is where you are from. Machines got their essential qualities from human, so machines come from man. Since machines come from man, they can be controlled, stopped or taken out of existence by man. Humans got their essential qualities from the heavens, so man comes from Heaven. Since man comes from Heaven, he can be controlled, stopped or taken out of existence from Heaven."

"Mejai," Holly sighed, "I can see how any machine can be controlled, stopped or taken out of existence completely by man. But there's no scientific proof of man being controlled from the heavens?"

"Do you know what the common hurdle is?"

"No," Holly replied.

"The common hurdle can be found in Genesis 3:17–19: '*In the sweat of thy face shall thou eat bread, till thou return to the ground*'. God imposed the common hurdle of man to control man, after man became disobedient and put the objective behind his creation into jeopardy. Genesis 3:17–19 is like stopping a machine from becoming useless.

"Go round and round the world and visit humans where they live. You will find no member of the human race can retrieve talent from his or her mind, body and spirit to enjoy life without sweat."

"Is that why it is called the common hurdle?" Holly asked.

"Yes. Still, Heaven has very little regard for humans' scientific proof."

"Why, Mejai?" Holly said.

"Humans can call something scientific proof today and

admit tomorrow or years later that they were totally wrong," the Mejai replied. "Go and check the history of science. You will find it is extremely dangerous to rely solely on the human mind when it comes to nature."

"But some scientists say nothing can be true, unless it can be scientifically proven," Holly said. .

"Scientists that tell you that nothing can be true without scientific proof are in total error. I'll tell you why. You cannot use science to prove what I dreamt about last night. You cannot use science to prove what my intentions are. You cannot use science to prove how many children will go hungry in the next hour. You can never use science to prove where humans came from.

"And, despite all the boasts and noises that you've been hearing, man can never use science to prove how man came to be. There is what can be proven by science. And there is what can be proven by philosophy. The closest you can get to prove how man came to be is through philosophy."

"Can you show us how?" Holly said.

"Hunger, thirst, boredom, and tiredness, to mention but a few, take man out peace. Out of peace is a temporary intrusion. Whatever can take man out of peace is a temporary intruder. But it cannot intrude on the peace of man, if man was not at peace in the first place.

"Nothing can yearn for what it did not know.
Man cannot long for what he never knew.
Man does things for only one reason, which is to return to peace.
Man will not do things just to return peace, if peace is not his only true home.

Man yearns for peace because man came from peace.
Man came from peace because God created man from His peace.

God gifted man peace to start from peace.
And to the peace that is God shall man return to learn his fate."

"The difference between God and man is contentment. Humans' contentment is prone to intrusions because hunger, thirst, tiredness, boredom and the rest can disturb humans and take them out of peace. God is contentment absolute because God cannot be disturbed by hunger, thirst, tiredness and all the things that can take humans out of peace.

"Not a single human creation has any of man's needs and wants. Therefore let it not surprise you that God the creator of man has none of man's needs and wants. Man cannot do without peace. Man always strives to get back to peace because God is peace and man came out of God. Peace is the only true home of man."

"Mejai," Holly sighed, "can we come out of God without leaving a hole in God?"

"Can a hole appear in the sea, if we fetch water from the ocean?"

"Oh my," Holly gasped.

Everybody laughed.

Then the Mejai said, "God is Spirit and Jesus told you so. God is infinitely more vast than all lands, seas and air on Earth put together. Men on Earth joke with God because they cannot imagine what God looks like. Your human creations have none of your needs and wants, so let it not surprise you that your maker has none of your human needs and wants. You live under God's breath known as air. God only need to withdraw His breath and you will all be dead. Ye are less than a grain of salt in God's eyes."

"My turn now," Fiffy said. "Mejai," she began, "how did one breath put into Adam by God turn into different talents in different humans?"

"Formation of variations in talents began in the womb of Eve, the mother of all mankind, not from the breath put in Adam," the Mejai replied.

"How did God do it?" Fiffy said.

"God lined Eve's womb with heavenly materials denied to all female animals, which is why all animals, lions and elephants included, have no variation in talent. What one lion cannot know every lion cannot know. What one elephant cannot do all elephants cannot do. What one whale cannot bring into existence every whale cannot bring into existence.

"God instituted the miracle of the pyramid of human gifts through Eve's womb alone. Everything to do with variations in talent starts in pregnancy. When your mother was pregnant with you she must have craved certain things, Fiffy."

"Yes. My mum said she craved the smell of sheep all the time when she was pregnant with me," Fiffy replied.

"What about you, Holly?" the Mejai said.

"My mum said she craved caramel when I was in her stomach," Holly replied.

"What about you, Anoushka?"

"My mother said she used to crave tripe and the smell of mud when I was inside her stomach," Anoushka replied.

"Your replies form only a tiny part of how Formation of Variations in Talents occurs in the womb. Through different cravings in pregnancy amongst other occurrences, variations of talents starts in the womb to form the pyramid of human gifts. The pyramid of human gifts is what gives us philosophers, artists, and scientists and so on and so forth. One pregnant woman would crave certain things that another pregnant woman cannot stand. One pregnant woman would like the smell of certain things that another pregnant woman would detest.

"Different yearnings, different cravings, and different behaviours amongst other occurrences during pregnancies give us variations in talent in the pyramid of human gifts. Through the womb of Eve, the first woman that ever lived, God sowed the seeds of all the talents that will combine to give mankind work, entertainment, security, protection, wealth, and dominion over all things on Earth. God is love. Through the pyramid of human gifts the love of God became manifest, except where men are so blinded by demons they cannot see a thing.

"During my time in the Royal Albert Hall yesterday, I gave you the materials for answering the questions, 'Who are we?' and 'Why are we here?'. I asked everybody to try and use the materials to answer the two questions that had dogged mankind since Babel, and put their answers in a brown envelope and send them. I then promised to put my own answers to the questions in a sealed and signed brown envelope and give it to Professor Huddleston before I leave these shores. I'll like to give my brown envelope to Professor Huddleston now with you as my witnesses."

Professor Huddleston stepped forward and received the Mejai's envelope.

Then Fiffy turned to the Mejai and said, "On behalf of the girls, thank you for answering all our questions, Mejai. But if our friends ask for your job title, what should we say?"

Everybody laughed.

Then the Mejai said, "Man creates things to make his life comfortable. The devil put things in the way of man's creations to make man's life miserable. Man will create something helpful today, and then the devil will focus on finding a hundred ways of rendering that human creation useless. Man operates in the open; the devil operates in the dark, so the devil has an unfair advantage. God sends our kind to earth to nullify the devil's unfair advantage when it becomes necessary.

"Our job is to spy on what the devil is doing in the dark to try and harm mankind. To carry out our mission, we have to allow ourselves to be dragged through mud, mysteries and strange journeys, which we do not like at all.

"But if we refuse to allow ourselves to be dragged through mud, mysteries and strange journeys, we cannot acquaint ourselves with what the devil is doing in the dark to thwart all your efforts and explain them to you in a language that you can understand. Then the devil will use his unfair advantage to defeat you and make your lives miserable in your homes, neighbourhoods, workplaces, villages, towns, cities, countries and continents.

"To try and stop us from knowing what he is doing in the dark to harm you, the devil throws mud at us during mysteries and strange journeys, hoping his mud and any stains of battle will sow seeds of doubts in your minds to make it hard for you to know which way to turn. Take heart. Without obstacles to overcome, you cannot reap rewards of that which is called Faith.

"God has sown the seeds of life for you to pick up its benefits. Let not mud, mysteries and strange journeys surrounding a tree get in the way of its benefits. Examine each fruit carefully to make sure the devil's fangs are not hidden in its flesh, then enjoy its benefits to help you help others, bearing in mind that, if there is any sense in wanting to live tomorrow, it makes more sense to want to live forever. Fifty years on Earth is less than a week in the Kingdom of Heaven."

With that, he went round and embraced them, one after the other. He embraced Deji-Vita last and whispered the day of his death in his ear.

Then soon he was gone.

Epilogue

LATE AT NIGHT, while the whole house was asleep, Deji-Vita found himself turning constantly in bed. He felt different in the head and, at one point, thought he'd crossed a line to become a lamb. Why this was the case, he could not tell, so he went down on his knees to pray.

"Why did you not tell me there's this amount of wealth waiting for me to inherit?" he said, after a long silence.

A voice replied, "There are things in this life that you cannot understand, if you have wealth or know you will inherit wealth."

"But I feel terrible now; all I think about is my wealth," Deji-Vita said.

"Jesus told you, '*It is easier for a camel to go through the eye of a needle than for a rich man to enter the Kingdom of God,*'" the voice replied.

"Then take the wealth back," said Deji-Vita. "I want to go back to the way I was. I want to finish what I started. I want to invent the spray that I saw in a dream; the spray that can kill poverty outright. I feel more comfortable in that role. I don't want to think about lawyers and accountants. I don't want a family of my own. I don't want to live long. There's nothing that you cannot help me achieve. Help me invent the miraculous spray that can kill poverty outright, then take my life and let me go."

"This is not about you," the voice replied. "This is about those whom God gave you life for. Awake from slumber. Rise in mind and think hard again. You will find more than the strength you need to cope and do well."

The next morning, Deji-Vita did not show up for breakfast, so Fiffy went to see him and found he was suffering from headaches.

"I know, I know," she said during the course of conversation, tears welling in her eyes, "To find and lose your only brother within hours, after so many years apart, is bound to take its toll. Let's go and see a doctor, after we've dealt with Dr Majid."

"Is Dr Majid coming here?"

"He's coming to see us girls. We told him everything at the airport and he's agreed to dance for the prophets…"

"No, Fiffy. You heard why he did what he did. He did it to help me."

"This is not about you, holy boy. This is not about you at all. This is about hundreds of millions of people that you were born to suffer and save from total waste. We are actors, Holly, Anoushka and I. We work with professional manufacturers of joy. We know how to generate publicity for a cause. We talked to Dr Majid about it and he's agreed to dance. We're going to tell the media why he must dance in all four corners of the world, which will give you a lot of publicity before you set foot in Africa…"

"Do I need publicity?"

"Remember the angry beasts with big horns that stood in your way in the dream that I had?"

"Yes?"

"Publicity will become the wind that lifts you high above their heads and take you to green pastures. Then you will work wonders. I know you will. You will be magnificent."

Deji-Vita ran into her arms and they embraced passionately. Then the voice said unto him, "Don't lose her."